CODE BLUE: ALIEN JAIL BREAK

CODE BLUE: ALIEN JAIL BREAK

UNLIKELY BOUNTYHUNTERS™ BOOK 1

MICHAEL TODD

DISRUPTIVE IMAGINATION

Copyright © 2021 LMBPN Publishing
Cover Art by Jake @ J Caleb Design
http://jcalebdesign.com / jcalebdesign@gmail.com
Cover copyright © LMBPN Publishing
A Michael Anderle Production

LMBPN Publishing
PMB 196, 2540 South Maryland Pkwy
Las Vegas, NV 89109

Version 1.01, June 2021
eBook ISBN: 978-1-64971-815-0
Print ISBN: 978-1-64971-816-7

THE CODE BLUE: ALIEN JAIL BREAK TEAM

Thanks to our Beta Team:
John Ashmore, Jim Caplan, Chrisa Changala, Larry Omans,
Kelly O'Donnell, Rachel Beckford

JIT Readers

Peter Manis
Dorothy Lloyd
Deb Mader
Dave Hicks
Debi Sateren
Zacc Pelter
Paul Westman
Jackey Hankard-Brodie

Editor
Skyhunter Editing Team

DEDICATION

*To Family, Friends and
Those Who Love
to Read.
May We All Enjoy Grace
to Live the Life We Are
Called.*

— Michael

CHAPTER ONE

"Did you get up early or did you stay up all night?"

John nodded from his chair and fired. He couldn't hear his mom, but he had no doubt what she was saying.

On screen, *Plodex* shot the mecha that was advancing down the catwalk. To either side was a drop of three hundred feet. The noise inside John's headphones drowned out everything his mother said. Vast cauldrons of boiling metal vied with the constant *hum* of rotors and pulleys. Some of them synced up with his mother's mouth so that she looked like she was a walking, talking factory. She made a gesture over both her ears.

"Yes, I hear you," John said.

She adjusted the orange vest and blue shirt she wore. Her mouth ran on as she wiped doughnut crumbs off, and she danced in place to get her uniform pants more securely over her rump. John was equally big below his belt. He'd done soccer and rugby in school and fit snugly in the gaming chair he'd bought himself the year before. He hoped he'd finished growing. Six-four was big enough.

The mecha was still advancing. Its every footfall *clanged* in his ears, and the charge of its weapon told him he had less than forty seconds to stop the thing, get shot, or jump to another catwalk below. His mom came up beside him. Her breasts, hair, and part of her face pushed in from the edge of the camera's view.

"Mom!"

"What? Are people watching?"

"Yeah, Mom! Only, like, five *hundred* of 'em! Stay off cam. *Please?*"

"Where do you see that?" She squinted at the enormous screen that hung from one wall of John's gaming-slash-bedroom and pointed. "Here?"

Plodex got a blast square to his chest. John retreated as far as he could, but he'd dropped onto this catwalk from one higher up and had practically nowhere to go. His LCV2 blaster was starting to misfire. *I'm not makin' a dent in that mecha anyway.* He paused the game. "I'm gonna take five, guys. Back soon."

"You're talkin' to *them*, right?" His mom pointed at the fluctuating number of viewers. "Are they here in Albuquerque?"

John untangled himself, stood, and stretched. "All over the world, Mom. Right now," he checked the time, "mostly China."

"They probably like seein' a big blond boy like you!" She inspected the shorts he wore. "You're gonna wear out the seat from sittin' all the time. I'll stop over at Target during my lunch break and get you a new pair. You still a size thirty-six?"

She pulled down the waistband of his shorts in back,

and John twisted away. "Mom! Yeah, thirty-six. Quit pickin' at me."

"Why don't you go to CNM, huh? There's still time to sign up for classes. You can study computers, maybe create one of these games instead of just playing them. That's where your friend Gage is, isn't he?" She looked around the room, then stuck her right index and middle finger into two glasses and clinked them together while her other hand gathered a plate and silverware.

"Yeah." John gripped carpet fibers with his toes and reached as far overhead as the ceiling allowed.

"What about that Hannah? Where's she at?"

"Boulder."

"She was a sweet girl."

"She cheated on me, Mom."

"Yeah, well, stuff happens, honey. You gotta get out in the game again. There any girls that play this stuff?"

"Lots of 'em, sure."

"Well, see? Maybe you could meet one of *them*. Take her out some place. It doesn't have to be fancy."

John cracked his knuckles and knees. *Hard to find a real girl with tits and a waist like Layla9.* "Chipotle?"

His mom frowned. She was almost six feet herself. "I said 'nice.' Anyway, sweetie, I gotta go to work. Stay outta your dad's way. He's in a pissy mood."

They heard his footsteps upstairs, then the door to the basement opened. "Vera? You down there?"

She gave John a quick kiss on the cheek, then trotted away. "Coming! What do ya want for breakfast?"

"He down there? Been playin' that goddamned console all night, hasn't he? Goddamn jerk-off is what he—"

The door shut and John checked his screen. A new subscriber. He sent the guy a thank-you emoji and texted Gage.

What U doing?
Shower U?
Mom harassment.

Gage sent him a selfie from the shower. There was lather piled atop his head and a big kissy-face below it.

Wanna hang?
Yup. 10?
15. Need to jerk.

John sent him a puking face and signed out of the game. He changed his underwear, pulled on new kicks, shorts with pockets, and a T-shirt that wasn't too tight across his chest. He flexed for a moment in the mirror hanging on the closet door, considered jerking his junk, then decided to wait until Obabebabe was playing, probably around seven o'clock. She always wore tank tops, and although she never showed face, she was one of the hottest girls on the site. She could kick ass at most games as well. Anything with a steering wheel and she was top-notch.

He snuck out the door to the patio as stealthily as he could, then cut across a few backyards and jogged to Gage's house on Amherst Drive SE. It felt good to run, especially while it was only around seventy degrees. He missed soccer and rugby.

He didn't miss the bullshit of high school. By the time

he'd graduated, he'd pretty much checked out. Nothing more to learn there, as he saw it. GPA of two-point-seven-five. He could've hacked his way into better grades. He'd done that for other students, anonymously, of course, but he didn't care enough to bother about his scores.

There was no money in being his own customer and definitely no challenge. He learned programming languages like most guys learned sports stats. Bard, Cozart, Griep. Python, Ruby, Swift. RBI, OBP, ITPHR. PHP, SQL, HTML.

His greatest achievement, however, had been Hannah. Not the girl, although he'd used it for her benefit, the hacking code he'd named in her honor.

It had let him into the school's grading program, the Department of Motor Vehicles, his dad's car insurance safe driver readout, all kinds of social media accounts, even the IRS and ICE. It had turned Gage's parents into naturalized citizens and let him peek at his Mom's breast cancer diagnosis before her oncologist saw it. He'd had it disguised as a silver and turquoise pendant that he could plug into any USB. It was powerful, versatile, and on his person twenty-four hours a day.

He let himself into Gage's house as quietly as he'd left his. They'd been friends for so long that John had the run of the place, but he didn't want to wake Mrs. Gonzalez or any of the little ones. The smallest, Toñito, was already up and quietly sucking on one finger in the hallway and drooling down his little chest. The diaper he wore looked dangerously full. He pointed at John and played with the pendant when John scooped him up. *Yup. Full.*

John grabbed a Pampers diaper from a container in a

hall closet, snatched several baby wipes as well, and headed into Gage's room.

"JoJACKo! My man!" Gage gave him a fist bump, took Toñito from him, and laid him on the rug to change his diaper, all while keeping his voice low. "Wanna break into a USSF base with me?"

CHAPTER TWO

"Gotta be this afternoon, *chavo*," John replied. "I'm bustin' into the White House this morning."

Gage removed his brother's diaper. They both gagged at the shitty mess inside it. John held out the room's wastebasket, and Gage dropped the filthy thing inside, then wiped Toñito quickly and got a new diaper in place without letting his brother pee all over. "Thanks, man."

They took the baby and the basket to the kitchen, emptied the latter into a big black garbage bag, and put that outdoors in a plastic bin. John thought the moon wouldn't be far enough away to get the smell out of his nose, but after they'd taken turns scrubbing in the kitchen sink, he felt better.

This part of the house was out of earshot of the bedrooms. Mr. Gonzalez had already gone to seek laborers outside the hardware store where John's mom worked. Gage got them both bowls of cereal, milk, and spoons, then fed his brother one Cheerio after another along with a bottle of juice.

"Seriously. I found a USSF base. We should go check it out."

"Let me guess. Secret facility with aliens way out in the desert by Roswell, yeah?"

"No, man, right here in Albuquerque."

John gobbled his Cinnamon Toast Crunch. "What? We never noticed the gigantic hangers and little green men as we rode the school bus?"

"'S not like that, Jojacko. It's *hidden in plain sight.*"

"As a giant plastic saguaro?"

Gage held out his phone. On it was a Google Earth view of the city's downtown. "Right here, on Central Avenue."

John peered at the white square rooftop. "Looks like any one of a thousand buildings, man."

"Exactly."

"What's it supposed to be?"

"A telemarketing hub for something called the Cooper Corporation."

"Sounds dull as fuck. What makes you think it's a secret *anything?*" John drank the milk at the bottom of his bowl.

"*La red oscura.* Source of all that's good and illegit."

"Dark web? You were lookin' for alien chick porn again, weren't you? Tentacles and shit."

"Nah. I'm into giantesses now. Big fifty-foot chicks that can stuff me up their—"

"Stop." John scrolled around the map display. "Where'd you get the idea this place is a USSF base?"

"Guy named Draylop, posts from Iraq...*maybe.* He's big into aliens, conspiracies, UFOs. It's him that says this is a hideout."

"No evidence, right?" John took possession of Toñito so Gage could finish his breakfast.

"That's where *we* come in. I told him we'd go by there, check it out."

"You are *loco*. Nothin' we can see from the street will mean anything. Only windows, concrete, the occasional shift change. Not worth my day."

"Like you got shit to do." Gage had stuffed his mouth. "We ain't gonna stand on the sidewalk. You and your jewelry are gonna get us *inside*."

Toñito played with the pendant in question. John was careful not to let him get drool or any half-masticated cereal into the universal serial bus. He dropped it inside his red and sand Zia sun t-shirt and amused the baby with a spoon instead. "They gotta have cameras everywhere. Sneakin' around is gonna land us in jail."

"So? We'll say we're applying for a job. We're enterprisin' young men, lookin' for scut work. That's more or less the truth."

John studied the map again. "This is only a mile from here."

"Less. We could be there in fifteen minutes."

"Okay. Why not? We'll wait until your mom's up, then head over."

"JoJACK the Hack!" Gage thrust his skinny brown arms into the air and overturned his bowl of cereal onto the towel he wore wrapped around his thin waist. Toñito found that very funny, so Gage did it two more times before getting up to trade his towel for clothes he could seek work in.

It was another hour and a half before the two teens got out of the Gonzalez residence. Lupe was a MILF, in John's opinion, although he'd never dare say that to Gage. The whole family—four sons and a daughter—had the same black hair, café eyes, and *dulce de leche* skin, but on Mama Gonzalez, it was all put together better.

John wished he weren't an only child and so pale. The entire Jacobs clan stood watch against melanoma. Squamous cell carcinoma had already taken bites out of his dad's ears and the nape of his mom's neck. John got checked out monthly by a dermatologist. Rugby and soccer had only increased his risk. *Better I had stuck to swimming. Or spelunking.*

Gage seemed to jump into the air about every five steps they took down Amherst. He'd always gotten excited easily. His face had frozen into a grin by third grade, and he talked non-stop as they walked.

"We'll head in the main doors and, like, announce ourselves to the receptionist or whoever, then excuse ourselves to go pee. There's gotta be an elevator near the bathroom. We'll swoop in there, and you use your pendant to see where the elevator can take us. I figure most of the secret stuff is underground, way down, labs and mummies, or whatever. Got it?"

"Got it. We're only takin' pictures, right? See what we can see, then post all that shit for your buddies on the dark web?"

"Absolutely. We'll trade photos. Draylop pretty much promised that. He says he's got proof of UFOs. Different ships. Different locations. Maybe even aliens, but he said those were pretty far off and hard to make out, so he's honest about it all."

When they got where they were going, they found the first hitch in their plan. "Thought you said this was a tele-marketing hub," John complained.

Gage checked his phone. "That's what it's marked as, yeah."

They stood across Central Avenue from a decently attractive, four-story building. It took up most of the block minus a small parking lot and a much smaller, hacienda-style building labeled Desert Developments. The place where they'd intended to apply for jobs, or at least pretend to, turned out to be a self-storage facility. Behind large glass windows were many non-descript doors, presumably opening into secure spaces where people could put the contents of *Abuelita's* house or that collection of cookware they'd bought on eBay.

"Nobody's in there, man. No receptionist, no phone banks. I bet there's not even a bathroom."

"Sure, that's how it looks, Jojacko, but don't you see how perfect this is for a secret base? It's even more boring than we thought it'd be. We gotta go in."

"It's not gonna lead to anything, Gage. Even if we get in the front door there, it's only one ten-by-ten cubicle after another, plus cameras."

Gage was already halfway across the street. When he reached the first of several unmarked, opaque doors, he waved John over. "Locked. Let's try that one."

John followed him to the next door and the next. There

were no keyholes, no keypads, no intercom to be buzzed in through.

They finally came to one door where the building was a simple red instead of gray. Here there was a 1-800 number to dial, the building's address and ostensibly its hours of operation, all stenciled on the inner side of glass panes. There was also a keypad.

Gage smiled even more excitedly now.

CHAPTER THREE

Meehixiheem played with her hair. *Looks dry. I need a swim and a chissatch oil bath.*

Unfortunately for her, the nearest source of chissatch oil was light-years away, in the Pnellu system. There, on Pnellu IV, in the city of Lagud, she'd found the very best spa, run by a Jaukh named Helkl. He was ugly, but he had refined tastes.

He'd beautifully decorated every surface in his establishment. Mists floated out of nozzles in the ceiling and the walls. They carried flavorings of lillichug spice or mettem cake right into one's mouth and nose so that walking through the spa nearly counted as a meal. Real meals, on the other hand, could consist of urwee cream and u-u eggs or sometimes fresh leaves of dewa mixed with jamec berries.

Undulating light displays vied with whole rooms of auske fabric to roll around in. As easily as one could purge oneself of all contaminants, there were wonderful things to put inside oneself. Meehixiheem especially liked veonk spheres. They were warm, slick, and vibrated in tune with one's heartbeat.

When X had become Ixi, and again when she became Meehixiheem, veonk spheres had been her chief means of celebration. Someday, when she became Sameehixiheemas, she hoped to be far away from this boring little room on this dull planet, someplace where veonks were readily available.

For now, however, she was still surrounded by concrete. The bed she lay on was crude and hard. It smelled of cleaning chemicals and the beings that kept her here.

They weren't bad looking: symmetrical, varied in color, mostly male. Meehixiheem had learned to recognize a few of them individually during the past fifteen planet rotations, but it was difficult. They didn't say much, and they almost always wore so much protective gear that she had trouble making out their facial features.

One male's eyes were small and dark. Another's were large and bright blue. That's what she called them: Darksmall and Bluebig. She'd told them *her* name many times, but they hadn't grasped it yet. She talked a *lot* when they were in her room, but either their translator matrix was non-functional, or she worried they didn't even have a translator matrix. She hated to think she might be the first off-worlder they'd ever seen. That would make getting home a whole lot harder.

She sat up and stretched until the top of her head bounced against the bottom of her spine. She slid off her bed onto the bare floor, stretched one leg in front of her and one behind her, then widened and contracted her pelvis.

Her clothes were nice, but she was very tired of wearing them. These were party wraps, diaphanous and seductive, made for low light and body rubbing. They looked gray in the light of her cell and provided next to no cushioning. In addition, they'd begun to tear here and there.

Her shoes held her feet at awkward angles because they were for the microgravity of a dance gathering. She would've taken them off by now, but they were of a piece with her body wraps; removing one piece would necessitate removing all of her clothing. She'd already noted the great curiosity Darksmall, and to a lesser extent Bluebig, displayed when they caught glimpses of her pelvic flap. No way was she going to be naked in front of her captors.

It was about the middle of a planet rotation, she guessed. A meal would come soon. She clasped her hands behind her back, raised them above her head, then brought them out in front of her and unclasped them.

Her fingertips had mostly lost the sheen she'd applied to them for the dance gathering. Only on the edges of her nails were there any sparkling remnants. Her scent was completely gone. It was an expensive perfume that her sire had given her years before called Tears of Tulangnalut. Now she only smelled of herself and not her cleanest self at that.

The male she called Greenolder and the only female she'd seen here had brought her a small metal tub of water during the first two rotations of her imprisonment. Later she'd been brought to this room in which one fixture supplied water and another used it to flush away body waste. At least that's what she guessed its function was.

She'd decided not to release anything until she was free. Who knew what these aliens would do with it. They'd surely study it, the idea of which revolted her. Maybe they wouldn't even recognize it as excrement and would smear it—

Ugh.

She was hungry now. They only provided food three times per rotation, so the nightside of this planet, which her people called Kdack 3a, was a hungry place. Her meals, although infrequent, were huge: fresh or steamed plants, some sort of animal lactate—which she hoped didn't come from the Kdackan females themselves—served cold in a separate container, and sometimes animal flesh, cooked.

Mostly she stuck to the grains they cooked in water. Next to bowls of that, they provided a simple plant sugar and a powdered brown spice that she ate by the spoonful. They'd seemed shocked by her appetite for the stuff. That made her worry that it was poison, but nothing nauseating had happened to her.

There were footsteps outside her cell. It was probably Bluebig and Darksmall. She wished she could communicate with them. She desperately wanted to know what had happened to the others on the ship. Had they died in the crash? Were they also under arrest or had they already been freed and returned to their government representatives?

Meehixiheem was no great pilot. She and the others

had been relying on Daukhl for that. He'd promised them fun on Kdack 3a, at least fun as Daukhl's species understood it. That could range from star-staring to sentient-hunting. Meehixiheem had only wanted to see the place.

She'd been on fourteen other worlds, but never this one. Now she regretted climbing into Daukhl's ship in the first place. He'd been completely intoxicated on hurnrern weed.

The door opened. As she'd suspected, it was Darksmall and Bluebig. They were covered cranium to hallux by blue, black, and white boots, uniforms, and transparent masks, but Bluebig smiled.

She smiled back and gave off the friendly scent. He seemed to respond to that. Tension in his buttocks pushed his groin forward. Meehixiheem copied his stance. Her blue skin deepened in shade, especially around her pelvis, and Bluebig said something to his companion.

Darksmall replied. He hit Bluebig's arm with his elbow and laughed briefly, then set down the platter bearing her meal. It was the flesh of an animal she hadn't seen before, maybe muscles from a bird's wing, plus steamed long green cylindrical plant pods. There was fruit juice as well. *Looks decent.*

Meehixiheem made a gesture of gratitude. She made a sort of pipe of her hands and moved them back and forth between her lower stomach and the Kdackans who fed her.

They watched carefully, and she thought they might be learning the gesture, so she repeated it several times while continuing to smile. She had an insight that Bluebig's buttocks and groin were a gesture used when offering food, so she pointed at him there and repeated the pipe-like gratuity movement, all the while drawing closer and closer to them.

I really should *become a xenoanthropologist as my sire has* suggested. *I clearly have a talent for it!*

Then Darksmall zapped her with an electric prod.

18

CHAPTER FOUR

The keypad had nowhere for John to plug his pendant in, but from his phone, he was able to find the most likely number of digits to push *and* the top ten most popular combinations. He wasn't merely a good computer engineer. He had a *knack* for things like this. In only three minutes, he'd guessed the correct entry code.

"All riiight!" Gage enthused. He slapped John on the back and followed him inside.

The place was air-conditioned and smelled a little stale. There were sounds from passing cars and their footsteps, but otherwise silence. Despite the quiet, John felt a tiny buzz in the floor. Gage confirmed he felt it too and they set off exploring.

They kept their voices down as they circled the entire street-level set of cubicles. When they came to an elevator, the only option was the up button. John's instinct was to start on the fourth floor, and he knuckled that button when they got inside the car.

"We gotta try to get into one of these cubicles," Gage

whispered. He looked up at John. His smile was gone, but he still seemed jumpy. Cameras covered each hallway, plus one presumably recording them inside the elevator, but so far no one had challenged their presence in the building.

John nodded and led his friend out when the doors opened. The fourth floor was nearly identical to the first except for no exit to the street. They walked away from Central Avenue and the road leading to it so that outside they could see some of the parking lot and a church.

John felt along the wall as they wandered. In some places, the buzz was stronger, in some weaker, but always there. He stopped Gage at the last door before the left turn to bring them back to the front of the storage facility. "This one."

Gage kept watch. He bounced in place and swiveled his head constantly, looking down both hallways they could see. "I think we should say we're looking to rent a storage unit," he whispered, "not jobs. I mean, there haven't been any 'No Trespassing' signs, right? They gotta make this place look legit, so they can hardly bar the public from comin' in here, right? We'll say we're lookin' to store, like, my, um, sports memorabilia here or something. We'll say we couldn't find any employees to show us a unit, so we found an unlocked one."

John nodded. This door required a keycard insertion. He kept a couple of blank ones in his wallet and had equipped his pendant to connect with them.

He took one out, hooked it up to his silver and turquoise hacker's tool with a retractable fiber optics cord, then inserted it into the reader. The pendant ran on super long-life batteries that were recharged both by a tiny solar panel on its front and by the motion of John walking. His chest was muscular—he could boost the pendant by making his pecs bounce.

The deciphering program got to work, and thirty seconds later it opened the door before them. They passed inside. It was approximately eight feet by eight feet, large enough to store a couch and lots of boxes, but maybe not as big as John had expected.

It also wasn't as rudimentary as he'd foreseen.

"Whoa! Pretty nice!" Gage shut the door behind them. "This ain't concrete, and the walls aren't cinder blocks. My *tío* rented one of these. It was secure, but damn, not like this! What is this?" He tapped the floor with his foot.

"Reinforced rubber over, I dunno, steel? It's not impossible that they built storage units with these materials, but why spend the money? Hey, look!" John crouched and tilted his head.

"What? I don't see nothin'."

"It's kinda scuffed right there." John pointed at the far wall and half-crawled closer. "Not like furniture, but like shoes. Plus, the buzz is stronger behind this wall."

"Probably big-ass air conditioners."

"No, people have, like, stood here or maybe walked through here." He touched the wall and about halfway up it, burnished steel plating suddenly lit up red.

"Oh, fuck!" Gage clawed at the door behind them. "That an alarm?"

"No." John stood. "It's a scanner. It's supposed to read code from, like, a badge."

Gage pressed his palms into his temples, then wiped them down his cheeks to his jaw. "Man, I didn't ... I didn't expect this to *be* anything. I'm not sure we should stay. What if they *shoot* us?"

"Don't be chicken shit. I'm gettin' into this." He pushed a couple of turquoise ovals on his pendant, and a red light came out of the center. It flickered up and down, left and right, over the panel they'd discovered. Suddenly and silently, half the wall opened. Beyond it was another corridor and more doors.

"Fuck me, John! I ain't goin' in there! Come on. Let's head home."

"Stay here or take off, bro. Jojacko is balls deep into this now."

John stepped forward, and the door slid shut behind him. It was apparent none of the "storage units" in the building would ever be rented by the public. It was all a front for whatever this place was.

He moved quietly but steadily forward. To his right and left the floor had periodic gaps that extended down at least one level. The walls emitted soft white light, as did the floor and ceiling.

There were no doors to his left but five to his right, spaced out from each other at regular distances. They each bore blue, black, and white labels. Some were blank, but others had alphanumeric codes on them. Those didn't mean anything to him at first, but after the third one he read he thought there were dates to be found in them. "12 May 1995. 1 Nov 2001. 17 Jul 2019. Hmm."

It was a big place and evidently important, but aside

from the buzz and his breathing, he didn't hear much, definitely not voices or other people's footsteps. *All automated? Controlled remotely?*

The remaining three doors in this stretch of corridor were unlabeled. He turned the corner and saw at least four more entries on the right but only one on the left. It stood beside a large glass window and behind *that* were two guys in blue, black, and white uniforms. They sat at a table and stuffed their mouths with sandwiches while they watched the TV next to them.

John immediately slid back around the corner. *United States Space Force? High-tech facility, but low-brow recruits.*

He took out his phone and started snapping pictures. There wasn't much to see beyond a well-lit corridor and some doors. He dared to extend his mobile around the corner and take a video of the guys in uniform, but that only looked like regular old enlistees chewing cheese and baloney with their mouths open. *Gotta find somethin' more... alien. Or at least more interesting.*

He walked back along the hallway until he came to the door labeled July seventeenth this year. *Two weeks ago. Gotta be somethin' cool in here.*

John examined the whole thing but saw no lock, handle, or LED. He did find scrape marks next to the label, blackish scratches in the white surface of the wall. He slid the tag to the left, found a button, and pushed it. The door opened and on a bed in front of him lay a woman with green hair, blue skin, and the best damn tits he'd ever seen.

CHAPTER FIVE

John was dumbfounded. The woman curled up defensively on the bed and said something he couldn't understand. She wrapped her arms tighter around her chest than looked physically possible and brought her knees well up to her cheekbones. He didn't move any closer, but he stared almost without blinking.

She blinked very little as well. Her eyes were large, and even from this distance, John could see that her pupils were horizontal black bars. She had no eyebrows, but the hair on her head was hay-like and stuck out in every direction. He tried to look non-threatening by holding his hands up in the air.

The woman noticed the phone he held and immediately leapt out of bed and snatched the device from him. She spoke again, more to herself than to him. He still understood none of it, but she didn't seem to care. Very quickly, she brought up the Internet and found YouTube. Then she began to film herself. He couldn't imagine why, but she went on for at least two minutes, then closed the cam and appeared to post the video.

"*Shu-u nep sikoris. Ne-ep don ta-am blustis mikellan?*"

Whatever that meant to her, she said it very earnestly. She began searching his pockets and wasn't shy about squeezing his ass cheeks and groin as she did so. It hurt, and the sound of pain John let out made her test his testicles again. "*Ka-a nep umora nekis.*"

She seemed to have learned something useful and followed up with a very hands-on examination of the rest of his body, all the while keeping up a steady stream of commentary. Finally, she stepped back and patted her chest with both hands. "*Meehixiheem.*"

John took that as an invitation to examine her body in turn. Perhaps this was how her people got to know each other or showed they were harmless. In either case, no sooner had he touched her breasts than she elbowed his jaw and knocked him back against the door. "*Re-edo shu-la memenis, vaika spu!*"

"Jesus fuck! I'm sorry! I don't speak blue girl!" He rubbed his jaw and wished he'd picked a different door to open. *But who knows what kinda alien might be next door? Acid-spitter or maybe some multi-fanged octopus.*

She repeated herself, "Meehixiheem," and tapped her chest again.

John tapped his chest. "Meehick'sa cream. Yeah, Meehick'sa cream."

She twisted her head far to one side like a confused dog. "Mee-hix-i-heem."

He repeated it correctly this time, but again she tilted

her head first to one side, then the other. She took hold of his wrists, brought his palms to his chest, and waited, but when he started with "Mee," she clamped her fingers over his lips. *"Ke-ke."*

He thought he finally understood, so he tapped his pecs and said, "Jojacko." It wasn't his real name, but this was such an unreal experience, he thought he'd be better off hiding his identity. If she could film something for YouTube, she could Google his address, and no way did he want her showing up at his house. His parents would be *pissed.*

"Jo-jac-ko," she practiced. This made sense to her, apparently. She stepped back and looked him over, then traced her fingers over the Zia sun on his T-shirt. *"Kdack?"*

"Kdack? Yeah, Kdack, I guess, if that's your word for sun."

She held up three fingers on one hand, and he noticed for the first time that she had the normal number, but two of them were thumbs. He took his phone back from her, told Google to bring up images of the sun, and showed it to her. "Kdack?"

She jutted her jaw out and back, out and back. "Kdack." She held up three long blue fingers again. John realized she smelled of berries or something. It was nice. "Kdack *mwaant."*

He took a chance and held up three of his fingers. "Mwaant."

She smiled. It was pretty human-looking except that her lower lip came up over her upper one and almost touched her nose. "Mwaant."

They spent a minute or two learning to count up to five in their respective languages. Hers were *u, dene, mwaant, sle,* and *furl* or something like that. She had lots of trouble saying "three" but did well with the others. *This is cool. Hangin' with an extraterrestrial hottie, doin' math.*

She laid her hand on the door behind him and made an opening gesture. *"Ngun totopes. Jojacko, ngun totopes"*

"Open it? Yeah, I can...I can do that." John fiddled with his pendant. He stopped when he noticed that she had started removing the wraps of cloth around her tits, hips, and legs, then sat and pulled off her weird-ass shoes. Her figure was excellent. Her nips were longish slits at the point where her breasts protruded the most, and if that was her pussy, a flap of dark blue skin that he longed to lift out of place someday covered it.

"Bezza ninoko ma-turturis." She looked expectantly at him, drew the Zia sun across her chest, and gestured with a sort of pulling motion. "Kdack, Jojacko! *Bezza ninoko!"*

John pulled his T-shirt up over his head and tossed it to her. She slipped it over her head and used one length of wrapping as a belt. When she stood again, it covered her to mid-thigh. *"Ngun totopes. Ngun sha-alme!"*

She joined him at the door, and he clicked the center of his pendant. The light it produced made the door slide open. She hurried him into the corridor, then led him left to where he'd entered this part of the facility. That door opened as well, and soon they were in the hallway that the outside world could see.

Gage was nowhere in sight. *Shit. He'll wish he'd gone with me for sure. He's gonna crap his pants just like Toñito.*

Meehixiheem hurried along the hall back to the elevator, and John kept up. When the car opened, she popped inside and pressed the lowest two buttons on the panel. He didn't know where they'd go once they'd reached Central Avenue. It'd be tough to hide a half-naked blue girl with goat-eyes from the passing cars.

When the door finally opened, however, they weren't at the bottom of the building he'd entered. Instead, they were at one end of a long, dimly lit hallway, which Meehix ran down immediately. John slowly understood she was heading to the building next door, Desert Development.

Through one more door, then up a staircase and they were in a hollow structure. Lights came on from the ceiling. Lights also came on from below an honest-to-God *U-Fucking-O!*

John was stupefied, but Meehix pulled him along until they were standing partly bent over underneath the craft. It was maybe twenty feet long but no wider than a fighter jet.

It was an odd mixture of materials and design. Some parts resembled steel. Others glowed like mother-of-pearl. Short tapered wings to either side of the craft and one on its top, but there were no rivets or bolts. John was so excited that he thought he might pee.

Meehix grabbed hold of his wrist and thrust the palm of his hand onto the ship's underbelly. A door opened immediately, and a staircase unfolded. She pushed him ahead of her, which meant he ended up in the pilot's seat.

She said a bunch of things he hadn't learned, then forced his hands onto cushion-like plates intended for people with only one thumb per hand. She sounded impatient, and when he heard the footsteps and voices outside the ship, he understood why: when the two guys eating sandwiches had finally stopped watching TV, they'd noticed that one of their prisoners was escaping.

Oh, shit!

CHAPTER SIX

Meehixiheem saw the men as well. She hoped they didn't have electric prods with them or anything worse. They were wildly unpredictable creatures. If they would shock her simply for saying thanks for a meal, there was no telling what they would do for escaping and *maybe* taking their ship.

"Shut the door, Jojacko." She tapped him on the shoulder and pointed at the opening behind them.

"Wu-ut? Aidoun ta nou wu-ut ta duu eer!"

"Shut the door! Come *on!* They're almost here."

He was practically drooling with stupidity. He kept feeling around in the control cushions. Lights came on, went off, came on, went off. The ship floated and dropped. Weapons fired up and cycled down. She'd be lucky if he didn't blow them up before the guards came on board.

"This hole! Press inside *this* hole!" She jabbed her finger inside a small round pit up and to the left of the pilot's seat. It didn't respond to her, as she'd expected. "This whole thing is keyed to Kdackan DNA! *You* have to do everything. Don't you get that?"

"Wu-ut?"

She took hold of his wrist and yanked his hand free of the control cushion. It gave out a kind of sucking sound, then reverted to the shape of a Kdackan hand with its four-fingers-one-thumb configuration. Then she seized his index finger and shoved it into the door control. He finally got the idea, and the ship sealed up.

Outside, Darksmall and Bluebig were arguing. Darksmall had drawn a weapon of some kind and now pointed it at the ship, specifically the window Meehixiheem was looking out. Bluebig pushed the other Kdackan's arms down and yelled.

Yeah, don't shoot the expensive spaceship, you fy-fy. Who knows how many of your planet's resources had to go into creating this thing. "Jojacko. We. Must. Leave."

He was as dense as ever. There had to be a translator function they could engage, but she didn't know where it might be.

Lots of this ship's design was familiar. The seats were Kdackan, but the control cushions were Jaukh, and her people used three wings on their craft. The translucent shell material was also theirs, but ugly Kdackan steel plates had been added, at least to the underside.

She thought the two small pits side by side near the place where the console met the front window were most likely a switch, but only if pressed jointly. She took hold of Jojacko's hand again—he'd been holding both of them safely in the air so as not to do anything fatal, she guessed

—and pressed his index and middle fingers inside. A circle of wavy blue lit up around the two pits.

"Translate between Dolurulod and Kdackan," she said as clearly as she could. The waves reacted to her voice. If this was the technology she was familiar with, one of the pits heard what was said and the other produced the translation. She thought she could see where this translator had been removed from another ship and inserted into this one. *Let's hope they didn't break it. Speaking of breaking, what's that noise?*

Meehixiheem shifted her attention to the side window where Bluebig was now banging against it with a staff and brush attachment. Darksmall had reached the staircase and was probably running for help. Bluebig said a lot of things. He wasn't wearing his protective helmet, she realized. He was quite handsome but apparently as dumb as Jojacko. She ignored him. "Say in Kdackan, 'We must leave.'"

The waves registered her request, and sounds came out of the other pit. She didn't understand them, of course. Jojacko apparently didn't either. He shrugged. *Maybe he means 'I'm stupid.' Maybe he means 'I don't know how.'*

The banging on the window stopped. Bluebig threw the brush tool to the floor and yelled at her. He looked very upset. *Maybe he needs an electric shock.*

Jojacko leaned forward and spoke into the two-pit control. "Aidouns pi-ika tshai ni-iz."

The device managed to translate some of that: "I don't speak."

She had *heard* him speak, so that was wrong. He'd talked in her cell as well. She remembered they'd exchanged words for numbers and counted to five: u, dene, mwaant, sle, fuural. There was a translation, but it didn't sound like any of the numbers he'd said earlier.

"Ais pi-iki ng gluhsha." He repeated *his* numbers. For some reason, he had to flip his fingers away from his palm as he did so.

There was an ominous sound from below the ship, then Bluebig said something very short and loud. *I think he hit his head. What a species!*

"U, dene, mwaant, sle, fuural." The device's pronunciation was good although it sounded like someone from Rerrennerrer or Suemmeus, not Meehixiheem's hometown. She decided she could live with that.

She leaned over his shoulder. *It is so cramped in here!* She wished they'd built a pleasure craft as Daukhl had. In it, there was enough room to walk around or even mate. "We must leave."

The device translated obediently and even began to sound like Meehixiheem herself. When Jojacko responded, it created a facsimile of his voice.

"I receive that, but I not know how fly. I have no carriage even."

Bluebig was making even more noise. There was metal banging below them. Then he appeared in the side window, walking away from the ship with a large coil of rope over his shoulder. He played it out as he walked. He'd clearly tied it to something, and Meehixiheem guessed that was the landing gear.

Jojacko said something. She ignored it and waited for the translation. "What thing he does? Question that rope?"

"You have to learn to fly this, Jojacko. Only a Kdackan can. Press into one of those pits on the right and tell the computer to teach you. We also have to open the roof, but first I have to untie Bluebig's rope."

The translation took a while, but he seemed to understand. He reached for the three red pits on the right, but she grabbed his hand and made him open the hatch first.

The stairs descended, and so did she. She tried to be sneaky, but Bluebig was walking backward as he fed out the rope and noticed her instantly.

He dropped the coil and bolted toward her. She found the knot he'd made in the landing gear and began to loosen it. It wasn't a simple knot, and he'd made it very tight. He was a lot stronger than she was and before she had even gotten one bit free, he tackled her.

Fortunately for her, the Dolurulod were as flexible as Kdackans were strong. He got her around the pelvis and thought that would bring her down, but she twisted almost one-eighty degrees and hung on with her hands. She got another bit of rope free.

He tugged on her bare legs, but they only stretched out, leaving her torso in place. That startled him, and she used the opportunity to wrap her knees around his neck, then squeeze with her ankles interlocked. The rope was coming free, and she had him nearly choked out. With one hand on the landing gear, she used the other to smack him hard on the ear. He fell unconscious, and she let him hit the floor.

Then Darksmall came back with marksmen.

CHAPTER SEVEN

Come on, Jojacko, you can do this. It's only an alien spacecraft. You've flown a dozen of these. In games.

John pressed three fingers of his right hand into the red-rimmed pits on the console. They formed a triangle and were about one knuckle deep each. When he'd touched their bottoms, the console lit up brightly around them. "I... I need to fly the ship."

Whether it was the wavy blue circle or the red triangle that heard him, he couldn't tell, but apparently, there was an internal translation after which a voice came at him from both sides of the seat he occupied. It didn't sound like Meehix or him, but it wasn't a horrible screech either.

"**Purpose explode engine digit penetrate pits.**" Two of the many white lights on the console lit up, one to his left and one to his right.

My purpose is definitely NOT to explode the engine! John heard Meehix grunt with air forced out of her lungs. He twisted around to see her struggling with the guy that had been banging the broom on the window. He was a big fucker, but John knew he could take him. He paused. Apparently, Meehix could take him as well. *That's good to know.*

She knocked her opponent out and dropped him hard, then undid the rope. There was a sharp, loud *crack* as he hit the floor. It reverberated around the building. *Funny. I wouldn't have guessed he'd make so much noise.*

Now Meehix made a noise as well, not a bang, but a whimper. They'd shot her! John rushed to close the hatch, and it lifted her into the ship. Another shot ricocheted off the landing gear, then many fast, pounding footsteps.

John saw at least three men with rifles and scopes taking up positions beside and in front of the ship. Shit had just gotten deadly serious. There was no telling whether bullets could break through the windows, but it was clear the soldiers had his brain in their sights. They might very well be willing to kill him and sacrifice a couple of panes of glass to do so.

John decided to "explode engine" after all.

He pushed his index fingers into the white pits, squeezed his eyes shut, and waited to die. What happened instead was a brief roar, then a loud and steady hum. The craft floated up, and the soldiers stepped back.

In the moment he'd bought himself and Meehix, he turned to check on her. She was in her seat now and tying the wrap she'd used as a belt around her leg wound. There was a lot of blood. At least he thought it was blood. It was very dark. She cried freely but kept wrapping and said only, "Go."

Where he should go was a mystery. This wasn't a huge hangar but rather a one-story building better suited to cubicles than capsules. As a first step, it was probably best to keep the soldiers dodging.

He laid his hands on the control cushions he'd been feeling up before. There was something intuitive about them and, he realized, *fucking sensual.* They were warm and pliant, sensitive to each motion of his fingers. He thought of Hannah, not the pendant on his bare chest, but the girlfriend he'd spent almost his entire senior year fingering and fucking. He was too busy and scared to get an erection, but *Man, I'm gonna explode my engine as soon as I fucking can!*

He lifted his hands slightly. The ship did the same. He tilted his hands to the right, and the craft did too. It was pretty easy to scatter the soldiers now.

He chased them slowly, rotated, and never gave them time to set up a good shot. He would've given them the finger except that he needed all ten inside the control cushions. There was a perfect sphere of movement possible to him, and he used it with increasing precision. It was almost *fun.*

Meehix said something, and he waited for the translation. "Open ceiling the."

Could he do that? Could the ship do that? He hoped the answer was "yes" and that the roof actually *could* be opened. As carefully as he could, he investigated the building's corners. There *did* seem to be levers and gears in place, but how to activate them?

Meehix looked at them as well. "Push down."

That was a *lot* more precise than he'd moved before. Could the nose of the ship even press hard enough without tearing right off? At what point would the soldiers decide it was better to kill him than lose the craft? He moved them forward until the ship began to scrape on the lever. It was too close to the wall to get any purchase on it. "Shit."

"I no shit. Why you say this thing? What stupid you do ship with? You want break?"

"Huh?" The translator sounded more and more like Meehix herself, and it had settled into English, but its grammar was still so bad it came off like the First Lady. "How else can I open the roof?"

The translator worked at saying that in "Bluegirlese" and sounded more and more like John himself, which he found freaky. Even freakier was the retort of bullets hitting the wall beyond the front window.

"Set the ship down and come out with your hands up! Now!"

That was one of the soldiers. He meant business. His squad was kneeling on either side of him, and all of them aimed for John. He could practically feel the muzzles against his forehead. "Ship," he said toward the red triangle of controls, "what weapons do you have?"

John bought it some time to come up with the answer by lifting his hands into sight and looking compliant. *Look scared too.* That was easy for him.

"Missiles lasers bombs sonics."

"Jojacko?" Meehix sounded scared as well. "Not give me them. Please."

"Ship, use sonics, but don't kill."

"Target is?"

John drew a deep breath. "All the people outside Ship... but inside this building." He'd had a horrible thought: What if this ship could kill everybody on Earth? What kind of "bombs" did it possess?

"Sonics ready say when."

John swallowed hard. "When!"

Nothing happened.

"Say when sonics."

It's not up for wordplay, I guess. "Use the sonics now!"

There was a very low-pitched, almost sub-audible *boom*, like when someone with way too many speakers in his car stops at a red light and decides to liven up the neighborhood. One soldier collapsed. Another threw his weapon to the side and puked. The one that had been yelling at John clapped his ears shut with one hand and his shoulder but still held his rifle.

"Ship! Use sonics again now!"

The second blast knocked them all out, even the guy with the pistol who'd stayed near the staircase.

John set the spacecraft down midway between the levers and opened the hatch. He ran down the stairs in one direction. Meehix, he was glad to see, limped off in the other direction. They reached their respective levers at basically the same time and pulled. The roof began to rise on its hinges. Sunlight poured in and sounds of metal grinding poured out.

John jogged to the ship. Meehix also did. She reached the staircase, but he fell for some reason. He then saw the soldier holding his ankle and a dagger.

CHAPTER EIGHT

The dagger plunged, and John kicked. Instead of sinking into flesh, the blade hit concrete. It didn't sever his femoral artery, but it did cut along the outside of his right thigh.

John kicked again. If *he* was gonna bleed, the soldier should too. John only wished he were wearing his cleats. Nevertheless, he got the soldier's lips and nose gushing.

They struggled over the dagger, but it turned out John outweighed the USSF serviceman by a good forty pounds and was very used to scrums. He came away with the blade and got to his feet.

The soldier dove after him, but John sidestepped him easily and got one of the other soldier's rifles. That made the bleeding man hesitate, and John walked backward away from him. When the soldier decided to act anyway, John fired a warning shot that broke close enough into the floor. *Take that, mecha!*

He walked up the staircase warily, put the rifle down, and slid into the pilot's seat.

"We go now?" Meehix asked.

"We go now." John pushed his hands into the control cushions and lifted. The ship rose higher than it had been able to before and sunlight streamed in from every window. There were two or three more rifle shots. One hit the craft's underbelly, but the others missed.

It turned out "Ship" could really book. John veered away from Desert Development and put the self-storage building between them and the soldiers, then hovered. "Should I take Central Avenue or what? Where are we going?"

"Far."

Duh. John steered the ship up to the stop sign. It was actually about twenty feet below them, but he looked left and right for an opening in traffic. He *created* one as cars came to sudden stops at the ship's appearance.

He hung a left, wishing he knew where the turn signals were or if Ship even had some. "This used to be Route 66, you know, like in the song. Still is, I guess, but people just call it Central now."

There were signal lights at the intersection with Morningside. John lifted the ship above them but kept following the street. He hoped they could, like, take a tour of the city and set down somewhere, free to go back to their regular lives. *I think I'm in shock.*

He was also thirsty. They flew past a 7-Eleven, and it tempted him to land and get a Pepsi, but *maybe it's better to find a convenience store farther away from the secret USSF base-slash-prison, huh?* "Ship, do you have anything to drink?"

Meehix made an impatient noise from behind, a sort of huff and *click* of her teeth. "Ship. Not restaurant."

A tube stretched out from the back of John's seat and curved around to his mouth.

"**Water.**"

Shows how much you know! John slurped from the tube. The water wasn't particularly fresh or even cold, but it slaked his thirst. It sounded like Meehix was drinking from her seat's line as well.

He'd gone in for a second drink when he noticed the helicopter. It was much higher than they were and bore the logo of a local TV news station on the side facing them. This was the one with the really hot weather chick. She always wore something low-cut.

John raised the ship to their level, and they came in closer. Somebody was filming them, and the reporter in the passenger seat was talking into his headset's microphone. It looked a lot like the headset John wore on Twitch. *Wish I could broadcast right now. That'd be wicked good for my number of followers.*

He hoped the reporter wasn't that dick former Marine that had joined the station back in January or February, but, yeah, that was him. *He has those high-end aviator sunglasses. Does the traffic report like he's in Kabul fucking Afghanistan. Trey McSwirley or something like that.* John gave him a chuck of the chin and hoped the rumors weren't true that he was putting it to the weather girl.

"Hey! Wave to the reporter!" He watched as Meehix listened to the translation. She looked confused, but then she made a gesture at the window. It was a kind of undulation of both hands that he eventually realized was meant to represent waves hitting a beach.

He laughed and did the same with his hands. They were

still in the control cushions, so the entire ship followed suit. It bobbed up and down. Straight ahead was downtown Albuquerque. It was probably time to show Dick McSwirley what Ship could do.

John shoved his hands forward, and the spacecraft zoomed away from the helicopter. "You been to Albuquerque before?"

Meehix puzzled over his question. "Fifteen planet rotations."

"First visit, huh? Hey, why did they have you in that cell?"

"Alien. You hate alien ess."

"I don't," John objected. "I don't hate anybody." *'Cept maybe that McSwirley if he's laying pipe in that Ashley.*

"No talk about my body. My body beautiful. I am no-difference you hate it or like it. Why is your Dolurulod so bad?"

"Huh? Whatever. Hey, there's the Rio Grande. See it?"

Meehix peered outside and down. "River. I see it." She checked her gunshot wound and hissed.

"It's not huge, I admit, but it's pretty cool. Over there is West Park and the country club. Buncha privileged white guys. I'm white, but I sure ain't privileged."

"Well, I mean, I *do* have privileges if you compare me with my friend Gage. His whole family struggles. They work really hard, and people still call them lazy to their face. I don't fucking get that. Hey! I should call him and tell him what's happening if he isn't already watching on TV. Hope they didn't capture him or nothin'. Ship, hover here."

"Hover."

John withdrew his hands from the control cushions and

wondered whether they had the same smell Hannah used to. He sniffed his fingers, but there was no particular scent on any of them. He hoped Meehix hadn't seen him do that.

He twisted around to make sure she remained focused on her wound. He looked at his. It had stopped bleeding, but still it hurt like a motherfucker. He pulled his cellphone out of his shorts and took a picture of it. *Wicked.*

He took several more photos of the console, the views out the windows, one of himself making the Vulcan salute, then another of him cracking up about that, and finally, one of Meehix on the sly. He kinda hoped he'd caught a shot up her skirt—his t-shirt—then felt bad about that and was glad she was too dark down there to see anything. *Send.*

WTF? Who dis? Jojacko?

The same.

W U at?

Waaay above downtown. Want me to come by?

Joder! No lie?

0 lie. Headin ur way. C U in 5.

John stuffed the phone back in his pocket. "Wanna go meet my friend Gage?"

"Friend? Soldier?"

"No, no soldier. He's a college student. Good guy. You'll like him."

John retook control of the ship. The news copter had caught up, and another was coming in from the south. He zoomed away so fast he almost missed Amherst. He sat the ship down in the middle of it and wanted to honk, but the only option seemed to be another sonics attack.

Gage ran out as the Air Force arrived.

CHAPTER NINE

John opened the hatch and Gage climbed up the stairs.

"John? What in the actual fuck is this? Who's *that?* What's going on? Who's in those helicopters?"

"Call me Jojacko, man. I'm undercover."

"Like fuck you are."

"No shit? How'd I look?"

"Scared as a kitten, if you want the truth. Ship is da bomb though. Wait. It don't got bombs, does it?"

"Get off the stairs. I'm closing up."

"Where the fuck am I supposed to go?"

"Crowd in." John pressed the pit that controlled the hatch. "Maybe you can stand on the stairs when they're closed. Meehix, this is my friend, Gage."

"Gay-jaw?" She looked from one man to the other.

"Gay jaw? What? I ain't gay. Tell her, man."

"He's totally gay, Meehix. Good eye."

"Meehixiheem. Mee-hix-i-heem." She thrust her breasts forward and tapped them.

"That's just her introducing herself. Don't, like, actually feel her up or anything."

Gage lifted his hands defensively. "No means no. I got it."

Now there were two helicopters above them, and one had a loudspeaker going. "Disembark with your hands up, or we *will* fire on you!"

"Oh, shit! Gotta go, man. Hang on to something."

"What am I s'posed to...?"

John thrust his hands into the control cushions and lifted. The two helicopters got dangerously close, both to him and to each other.

"Land your craft NOW!"

John tried retreating down the street, but the copters weren't easy to shake. He knocked through the top branches of a tree and scared everybody on board including himself. Gage let out a yelp.

Meehix fastened her seatbelt with a metallic *click* and John spared a hand to do the same. "Hang on!" He reversed down Amherst fast, did a sudden flip that sent Gage hard onto the ship's roof, then sped off upside down at top speed. Once they'd escaped the helicopters, he turned the craft upright. Gage fell again with a bang.

"Ow! Fuck! I bit my tongue!"

"We need speed, man. Hang on as good as you can."

"Wait. I think there's a fold-down seat back here." There were sounds of scuffling along the floor, then the creak of metal and the compression of a seat made of foam or something. "There. I'm clicked in, man. Let 'er rip."

As long as John was pressing forward, the ship accelerated. He headed south away from the city at about three hundred feet up. He still had no idea where they should go. He decided Roswell was a logical destination. "Hey, Meehix, how do I tell it to fly somewhere specific?"

"Ship? Tell it."

John leaned in. "Ship, fly to Roswell, uh, New Mexico. Gage, is there another Roswell in the US?"

"Beats the shit outta me. Why you wanna go there?"

"She was arrested there. Actually, I don't know *where* they arrested her, but that storage facility, you were right, or Dayslip was right-"

"*Draylop*, man."

"Whatever. He was right. It *was* a storage facility, but not for comic collections or old *Playboys*. For aliens."

"You saw aliens there?"

"Just her. Only door I opened."

"Pretty lucky. Coulda been a Gorn."

"Gorn are ugly," Meehix added. "Slimy."

The two men looked. It was impossible to tell whether she was joking. "Anyway—" John began. Ship interrupted.

"Roswell where? No star is Roswell."

"Uh...what're the coordinates for Roswell, Gage?"

"I dunno. Go out I-40 East to Clines Corners, then Highway 285 South. You been there. I know you have."

"Yeah, but we don't wanna waste time following roads. Plus, people seem to freak out when they see this ship. We might cause accidents. We fly straight there over the desert, right?"

"Okay, okay," Gage was apparently checking his phone. "Thirty-three degrees, twenty-three minutes, fourteen seconds north by one hundred four degrees, thirty-one minutes, forty-one seconds west. That what you want?"

John repeated the location to the ship, and it banked hard to starboard. He raised the craft to what he figured was a proper altitude. Outside the windows, roads shrank away to thin lines, and scrub brush became tiny dots of green or brown flashing by. "Ship, when will we arrive?"

"Forty-six minutes after."

"After what?" Gage asked.

John found that his seat could swivel around if he pushed on the floor hard enough with his feet. "It has trouble with prepositions, I think."

"So, tell me all about the blue girl."

Her hair stood on end, and she made a sort of snarl, then slapped her chest again. "I am not blue girl. I am Meehixiheem. Gay-jaw tan boy."

"Sorry."

John told him all that had happened at the storage facility, and Gage apologized for chickening out. He'd left the building without trouble and gone home. "Man, I suck. I shoulda stayed with you and seen it through."

"Don't sweat it, bro. Turned out okay and now we got this sweet ship."

"So," Gage turned to the alien, "where you from?"

She waited while the translator added him to its matrix, then answered. "City Vevev on Dolurulod."

"That's the name of her language too," John asserted. He liked knowing more than his college-bound friend.

"No," Meehix exhaled with a quick and loud vibration of her lips, then swiveled her seat. "Dolurulod equal our planet. Dolurulod equal our language. Kdackan know zero things."

"How did you get here?" Gage couldn't help looking at her body now that she half-faced him.

In the shattered English that the translator could manage, Meehix told them both about Daukhl, Tseetsay, and Obro, how they'd partied together, then took a trip to Earth and crashed. Males had come and put her on this ship, then confined her where Jojacko had found her. "Daukhl ship bigger. Better ship. No stench."

John almost took offense at that. He thought he'd provided her with a pretty decent getaway vehicle. *Haven't crashed yet, which is more than you can say for your bigger, better fuck buddy Daukh.*

Meehix took Gage's cellphone from him and brought up YouTube. She very quickly found the short video she'd posted earlier. It had nineteen views already.

"You, like, an influencer?" Gage asked.

She ignored him and scrolled through the comments. "No Dolurulod see? We much watch Kdack 3a."

"Sorry you're not gettin' the likes you expected." John wondered whether an alien could be basically a very shallow person.

Meehix replayed the video after commanding the translator. When they next listened, it dubbed her in English. "Please help. We crashed. Now Kdackans prison me. I try escape. Please find. Others died? Prisoned? I am Meehixiheem, Vevev. My sire important rich. Pay."

She looked distraught. There were crinkles where her eyebrows should be. *Not shallow. Worried and scared.* "We'll get you home, won't we, Gay-jaw?"

"Really don't call me that, man, but, yeah, we'll get you home." He gave her a thumbs-up, which she clearly didn't understand. "So, pay? How much? You Dolurulodans use Bitcoin?"

"Jeez, guy, why you gotta focus on that?"

"Community college costs, Jojacko. *La familia Gonzalez* ain't exactly rollin' in dough."

"Hey, speakin' of our folks, think we should call them?" John pulled out his phone again. "Maybe warn them we might not be home, uh, tonight."

They both made calls. Gage spoke Spanish with his mom. She sounded panicked at the way he'd run out of the house. Cops were outside, plus Air Force guys. John's mom still hadn't picked up when they felt the explosion of the first incoming missile.

CHAPTER TEN

"Fuck fuck fuck fuck FUCK!" John's phone tumbled out of his hand. Meehix and Gage both screamed. John swiveled back around to face the front window and slammed his hands into the control cushions. "Ship! What was that?"

"One that was missile."

"One?" John couldn't see anything but sky and desert.

"Two number missile come now."

"Evade! Evade missile!" He moaned as the whole craft tilted up and his phone clattered to the back. Gage said "ouch" when it hit him, and the desert started to fall away below. They passed through a stray cloud that turned bright orange with another detonation. John pushed for more acceleration and began to black out.

"Three missile. Missile three number."

"Ship," John said as loudly as he could manage, what with the passing out and *gee*'s they were pulling, "put us into orbit."

By the time the sky turned black, everything had gone black for John.

When he came to a minute—*five minutes? Ten?*—later, he could see most of the California coast, both Alta and Baja. It was a clear and sunny day across most of the western United States. It was very, *very* bright inside the spacecraft. John wondered how much radiation this exposed them to. Was this spaceship, like, actually prepared for space? "Ship, how high are we?"

"Hi."

"I mean, what is our altitude?"

"Four thousand nine klau units."

"Uh, how many miles is that? Convert klau units into miles."

"I can see for miles and miles and miles and miles and miles."

This time it wasn't Ship's voice but the actual song and music. John wondered why this translator-slash-computer wasn't more used to English if the USSF used it. "Who sang that?"

"Who."

"Yes. Who?"

"Who sang that."

This ship is clearly *not ready for space. It's spacey.*

"John? Are we...are we in space? My head hurts, and I think I'm gonna hurl. Is this *your* phone? It's cracked, man. Hey! Look at your girl! Her arms are floatin'. *My* arms are floatin'! Look!"

John swiveled again. He realized he was weightless as well, but his arms didn't start floating until he'd taken them out of the anchor of the control cushions. "Cool."

"Look at her hair. Hah! It's all, like, every which way. Is mine like that?" Gage felt around his head, then got his camera ready and started taking selfies. He also aimed his camera out the port and starboard windows. "I gotta send these to my folks. They're gonna *cagar* like Toñito, man!"

"I'm tryin' to figure out how many miles up we are, but the computer is broke or something."

"Miles? Get with the program, Jojacko. Use kilometers, man, like the rest of the fucking world."

Over his shoulder, John addressed the ship. "Uh, Ship, calculate our altitude in kilometers."

There was a pause while the work went on. **"Two thousand sixty-eight kilometer units."**

"Sounds like orbit to me." Gage pointed the camera at John. "Flex, man. Show the world your guns in spaaace!"

John complied and smiled. It was pretty damn awesome what they were doing. He also had to worry about the radiation though. *I ain't even wearin' a shirt. My nips are gonna fry.*

"Your girl okay? She's lookin' zoned out."

"I travel much. Space unimpress." She blinked and took in the view with no discernible expression.

Gage spun John's phone through the air. John caught it and was about to redial his mom when he thought of something.

"Ship, can you transmit cell phone signals to Earth from here?"

"Transmit many signals. What is cell?"

"Uh, a communications device. Uses frequencies measured in hertz."

"Hurts?"

John floundered, unsure how to explain the difference between the similar-sounding words.

"Try it, man," Gage broke in. "Easiest way to find out."

John shrugged and redialed his mom while looking at the West Coast move east. Thankfully, the phone still worked despite its cracked screen. More surprising, the call connected. *Ship must've detected the frequencies and boosted them somehow. Not gonna ask questions.* "Mom?"

"Honey, I'm on break. I can't talk long. You didn't go back to bed, did you? You're getting your days and nights all mixed up."

"Mom, look where *I* am." John took a photo of himself and the view of the Pacific Ocean. "See it?"

"Oh, is that your TV screen? Is that supposed to be Vulcan or something? I can't keep up with all the games you play."

"No, Mom. It's real. I'm in orbit!"

"Okay, honey, I gotta go back to work. Hiram is all over us these days not to, you know, extend our break times. Will you thaw them steaks I bought?"

"I, uh, won't be home for supper. Me and Gage are up to somethin'. WAY up to somethin'."

"Hi, Mrs. Jacobs!"

"Gotta go, sweetheart. Stay outta trouble. Your dad, you know, he gets…well, we'll talk when I get home."

John ended the call and secured the phone in his pocket. He was both chilled and hot where the sun was hitting him. "Meehix?"

She crossed her legs like a yoga master and breathed deeply. "Meehixiheem. You learn that."

"Meehixiheem, uh, radiation?" John pointed toward the sun.

She looked at it as well, a whole lot longer than John could have endured. "Ask ship."

"Ship, are we, like, protected against radiation up here?"

"Radiation lethal magnet meadow."

"Can you protect us from radiation lethal? Ship, can you create a magnetic field?"

There was more internal processing. **"Yes."**

"Well, do that." John hoped the windows would dim as well. There was a new hum in the floor and sides of the craft, but otherwise, it was impossible to know whether something had happened. "Meehixiheem, will that work?"

She jutted her jaw forward, then pulled it back. John assumed that was her people's version of a shrug because she said nothing else. "How long you guys wanna stay up here?"

"Aw, man, can we go to the moon? I'd fuckin' *love* to, like, write my name in moon dust."

"I dunno, Gage. Maybe we'd better take things slow, okay? I don't even know how far the moon is. It's, like, two hundred thousand miles away, isn't it? I at least wanna go home and grab a shirt, maybe some pants."

"Be prepared, huh? Good Boy Scout you are."

John gave him a three-fingered salute. "Where all have you been, Meehixiheem? This is your first trip to Earth, right?"

"Dolurulod," she pressed her index finger to the nearer of her two thumbs, "Pnellu IV, Pnellu VI, Pnellu IV better. Go there. Tozezzezot, Wrn, Uklad III, Nubaat, Rubaat, Swissa-Vyn, other. My sire take me Laulaulau young. I remember zero thing Laulaulau." She jutted out her jaw again.

John had not been able to keep count. She talked quickly, and the *clicking* of her fingers together had distracted him. Still, it was impressive. He was amazed there were all those worlds worth visiting. "Wow. Uh, why did you come to Earth?"

"Rth?"

"What'd you call it? Kdack? Why come here?"

Again the jaw. "Pretty. Water. We watch Kdackan plural. Air thing tornado. YouTube. Jaaazz. Billie Holliday."

"Who's he?" Gage asked.

John shrugged. "I think he's in that one band, Running Toilets, or something. So, you like our planet?"

Meehix pondered. "Primitive. Hostile. Fun. Easy." She flipped her hands palm up, palm down. "Dolurulod better interest. We have beauty nature, beauty people, beauty music. Come there."

"Ship, can we go to Dolurulod?"

"Star planet yes."

"How long to get there?"

"Temporal units nine thousand nine hundred near number."

"Uh," Gage spoke up, "however long that is in hours and days, sounds like we'd better get snacks."

CHAPTER ELEVEN

"You got money on ya?" John asked.

Gage started to check his wallet, but he got it out of his shorts too fast, and it spun away from him in the air. Meehix caught it, stared at it, then began exploring it.

She pulled out Gage's license to drive and compared his photo to his face. "Gay-jaw." She tossed it away indifferently. She showed even less interest in his community college ID, his Social Security card, and his newly acquired voter identification. She did ponder the twenty-one dollars he had and pronounced that neither Andrew Jackson nor George Washington was Gay-jaw.

She let go of his wallet entirely once she had found the rather tattered condom package he carried with him at all times. Gage objected when she tore the foil open and pulled out the latex contraceptive, but she ignored him, stuck two of her fingers in the tip, and rolled it down over them. "Penis?"

Gage sort of blushed and nodded. It didn't help that she started convulsing her shoulders back and forth and squeezed her eyes shut in what they realized was Doluru-lodan laughter. Gage unbuckled himself and set about gathering up his belongings as they migrated lazily around the cabin. "Yeah, well, I'm sure blue men are *huge*, huh?"

Meehix snorted, then tried fitting her whole hand inside the condom. It burst, and she convulsed even harder. She gave off a sort of humming and wheezing sound at the same time.

"I've seen it," John defended him. "It's an absolute *terror* of a cock." He fist-bumped his buddy.

Gage thanked him without complete trust in his sincerity, then sat again. "You wanna go back to Albuquerque then? Hit up that 7-Eleven?"

"Nah." John looked out the window. "I think we should stay away from there for a while until things cool down with the USSF. How 'bout Hawaii? Ever been?"

"Nope. You?"

"Never. I'd love to see it though. Wish I had a surfboard. What'll we do with Meehix...iheem?"

"I go Hawaii. Why I do not go? I go fourteen star-planets. I go Hawaii. How far?"

"Well," John pointed toward the Pacific, "it's coming up now."

They spent a little while taking more photos and teaching Ship how to tell the time in seconds, minutes, hours, days, et cetera. It turned out that Ship had a camera it could use to look at Gage's cellphone and it learned quickly. They decided they would land in Puu Ualakaa State Park and hike into Honolulu.

"Only two problems." John made a "V" with his index and middle fingers. "How do we hide Ship—"

"Hey, let's call her Shippewa!" Gage interrupted.

"—Shippewa, and, number two, how do we disguise Meehixiheem?"

"Why disguise? I am number one beauty on Kdack. I am zero Jaukh."

"You are beautiful, definitely, but Kdackans don't know people live on other star-planets. They would stare and maybe be afraid."

Meehixiheem cocked her head and counted on her fingers. "You stupid. Thirty-six people star-planetsss. All-star swirl is..." She stretched her legs as far apart as they would go. That afforded both young men an unobstructed view of something alien but spellbinding. Gage's tongue lolled out. John coughed.

"Um, *enormous?*" he suggested.

"Een-or-muss." Meehix tried the word out in English. "Een-or-muss. Yes."

"A hundred thousand light-years across," Gage added.

"How'd you know that, man?"

"I actually *learn* from my games, Jojacko. I don't just *shoot* things."

"Hey, Shippewa, how many Klau units is this galaxy in length?"

The ship's tri-camera swirled to focus on John's face. **"Four million."**

"Een-or-muss." Meehix smiled with her lower lip on top of the upper.

"Let's focus on Honolulu, bro. I'm cravin' Pringles."

"Okay, okay. Shippewa, can you become, like, invisible?"

"No."

"Can you disguise yourself?"

"Yes."

Gage gave the tri-camera two thumbs up. "Tell it to look like the Tardis, man."

"Aw, *chavo*, be serious. I think we oughta try for, like, foliage or whatever. Shippewa, can you disguise yourself as plant life?"

"Yes."

They pulled up a map of Honolulu and eventually settled on an area near the Hawaii Nature Center. It looked decently dense, and they gave Shippewa the coordinates. "Get us there as fast as you can."

That turned out to be a harrowing suggestion. Before they were ready, Shippewa plunged into the atmosphere. The whole cabin heated up and the front end of the spacecraft almost glowed.

"Oh shit!" John braced himself on the armrest of the pilot's seat. "Shippewa! Don't let us burn up!"

The ship tilted around so that different parts of it bore the brunt of contact with the atmosphere. When they were actually upside down, they landed.

John had to tell Shippewa to turn over, and this time even Meehix looked ready to puke. He wondered what her vomit would resemble, then had to rush to open the hatch so he could throw up outside. *I don't even have a shirt to wipe my mouth on.* He chose the large leaf of an innocuous-looking fern or something and cleaned himself up.

The others joined him. Gage was unsteady and almost tumbled down the hill they were on. Meehix strode down the stairs confidently and breathed deeply. Right into John's face, she said, "You pilot stupid."

"You're welcome," John replied. "If you don't like it, *you* can pilot from now on. Oh, that's right. You got them two thumbs, and Shippewa won't respond to you."

She walked off to explore. John and Gage clapped each other on the backs. "Am I wrong or is she kinda ungrateful?" Gage asked.

"You're not wrong, man. I'd say I shoulda left her in her cell, but, yeah, that wasn't cool of the USSF. Why arrest her? She didn't do anything wrong."

"You sure about that?" Gage watched her walk away. "Maybe they arrested her 'cause she killed somebody. Maybe it wasn't only that she came here, like, illegally."

John looked at her himself. She plucked flowers and smelled them, scooped up a caterpillar, and chewed it. He had only her word that she'd crashed here with other drunken partiers.

Maybe she was an advanced guard of an invasion or something. For all he knew, her "important rich" sire was a tyrant who planned to subjugate Earth. *This is like Spydome: The Uprising. I only got to level three before someone killed my agent, all 'cause he...I chose to romance the three-titted chick.* "We'll keep an eye on her, aight?"

Gage nodded. "How're we gonna get back in if you close this hatch?"

"I touched it before, and it opened. It should do the same when we come back."

"Won't it do the same for any human?"

"I dunno. Test it out." John watched as Gage lifted the staircase. It was self-powered once he'd laid his hands on its underside. With a *whoomp*, it shut entirely, then the whole craft shimmered and looked like another stretch of plants and flowers around it.

They tromped off and realized they'd lost sight of Meehix. "Fuck! Where'd she go?"

Eventually, they found her in a particularly off-the-beaten-path area where she had squatted. She swatted at both of them and said something unintelligible. Her intention was clear, however. She was defecating and wanted privacy.

Both men hurried away. They found privacy themselves, unzipped, and let loose with streams that John thought were part urine, but mostly adrenaline. He eyed Gage and joked, "*Terror* of a cock."

Somebody screamed downhill.

CHAPTER TWELVE

John and Gage zipped up and hurried toward the sound. About fifty feet away, Meehix stood facing a mother and daughter. The mother had her hand clamped over the girl's mouth. Apparently she'd been the one to scream.

"Hi!" John waved cheerily. "How are you two? Great day, huh?'

The little girl pointed at Meehix and looked up at her mom, then peeled the hand away from her mouth. "What's wrong with her?"

"Oh, uh, nothing's wrong with her." John gave Meehix a sideways hug. "She's just a little different. You know, punk."

The mother seemed to understand. She nodded vaguely. "Sorry. Lisa was taken by surprise when she came out of the woods there. She's not normally like this."

"No problem." John waved, dismissing the incident. "Happens all the time, doesn't it, honey?"

Meehix responded to his squeeze and nod by mimicking the last gesture. "Een-or-muss."

John was glad to see Meehix had the good sense to keep her hands behind her back.

"Is that a…a tattoo?" the mother asked.

"Uh, some of it, yeah, but she's also…uh," he consulted his phone for 'blue people' and came back with a Kentucky clan that suffered from methemoglobinemia, "See? She's from Kentucky, and it's just a genetic thing." He stepped forward and shared his phone screen with the two onlookers.

The daughter was very curious. She examined the photos, then turned and buried her face in her mother's side.

"Are you wearing contacts?" the mother asked Meehix directly, "because it looks like, you know, your pupils are…" She made a horizontal movement with her hands.

"Yeah," John answered her, "contacts. Two, right, honey?" He held up two fingers.

"Tu-u." Meehix still didn't show her hands. "Een-or-muss."

"Well, we should be going," the mother said. She gave her daughter a reassuring hug. "I'm sorry. She's at that age where she doesn't have any filter. You two don't have any kids, do you?"

"Oh, haha, no. No kids."

"That's probably, well, you know. None of my business. Have a good day. It's a beautiful one. Bye."

They wandered off. John waved goodbye, then dropped the act and said to Meehix, "We gotta get you some clothes."

"And sunglasses," Gage added.

"Yeah. Maybe a hat too."

"Think we got enough money for all that?"

"We'll buy cheap. Okay, Meehixiheem?"

She'd been listening closely, but without Shippewa's translation service, she clearly didn't understand anything beyond her name. "*Sel-uutnakis mor-e vau em?*"

John took hold of Gage's shorts by one belt loop and tugged. "Shorts." Then he pretended they reached to his ankles and pointed at her. "Pants."

"Puh-hantsss."

"Shoes."

"Shuuza."

"Hat." John mimicked donning and doffing a bowler.

This puzzled Meehix. She took hold of her hair and tugged it. "Hae-aet."

"Well, we'll get it and show you."

Under his breath, Gage said, "We should get her a thong or something too, man. I mean, you know, she is *fiiine* down there, but she can't be showin' Heaven's Gate to just anybody."

John elbowed his arm. "She won't. She'll have pants on. Don't be crude, dude."

"Jus' sayin'. We leave her here while we go get shit or take her with us?"

John consulted his phone. "Look. There's a clothing store just, like, a mile away on South King Street."

"I dunno, bro. I think, if we take her with us, we're askin' for more screamin'."

"Maybe you're right, but how we gonna tell her?"

"Just, like, tell her. Make her sit down or put her back on the ship."

John tried exactly that for a couple of minutes, but

Meehix was as stubborn as she was alien. John didn't know whether that was a Dolurulodan characteristic or only hers. Maybe growing up with an "important rich" sire had made her a spoiled rotten brat.

In either case, she wouldn't stay put and sometimes led the way. It was all they could do, once they'd reached the nearest road, to tug her in the direction of the store. She stopped and examined anything that interested her. She did shy away from a tiny dog that ran up, even though it was sweet-natured and accepted pats from both John and Gage. Meehix half-climbed a tree to escape it and thereby showed off "Heaven's Gate" again.

They cut time off their walk by sprinting through some people's yards and in about thirty minutes total, came to the store they'd been seeking. John was very apprehensive about bringing her inside, but Meehix was undaunted. She stepped in front of the door, it slid apart automatically, and she strode in. *She's clearly a pampered princess on her world. God fucking help us.*

There weren't many people there, but those who saw her did double-takes. John and Gage made the best of it by smiling, waving, and acting natural while Meehix perused the offerings. However alien Earth might be for her, shopping was obviously something she'd done a lot of.

She slid dresses along the racks they hung on, held some up to her, draped others on John or Gage's shoulders, then moved on to hats and shoes. The young men tried to entice her toward clothing that covered up the maximum amount of skin, but Meehix favored sundresses that left her shoulders and arms bare.

"Ya gotta admit," Gage offered, "she has good taste."

John agreed. She'd picked out a mid-calf sundress that fit her figure *very nicely*. It left her skin uncovered in many places, but it was so nearly the same color that it gave the illusion of being almost Victorian in its modesty.

To these, she added a floppy hat, sandals, and under duress from the human males, a pair of dark spider-web style gloves. They were difficult for her to put on since her index finger ran parallel to her thumb, but she managed. Not without complaining, however. *"Keke ju* stupid *nalho!"*

They brought the apparel to the checkout counter and threw in a pair of sunglasses from a whirling display case. Meehix rejected them, however, and picked her pair with a scowl at the men.

"$52.98, please."

That was a lot more than John had on him, but Gage came to the rescue with his debit card. "You gonna owe me, bro. And sis." He showed his ID as well. They got everything bagged up and pulled Meehix away from another display table of purses.

Once they got outside, they found the most secluded spot they could between a Dumpster and the concrete block wall that surrounded it on three sides. John and Gage turned their backs to Meehix and gave her additional privacy. She tossed John's Zia sun t-shirt over his shoulder and got dressed, then pushed between them and spun like a model. She smiled "een-or-muss" as they clapped and made a weird sort of "fuck me" motion with her hands in front of her belly.

"Jesus, John, are we gonna, like, lay her at some point?"

"Let's just 'lei' her instead, all right, bro?" John mimicked putting wreaths of flowers around his neck.

"Good idea. I wonder where we can get those in Hawaii." Gage stuck his tongue in his cheek. Using John's phone, they all set off toward the ocean.

Well behind them, but also in motion, USSF Lieutenant Brian Kekoa whispered into his cellphone, "Subjects are proceeding *makai* down Makahiki Way."

"Follow but do not approach, Lieutenant. We will intercept them on the beach."

CHAPTER THIRTEEN

The three of them, almost arm-in-arm, walked jauntily to the Ala Wai Community Park, situated on the Ala Wai Canal. They tried to keep their distance from other people, but even when pretty close up, Meehix didn't garner as much staring as she had before. John had put his t-shirt on, but he took it off again and stuffed one end of it in his shorts at the small of his back in hopes of distracting onlookers.

He knew he looked good: tall, very muscular, thick blonde hair that could almost bear a ponytail. When he put his hands on top of his head, the view helped keep the alien girl unnoticed. Gage took off his shirt and mimicked John. He was shorter and much thinner, but he had a treasure trail and a lot more swagger when he wanted it. He laughed at John and himself.

"Struttin' in Hawaaaii," he drawled. "Checkin' out the hula girls."

"Hula?" Meehix repeated. Gage did a short, inauthentic dance full of wavy arms and swaying hips. He had sweet moves, even if he usually reserved them for *quinceañeras*. Meehix mimicked him gracefully and smiled. She managed to look both alien and native at the same time.

John wished they had a language in common. He knew nothing of hers beyond the numbers one through five, and she seemed fixated on using "een-or-muss" in every situation. He had a flash of inspiration and asked Google what the Hawaiian word for water was. It turned out to be *wai*.

He crouched at the edge of the canal and scooped some into his palm, then held it out for the other two. "*Wai*." They repeated the word. He threw his scoop back into the canal and repeated it. Meehix did the same with great delight, then looked at him.

Next up was tree: *kumulāʻau*. They each touched and named the ones around them. Then in quick succession came path "*ala ala*," light "*kukui*," shadow "*malu*," fence "*pā*," followed by shorts "*hikō*," pants "*ʻōpua*," dress "*ʻaʻahu*," hat "*pāpale*," sunglasses "*nā pōkole*," and finally cell phone "*kelepono paʻa lima*."

Using a guy standing about fifty feet from them where the path bent away from the canal, John learned and taught "*kāne*," man. Meehix took that word, pointed toward the guy in the blue, black, and white shirt, then touched both John and Gage on the chest.

"*Kāne*." She touched herself and waited for John to use his cell phone.

"*Wahine*," he supplied. "Meehixiheem *he wahine ia*. Jojacko *a me* Gay-jaw *nā kāne*."

"Still not funny, *kāne*. Hey, where did *o ke kanaka* go?" Gage pointed down the path.

John consulted Google. "*Aia i hea ke kanaka?*" He made a

dramatic show of looking for Mr. Blue Black White. Meehix caught on, but after looking, she only jutted her jaw out and back.

"*A'ole maopopo ia'u,*" she learned to say.

John jutted his jaw out and back, then translated that into a human shrug. *I don't know either.* He then made a face of great fear and set off running. "*Holo!*"

Meehix and Gage ran along with him, yelling "Holo, holo, holo!" until they had reached a *pā* where construction blocked the *ala ala*. A sign told them to detour over to Hihiwai Street. John read the name out loud and taught Meehix what sound each letter represented. He'd had some training in deciphering alien languages during his games and was proud to use that skill in real life now.

They then found the street in question and were surprised to see Mr. Blue Black White on the other sidewalk. He was talking into a cell phone and watching them while pretending not to.

"O ke kanaka!" Meehix pointed excitedly. She learned blue "*polū*," black "*ele'ele,*" and white "*ke'oke'o,*" then shouted them across the street. The man immediately hung up and hurried in the opposite direction.

"Weird," John said with an exaggerated expression, "*Aniani.*" It struck him where he'd seen that combination before, and he hurried to tell Meehix and Gage who he thought the man might be working for. He brought up an image of the storage facility in Albuquerque, then said, "Kāne polū, ele'ele, ke'oke'o."

"Aniani," Meehix agreed. She looked back toward where the man had gone. John wanted to *holo* away, but Meehix instead set off fast in the man's direction.

"Wow," Gage huffed as the men struggled to keep up, "when she wants to *holo* she can really book, huh?"

"Yeah. You've seen how fucking flexible she is. I guess she can use that for fighting *and* speeding along. Come on!"

They redoubled their efforts and began to catch up with her. In one hand she held up the bottom of her dress. In the other, she kept her hat on her head. She saw her prey running a half-block away. "O ke kanaka!"

The man had to be young and fit, but he wasn't double-jointed. In short order, Meehix had jumped *high* and come down on his back *hard*. That knocked him face-first to the sidewalk.

He fought back, but she dodged and swatted, dodged and swatted. He managed to get one good punch in on her jaw. She reeled with the blow, but right after that, John was on top of him, iron thighs on either side of his head and one big fist ready to deliver enough force to knock some teeth down his throat. "You're USSF, aren't you, motherfucker?"

Gage sat heavily on the man's knees, Meehix straddled his hips, and John bounced on his chest until the man gasped, "Christ! Yes! Let me the fuck up!"

"How'd you know we were here?"

"Ow! Fuck, man! You stole a multibillion-dollar alien spaceship, and you think we wouldn't be able to *trace* it? You are in such shit!"

"Meehixiheem, 'ōpua kelepono pa'a lima."

She dug around, found it in one of the man's pockets, and handed it over.

"We'll be takin' this," John told the guy. "I don't wanna

knock you out, man, but whoever you were talking to, they're tryin' to catch us, right?"

"They're at the beach, man. They're waiting for you there."

"Why'd you give 'em up so easy?"

"Fuck, man, you think I ever get to go up in one of their ships? I never even get to *see* one. *Or* aliens. Any they catch, they lock up.

"They confiscate ships, whatever technology they get, and they adapt it for humans, but never me, man! I'm just a fucking grunt. This is the biggest mission I've ever had with them and I been at this for ten fucking years! You're hurting my chest, man."

John felt sorry for the guy and lifted his ass, but now they had to hightail it back to Shippewa, find whatever tracer was on board, and get the hell outta Dodge. "Whadda we fuckin' do with him, Gage?"

"Gag him and throw him in a Dumpster."

"Meehixiheem? O ke kanaka?" He shrugged and tried to will her to understand his dilemma.

She mimicked an electric prod to the man's belly. "Zzzzz."

Without more debate or warning, John lifted the man's head and knocked it against the sidewalk once. It maybe didn't render him unconscious, but it certainly dazed him well. He got up, had Gage help him carry the guy behind some shrubs, and made him as comfortable as possible.

Then they ran.

CHAPTER FOURTEEN

They retraced their steps back into the Puu Ualakaa State Park. John began to shake off the illusion he'd had about all this being just a lark. He'd broken into a USSF facility, helped a prisoner escape, stolen government property, fled the authorities, harbored a fugitive, and now assaulted an agent of the military. *Actually, a* second *agent.*

Gage looked scared. He kept meeting John's eyes as they ran, maybe looking for guidance. He and John had always been more or less on equal footing as friends, but now John felt like a leader. It was *his* responsibility to safeguard both his best bro *and* the alien princess he'd sprung from prison. What that would mean, he didn't know.

It was unclear how precisely the USSF could trace their spaceship. They'd fired on it back in New Mexico, probably had seen that it escaped into orbit, and knew that it had landed in Honolulu. They presumably knew who John and Gage were. Maybe they'd already taken both their families into custody.

John hated the idea that the Gonzalezes were facing

trouble. They were such decent people. Maybe their status as citizens was now being looked into closely. The government might detect that John had hacked the system to establish all the Gonzalez family as bona fide Americans.

What agents might be doing to his mom and dad was likewise terrifying. They couldn't deport them, but interrogation seemed certain. His poor mother wouldn't have any idea what this was about. If agents nabbed her at work, she'd swear up and down that John was at home or with his Mexican friend playing some computer game. John's dad was more belligerent and didn't trust the government to fix their street, let alone investigate his son.

John wiped his face as they ran. Part of that was sweat, and part was tears. He was only eighteen and earlier this morning had never contemplated being on the lam from any authorities outside mecha police in his fave game.

He stopped Gage and Meehix, then pushed them into a clump of trees. All their jauntiness was gone, and they didn't question him as he laid a finger over his lips. They understood the need for stealth now.

Up ahead was an overlook where people watched the sunsets of Hawaii, but right now it hosted two men and one woman in blue, black, and white shirts. Each wore sunglasses, but they were hours away from twilight.

John signaled the others to follow him through what cover they had. They circled behind the overlook, keeping low and listening for any sounds of trouble. The three agents talked into their cellphones in short bursts. If they were trying to pinpoint the ship, they hadn't succeeded yet.

John got the others to move even more slowly and carefully. He had a good idea of where Shippewa was. He hoped nobody from the USSF realized she could disguise herself.

There was no telling how long the Space Force had possession of the alien craft. They'd been able to install human devices on the ship's underbelly and had transported Meehix away from her crash site in it, but the translator matrix wasn't yet fluent in English, which might mean nobody had trained it in the language. Maybe they didn't even realize such a function was possible.

Pilots had logically communicated with their control towers—if that's what they had—in English. They'd only used English with each other too.

Keeping the ship in a fake Desert Developments building next to their prison was like cop cars parked in a lot next to the police station, except that cop cars were public knowledge. They had markings. Shippewa was *hidden* but readily available when needed.

Probably she was only launched at night and at high speeds, sent out on a mission, then rush-landed back under the movable roof. *Nah, they have to know she can disguise herself. Even at night, people would notice a spaceship lifting off from Central Avenue.*

Knowing she could disguise herself didn't necessarily mean they could *detect* her in disguise. That gave John and his group a chance. They snuck past a parking lot, then veered left. They came within sight of a trail John knew they hadn't used before, so Shippewa was to the right of that. He led the others that way. *On the side of a hill, below this trail, well camouflaged as another clump of bushes and flowers.*

Two more agents suddenly appeared on the trail. They

were also in blue, black, and white, but instead of cell-phones, they carried iPads and listened to them through earbuds. The man aimed his to his right, the female aimed hers to her left.

John lay flat on the ground as they passed. Meehix and Gage did the same. John heard Gage starting to wheeze. He reached back, took his buddy's hand, and squeezed it with reassurance.

They crawled forward and slinked farther off the trail down the hill. John hoped they were getting closer, but this wasn't the angle from which he'd last seen Shippewa. It would be hard to recognize her surroundings. Only when he smacked his head on something that looked like a leaf but felt like metal did he realize they had reached their destination.

"Careful," he whispered to the others. Maybe Meehix didn't know the word, but she got the idea.

John felt along the short port wing of the ship, getting a good sense of where it was. There was free space between the hill and the hull. He bellied down until he figured he was underneath Shippewa and stood very slowly with his palms stretched above him. He made contact and felt a wave of relief, then helped Meehix and Gage join him.

Equally carefully, he found the outlines of the staircase and gave it a slight push. It released and descended. Meehix and Gage scurried up it into safety, but another agent suddenly rushed John. This one was much bigger than the guy the three of them had tackled in the city.

He knocked John down against the staircase, giving him at least the blow to the head John had given Mr. I'm-Just-a-Grunt. There was blood and a sudden departure of air from his lungs, but this was still hardly the worst tackle he'd suffered in rugby. John gave the guy an elbow to the jaw, another one, and a really unmanly knee to the groin.

That did the agent no good, but he hadn't given up. He punched his elbow into John's belly and slammed his fist down on John's sternum. John returned that with a hard clap to both the man's ears.

His sunglasses flew off, and John saw fury and determination in his opponent's eyes. He *hated* John. That was something the younger man had never dealt with on the rugby paddock. It made him feel weak and in the wrong.

"Over here!" the man shouted. John couldn't be sure, but he imagined he heard rustling in the undergrowth, other shouts, and footfalls. He had to end this fight *right fucking now!*

Since he was already bleeding, he didn't care how his head would suffer from the smash it gave the agent's upper lip, philtrum, and nose, but the man reeled backward from the blow. John capitalized on that by bringing both feet up to the man's chest and throwing him away with all the power his legs could muster.

"Stop!" somebody shouted.

John didn't stop.

CHAPTER FIFTEEN

John hurried to the stair control pit and closed it. He could barely see it for all the tears he'd started welling up with, but if he and Gage could open the hatch, it was likely any other human could too, especially USSF personnel. His jaw trembled, and he let out a sob he didn't mean to.

"You okay, Jojacko? You're bleedin', bro."

"I know, yeah. We gotta get outta here though. It's just, I been in dust-ups before, like, tempers flare in a game or whatever, but that guy, I think he wanted to *kill* me, ya know?" John cried harder.

"You saved us all, man. Love ya. Sorry I got you into all this. Stupid me, huh?"

John sat down. "You didn't force me into anything. I *wanted* the adventure. It got bigger than either of us expected. Strap in."

The translator matrix told Meehix what to do as well, and John addressed the ship. He was shaking with shock now. "Shippewa, are you awake?"

"Function ship."

"Good. We're lifting off." John laid his hands into the controls. There was no time to teach Shippewa the coordinates of a destination. He'd have to wing it, but he had an idea already: someplace the US government couldn't go, at least not easily or officially.

The spacecraft got airborne, brushing aside small branches, leaves, and a few rocks. John realized they were probably still disguised that way. "Shippewa, disguise yourself as a cloud. Can you do that?"

"Cloud cover."

Sure. That'll do.

Below and around them, Hawaii shrank until it became a streak of brown and green in a vastness of *wai uliuli.*

"I hope we get to come back someday," Gage said.

"Me too."

"Hawaii een-or-muss beautiful," Meehix added.

They floated up, apparently alone and undetected. John pushed the ship higher until he could see Japan. Beyond it were North and South Korea. Below and to its left was China. *Definitely don't want China. They got jets, and they wouldn't be friendly.*

"Ever heard of Ulaanbaatar?" he asked the others.

"That's Mongolia, right?"

"Outer fuckin' Mongolia, yup. That's where we're heading.

"Why?" Meehix asked. "We go Dolurulod!"

"Yes, and we probably *will.* I know you wanna go home, but first, we need things, and I need to *do* something before we leave good ol' Earth. Gage?"

"Yeah?"

"You don't have to come with us, bro. I can take you

somewhere, *anywhere*, and you can get home. I can't, like, guarantee everything will be cool, but I also can't guarantee how long it'll take to see Meehixiheem back to her planet."

"I'm in it to win it, Jojacko. Community college can wait. Meehixiheem, they got education where you're from?"

She scoffed. "Dolurulod best. Smart we beautiful. Rich. You see. I study art!"

"Art degree, huh?" Gage whistled. "Well, that's guaranteed employment then."

John chuckled and told Shippewa exactly where to go and asked the distance in kilometers, which turned out to be eight thousand, six hundred fifty-six. "Can you get us there in three hours?"

"Three hours."

John hoped that was an agreement, not a question. "Go." Shippewa took over, and he removed his hands from the controls, then spun his chair around. "How much cash you got?"

Gage checked his wallet. "Well, if I dip into my secret stash that even Meehixiheem didn't discover, I got a hundred."

"We wanna buy warmer clothes, supplies, stuff like that."

"Ask Shippewa exactly how long we're talking about, okay? I'm not down for spending a year in here."

"Me neither. Ship, how many hours to Dolurulod?"

"9.461e+13."

John asked Gage, "You understand that?"

"Not a clue, dude. *Wahine polū?*"

Meehixiheem made a sort of motorboat sound with her lips. "Dolurulod too far, *kāne* stupid."

Gage Googled the word and taught it to her: *hūpō*.

"*Kāne hūpō*. We go moon. Hawaii?"

Gage gave her that as well: Mahina.

She held up her fists, identifying the nearer as Hawaii and the further as Mahina, then she stuck a foot into the air beyond that and said, "Door. Dolurulod, Jaukh, Wrn, Pnellu and and and."

John got the word for door off his cell phone and pointed at her toe. "*Puka*. Puka Dolurulod, Wrn, and and and?"

Meehix brought all her limbs back together. "Yes."

"Cool."

"Way cool," Gage agreed.

They spent the rest of their three-hour trip teaching themselves more potentially useful Hawaiian words and exploring every nook and cranny on board. There wasn't much, but they determined they had enough *wai* to drink and, embarrassingly close to Gage's head, a larger pit indentation where they could pee that *wai* away as needed.

"You better not shake any of that onto me, bro. I will *not* be cool with that."

"I wonder whether it goes outside or, like, gets recycled." John tried peering into the pit. "It sort of seems there's a vacuum effect in there."

"Better not be *too* vacuum-y or else it'll pull your *pinga* right off."

"I could do with some *pinga* pulling. Missed my mid-afternoon sesh." John made a jacking-off gesture.

"*Mahalo?*" Meehix asked. "Mahalo for what?"

"I tell you, bro," Gage whispered, "we're gonna miss that condom."

As they descended toward Ulaanbaatar, they didn't see any kind of jungle to hide Shippewa in. They kept her in sky-slash-cloud mode until they were low enough to see storefronts.

"Hey! There's a Ramada Inn!" Gage pointed out the port window.

"Bingo!" John pointed to starboard. "A mall and a place to park."

He took the ship over a kind of abandoned-looking parcel of land, told Shippewa to disguise herself as shrubs and a fence, then landed her with a brief *whoosh* of air so that the staircase would be nearly out of sight. Dust swirled around, but only one guy seemed to half-notice. Meehix put her sandals back on.

"No, Meehixiheem. *A'ole*. You stay here. Me and Gage'll stand out plenty. I don't think the good people of Ulaanbaatar can handle a *wahine polū* with four thumbs."

"Shopping!" She pouted. *That* expression was exactly like a human's. John was resolute, however. "*Kāne hūpō. Jojacko hūpō.* Buy *nā pāpale nani*." She pointed out the window at a couple of women strolling down the sidewalk.

"Will do. *Lole nani* for Meehixiheem. I promise."

The men put on as much clothing as they had and hurried down the staircase, then closed it. It didn't look like any other men were wearing shorts. It was August there too, of course, but cooler than New Mexico, and maybe a lot more conservative. "In. Out. Fast. Yeah?"

Gage nodded, and John led him through an opening in the tumble-down wooden fence. They walked casually but quickly toward the mall. "It's a lot more modern than I figured, Jojacko. Guess I thought we'd see more yaks."

"Lots more pollution and thin air than *I* figured. More English too."

They dashed up a concrete staircase under the word Supermarket. It hung on the side of a four or five-story slate-gray building topped off by Grand Plaza. There were tall glass walls mostly covered up by advertisements for women's clothing, computer laptops, and smokes. They passed through one of the entrance doors, reminded themselves of the word *puka*, and dove into a store with racks and shelves of women's wear.

"John, this is as scary as any alien world. Look! Thongs!"

CHAPTER SIXTEEN

The young men moved cautiously into the store. Two young women without smiles stood behind the cash register and watched them. "Let's be extra quick, Gage."

"Okay, but you know if we buy something crappy, Meehix will probably tear it in two."

"I'll go look at pants. You go for shoes and socks."

"No way! We'll come back with shit that's totally unco-ordinated!"

"All right, all right. On safari together then." He held out his fist, and Gage knocked it down with his own, then got the same treatment in return. "Hey, this looks cool."

Gage looked over the dress John had lifted off the rack. It was as dark blue as Meehix herself. "I dunno, man. I think she'd blend in with that too much. *This* one's better."

He held up a gray silk and cotton knee-length dress with yellow flower prints at each shoulder. The collar was a wrap of yellow with buttons that stretched out over the right breast.

"That definitely says Mongolia to me." John pursed his lips in approval.

"May I help you?"

They whirled to one of the cash register women who'd come up behind them silently. She was very pretty, slim, and not a hair was out of place. "Um, we're buying for my...girlfriend. It's a gift."

"Is she my size?"

"Maybe a little taller?" Gage answered, looking the woman up and down. "We haven't seen her in high heels yet."

"I think she can wear this then." The clerk held the dress up to herself and modeled it for them front and back.

"Can we, um, get shoes and, uh, pantyhose to go with that?" John ventured. He knew he was blushing. It was pretty much his natural when talking to Earth girls.

"Certainly. Right this way."

"Your English is great," he commented. *I wish it was you we were taking home to outer space.*

"Thank you. Here are..." she scanned the shoes on display, "a very nice pair to go with this dress. Not too elegant, but not shabby. Sort of everyday chic. You don't know her size, do you?"

They apologized.

"It doesn't matter. My feet are twenty-two centimeters. Is your girlfriend bigger?"

John tried to imagine Meehixiheem's feet. "Bigger. She's around five-foot-nine, and that's..." he waited to Google the conversion, "a hundred seventy-five centimeters. I'd say her feet are...twenty-five centimeters long?"

The clerk calculated the length of her feet in centimeters, came up with a number, then chose a pair of shoes. "I recommend these."

John took them and smiled. "Not so scary, huh?"

Gage still looked dubious. "We haven't gotten through pantyhose yet, man. Still lots to fear."

In about twenty-five minutes, they had completed their purchases. John was happy with them and confident Meehix would like them too. The clerk rang up the total, saw that Gage had a hundred dollar bill to pay with, and looked a bit dismayed. "Do you perhaps have a credit card?"

"Uh, yeah." Gage brought out his VISA, signed for their stuff, and made John carry the bags. As they left the store, he said, "Mongolia's cheap, bro. Cheaper than Mexico even."

"Lucky for us. Let's go in there and get stuff for ourselves. I definitely wanna get outta these shorts, maybe buy some new underwear too."

"Don't model that for me, Jojacko, and don't ask the clerk to either."

They entered a store that sold much more traditional Mongolian garb and wandered through shelves and hangers of shirts, pants, boots, and hats. "These are awesome! I'm gonna try these two on. Got something for yourself?"

"Still looking, man. It's gotta be stylin'."

John went up to the man behind the counter. He seemed as young as the female clerk they'd dealt with, but he didn't have nearly as much capacity with English, so John resorted to gestures. The man understood and pointed him toward a changing room down a short hallway. In another half-hour, both he and Gage had found outfits, paid for them, and changed into them.

John had a cotton and silk tunic called a *deel* by the clerk. It had a silver square of an embroidered hawk and leaves on its chest, plus a brown long-sleeve undershirt and brown pants. Along with it came a sort of skull cap with an extended neck cover in back. He stuck with his kicks but also bought a pair of gray sheep's wool long underwear, a black belt, and some socks.

Gage chose a light brown *deel* with a very dark brown undershirt and pants. "We look totally badass," he said. "I wanted the whole suit of armor over there, but, you know, restraint."

"Good call. Ready?"

"Yeah. Hope your girl likes her stuff. Maybe we should buy padding."

"She's not, ya know, my girl." They exited the store and found the supermarket. Another twenty minutes and they had bags of edibles that would last for lightyears. Out on the street again, their clothes were a bit too much for the heat, but space promised to be pretty chilly, John thought.

Meehix was indeed pleased by their choices. She tapped each of them on the cheek and changed while they turned away. The dress, shoes, and pants fit well, although John suspected she could grow or shrink a little as needed. She examined their food and dug into a container of dried fruit.

"Okay," John said, "before we go, we should say goodbye to our families."

"We'll be back, man."

"But who knows when, yeah? Take care of it. I also

wanna put something up on YouTube." John turned to the console and started recording himself. "Hi, Mom. Hi, Dad. This is John.

"To all my Twitch fans out there, yeah, this is Jojacko. I'm about to head out into space. No lie. This is a bonafide spaceship. It's sort of one of ours. I mean, the United States Space Force confiscated this from some extraterrestrial man or woman. I'm not sure when, and they probably imprisoned them or experimented on them.

"This woman," he showed them Meehix, "was a prisoner in Albuquerque in what purports to be a storage facility on Central Avenue. Check it out, like, lots of you. Expose these fuckers. It ain't right.

"I wanna found a group, like, *Save the Aliens on Earth*, and I need all of you to help me. Share what you know or even what you suspect. I got this ship outta a building labeled Desert Development, so peek in their windows too. I know you can do it. Just don't get hurt. These USSF guys have been after us *hard*, so, like, use your heads.

"Yeah, I busted out their prisoner. I think she's maybe an alien princess from a planet called Dolurulod. She's pretty cool. I stole this ship. I'm upfront about that 'cause I need it to take her home. She said she came to Earth with three others. Try to find 'em, okay? Might be dead. Might be in jail. Shake shit up, folks.

"Meanwhile, we're heading up, out into the big ink. Don't know when we'll be back. Hey, if you wanna make donations, that's cool. I'm definitely into for-profit activism and awareness. Anyway, guess I'll sign off. Probably won't be in contact again until I get back to Earth. Meehixiheem's people call it Kdack 3a. Cool, huh?

"Mom and Dad, I love you lots. Hope you're okay, not in custody. Give them all shades of hell, Dad. Mom, don't worry. I got food, warm clothes, and the best friends you could ever want to explore the cosmos. Peace out, everybody."

Gage was done with his phone call as well. "Bad news, guy. I gotta go home."

CHAPTER SEVENTEEN

"What are you talking about?"

John felt a wave of vertigo wash over him as he tried to comprehend the words "*I gotta go home.*" He wiped sticky blood from his forehead and wondered if he might need stitches. That agent cracked him harder than he thought. The knife cut on his leg stung too, and he could see a line of dried blood on his new Mongolian pants.

"What happened to 'I'm in it to win it?' This is big, Gage. It's not a soccer game where you take your ball and go home. What did Lupe threaten to do? *Ground* you?"

"That's not funny."

Gage held up his cellphone. There was a single text message on its face. If a text could ever look pitiful and helpless, it was this one. All it said was **Por favor ven a casa.**

"*Please come home?*" John was incredulous. "Lupe wrote that?"

"No. Not my mother. My sister."

Meehix paused her chewing of dried apricots. The

translator was still garbling portions of their conversation, but she could tell by Gage's tone of voice that something negative was going down.

John understood immediately. Gage loved his family, took care of his brothers like a mama bear, changed Toñito's shitty diapers despite the intolerable stench...but his *little sister*. If ever there was anyone Gage would trade the sun, moon, and stars for it was *Isabella*, the wide-eyed, innocent waif that looked up to her older brother as if he was God incarnate.

"Well...I mean..." John tried to reason, "she'll get over it. I mean, it's not like we'll be gone forever."

"We *could* be gone forever. We're lucky we're not dead already. I can't do that to her."

John slumped in the control seat. His head throbbed, his stomach ached, and the hard reality of their situation began to weigh on him. *It's all fun and games until somebody dies.*

At first, it was like a fantasy vacation, complete with exotic locales, shopping sprees, a sexy Dolurulod, and a cool, talking spaceship. Now they were back to familial responsibility, diapers, and possibly prison, the thought of which gave him another point to argue.

"If you go back, you could spend the rest of your life locked up, man."

"At least jail has visiting hours. *Death don't.*"

Meehix's voice—clear, firm, and without any more linguistic encumbrances—suddenly burst forth from where she sat in the back of the cramped cabin.

"Do you think we could nix the weepy soy-boy routine and get down to business? Or do I have to fight this whole battle by myself now?"

John and Gage looked at Meehix as if a Playboy center-fold had spontaneously recited the periodic table amid a good wank.

"What's going on?" John was completely baffled. "*Now you speak perfect English?*"

"**Dolurulod-Kdackan translation singularity achieved**," Shippewa announced through the audio system.

Meehix sealed up the bag of dehydrated fruit.

"No, dummy. The translator finally caught up with our jibber-jabbering. Ever since I ordered it to translate between Dolurulod and Kdackan, it's been cross-referencing billions of Earth communications with the Dolurulod quantum library storage banks on the ship. You Earthlings talk like your mouths are full of dried apricots. It takes a while to build an accurate quantum network to translate your language into Dolurulod and vice versa."

"Well...damn," John said, "that's cool. I guess. So no more miscommunications."

"Nope. And let me start by communicating clearly that *you fly a starship like a goddamn fuck-tard.*"

"Man," Gage said, "that translator is *good.*"

"Well, let me start by communicating clearly to you. *This...*" John made a jacking-off motion, "means wankin' your pole. *Not* 'thank you.'"

"Oh," Meehix said meekly. "That explains a lot."

"I'd suggest you stop tapping your tits every time you meet somebody. They can take that the wrong way too."

Gage's cellphone rang. "Uh-oh."

"Your mom again?"

"Yeah." Gage let it ring two more times. "I better answer it." He hit the button. *"Hola?"*

"Gage?" a little voice responded. The volume was up high enough for John to overhear and for the translator to relay to Meehix. "When you coming home, Gage?"

Gage choked up. *"Nena,* what you doing on the phone? Where's mama?"

"When you coming home, Gage?" Isabella whimpered.

Gage covered his eyes with his free hand. John and Meehix looked away.

"Right now, bebita, right now. I'll be home soon. You stay with mama 'til I get there."

"You come home, Gage. You come home *now.* Toñito's diaper is full."

"I will. I will. I'm…I'm on my way, baby." He hung up and wiped his eyes.

John didn't know what to think. He was still half-pissed at Gage since this whole plight was his idea to begin with, but he really couldn't blame him entirely since Gage wanted to quit way before things got gnarly. John's blatant disregard of the dangers involved got them where they were now, not only Gage. *Fuck.*

"Okay. We'll fly you back to Albuquerque. On one condition."

"Name it."

"Assuming you don't get arrested two seconds after we drop you off, you help us any way you can. Get the *Save the Aliens on Earth* group going online. Throw the Space Force off our trail. Finish what you started. Family is one thing, but we're family too…right?"

"You know it, Jojacko." They fist-bumped and all the

tension of the last few minutes evaporated. "If you get a rich reward from her sire on Dolurulod, you split it with me, right?"

"Deal."

Gage found his grin again,

"Sweet, very sweet," Meehix said weakly from her place on the floor. "You two lovebirds are giving me a hard-on. Problem is, I'm not going to stay hard for long."

Gage and John looked down at her.

"Oh shit!" John said.

Meehix was sitting in an *enormous* pool of her blood.

CHAPTER EIGHTEEN

"What happened?" John crouched next to her.

"I got shot in the leg, remember? Bullets tend to cause blood loss. That's kind of what they do."

"I know, but I thought you were okay."

"I think I tore something open with all the running around and beating on agents and whatnot."

"We need to get you to a doctor."

"You need to get me to *Dolurulod*. How are you going to explain *me* to an Earth doctor? I'll end up back in a cell off Central Avenue before he finishes tying off the last stitch."

John pulled off his cotton and silk tunic and ripped it into long strips. Then he untied the blood-soaked wrap Meehix had cinched around the wound earlier.

Blood—like black Kool-Aid—pulsed out of one of the two holes in her thigh. They were entrance and exit wounds, each about the diameter of a pencil. *Must be an artery, or at least the Dolurulod equivalent of one.*

He wrapped the fresh cloth around her leg and tied a

new knot. His eyes wandered. Even in dire circumstances, he found it difficult not to lust after that amazing body. Boy, she always smelled good too.

"This might hurt," he said.

"No shit." Meehix whimpered as he pulled the knot tight.

"How much blood can you people lose and still live?"

"Uhm...*we people* can lose about two gallons before we die. How much can *you people* lose?"

John wiped black, vital fluid off his hands and onto his pants.

"Sorry. Didn't mean to sound like a bigot."

Meehix stared John right in the eyes. Her expression was a sly smile crossed with flirtatious overtones. How would the translator translate *that*? *Intra*species communication was hard enough but *inter*species? Geez, that complicated life. *It's a wonder we don't give up on ever connecting, and all become hermits,* John mused.

"Can you set me in a chair? If I could elevate my leg, it might slow the bleeding."

They lifted her to a sitting position and raised her leg. John almost slipped on the blood puddle and made a mental note to get the ship cleaned up as soon as they had the means. There was wet Dolurulod blood on the floor, dried Dolurulod blood on the seat from earlier, bags of snacks scattered around, and now Meehix's gray silk dress and pants looked like she worked at a Jiffy Lube. What a mess.

John crouched in front of Meehix. He reached out and took her by her double-thumbed hands. At first, she pulled them back but relaxed when she met his round pupils with her horizontal ones.

"Now that we can *talk*, I mean, *really talk*, and understand every word," he said, "I wanna know something, straight up, no bullshit."

"All right. No bullshit."

John noted that the translator had not only jacked itself up to an extremely high grammatical accuracy level but also improved the subtle nuances of inflection and tone. Meehix no longer sounded like a childish, ignorant alien but more like a sophisticated human phone-sex girl with a bit of attitude.

"You're not gonna turn around and kill me as soon as we get you home, are you? I mean, they didn't have you in that cell because you're leading an invasion or because you eat humans or anything weird like that, right?"

Meehix squeezed his hands affectionately.

"John, I'm only a rich girl from the city of Vevev looking for fun in all the wrong places. You get me home and into a chissatch oil bath and we'll be best friends forever...maybe more."

"Nice." John smiled. He believed her. Some communication went beyond translators. He rose to his feet.

"Shippewa!"

"Yes John?"

"Is there a tracking device on you, and if so, where, and how do I remove it?"

"Yes, John. A USSF tracking device is attached to the exterior steel plates that they added to my forward hull. Its appearance is that of a gray plastic donut, and it is

magnetically affixed. You should be able to remove it using only your hands and physical effort."

"Bingo!" John said. "Gage, if you wouldn't mind straightening up the cabin a little, I'll get rid of that tracker, and we'll hit the road."

"Cool beans," Gage said.

John extended the staircase and jumped down. Gage started organizing the bags of food into the back of the cabin.

"So, *Gay-jaw*, you're not going with us, huh?"

Gage gave her a serious look despite the *Gay-jaw* crack.

"You know the expression, *blood is thicker than water?*"

"Not my blood."

"Yeah, I guess that wouldn't translate well in Dolurulod." He thought for a moment. "Do you have babies on Dolurulod? Little ones?"

"Yes, but we hatch from eggs."

"Well, I still have a lot of eggs to hatch."

"I get it." She smiled and did one of her weird lip things.

John crouched under the ship, searching. The wind had picked up, and little dust devils swirled around here and there. With the craft still disguised as shrubs and a fence, he had to feel around where the steel plates were supposed to be.

He noticed the same man who watched Meehix put on her sandals earlier, watching *him* now. John realized he must look ridiculous, feeling around with his hands on a bunch of shrubs and a fence.

He could feel the surface of the ship and the plates, but no donut.

"Shippewa? Can you hear me out here?"

"**Yes, John. I can hear you.**" Shippewa's voice sounded as if it was right next to him. *Cool,* he thought.

"I can't find the tracking device. Can you unhide your forward hull?"

"**Yes, John but I would not advise it at the moment. Two police vehicles are approaching from the southwest. At their current speed, they will arrive in less than one minute. The man watching you from across the lot contacted the authorities on his cell phone. I would have told you earlier, but I wasn't certain at the time if it would become an issue.**"

"Shit! It's an issue."

John saw a cloud of dust on the other side of the building nearest the lot. The man watching him ran toward the dust and began waving his hands and shouting.

"Shippewa, how close am I to the tracker?"

"**Move your right hand farther right. Warmer. Warmer. Bingo!**"

"Got it!"

John grabbed the tracker with both hands and pried his fingers under the edges. The two police vehicles rounded the corner, and the man pointed at John, yelling something in Mongolian. John pulled the tracker as hard as he could, and it finally came loose.

As soon as it was off the ship, he could see it—a gray, plastic donut, like a baby's chew toy, only heavy, like it was full of lead. He tossed it like a Frisbee and ran to the stairs. He was about to run up when he felt something in his pants pocket. It was the cell phone he snagged from the agent in Hawaii.

"Shit! Better dump that too."

He dropped it in the dust and smashed it with all of his six-foot-four weight. The cops started shouting at him as soon as they jumped out of their vehicles.

"Power it up, Shippewa! We gotta roll!"

"Ready for lift-off, John."

CHAPTER NINETEEN

An hour later, Shippewa glided effortlessly above the clouds, disguised *as* a cloud.

John was in the control seat wiping dried blood off his head with a piece of his shredded tunic he'd soaked in water. Gage was munching on snacks next to him. Meehix was lying in the back, apparently asleep. She didn't look sick or on the verge of death or anything, but John noted that black blood soaked the cloth around her thigh again. *Not cool.*

"Hey, Shippewa."

"Yes, John?"

"If you detect any threats, or, you know, think you have information on something that might help us in any way to, uh, *succeed* in whatever we're doing, feel free to let us know, will ya?"

"Will do, John."

"Don't be afraid to speak up."

"I won't be afraid to speak up, John. Speaking of which, we will be directly over the city of Albuquerque,

New Mexico, in three minutes. Altitude twenty-five thousand feet."

"Cool. Thanks, Ship. I appreciate the Imperial system conversion."

"**Not a problem, John.**"

"Where you gonna drop me?" Gage asked.

"I've been thinking about that. Even if the cops split, they'd still probably have our houses under surveillance. Better to drop you off on the edge of town. Can you snag a Lyft?

"Yeah, no big deal. Kinda wanted to make a grand entrance on a UFO, but I get it."

John tossed the bloody rag on the floor.

"Gonna miss you, buddy."

"Ditto."

They didn't know what else to say. Then Gage thought of something.

"If you bang Meehix, shoot me some video."

"Pervert."

"Gotta love that dark web alien-chick porn."

"That reminds me," John said, "you got an email address for that Draylop guy?"

"No, but I can get to him through the web. Why?"

"Don't send him any pictures yet. Don't even tell him what's going on. I want to know more about him before trading any info."

"He's cool, man. I think he's legit."

John thought for a minute.

"Shippewa?"

"**Yes, John?**"

"Can you get me all the information you can about this

Draylop character Gage has been talking to on the dark web?"

"**I can try, John, but it may take some time. It will require remote access to highly secure and encrypted Earth computer systems. Also, I will require consistent and uninterrupted signal strength, which could fluctuate depending on my physical location.**"

John reached into his shirt neck and pulled out Hannah.

"Can you scan this," he held up the pendant, "and extract the code inside?"

"**Scanning.**" Shippewa paused for a moment. "**I have successfully extracted the code.**"

"Could it be helpful?"

"**Yes. I believe it could. May I ask where you got it?**"

"I wrote it."

"**Nice job.**"

"Thanks. Let me know if you find anything on Draylop."

"**Will do, John. By the way, we are over Albuquerque, New Mexico. Would you like to pilot now?**"

"Sure."

John slid his hands into the "boner-maker" controls—as he now referred to them—and brought the ship down fast. *Best to keep things speedy. Less chance of being seen.*

"Try to match your color to the surrounding sky, Ship."

"**Already on it, John.**"

John set Shippewa down quickly on a rocky plateau near a highway on the edge of town. They landed without a hitch. Meehix awoke.

"What's going on?" she asked blearily.

"Say goodbye to *Gay-jaw*," John said.

"Fuck you, you lucky bastard. You got the spaceship, the girl...damn. Sometimes I wish I was you. Only smaller."

"I *never* wish I was you."

They hugged.

"Bye, Gage," John said. "I'll be in touch."

"I hope so, buddy. Don't get laser-blasted or anally probed or anything."

"Bye, *Gage*," Meehix said. "Do I get a hug too?"

Gage grinned and leaned over to embrace her. Meehix grabbed him by the face and kissed him right on the mouth. It was a deep, wet, alien, *French* kiss. She released him and licked her blue lips. Gage looked like he'd just smoked a bag of hurnrern weed.

"Wow." Gage's head still spun. "You taste like strawberry ice cream."

"Oh, I'm full of flavors."

"Motherfucker," John interjected. "Get outta here before you embarrass the human race."

Gage smiled ear-to-ear and extended the stairway.

"If you get sick of him," Gage said to Meehix, "you know where I live."

"I *don't* know where you live."

"Tell her where I live, Jojacko!"

He disappeared down the ladder. John went to the starboard porthole and watched him as he ran down the plateau toward the highway. He glanced at Meehix.

"Is there something I should know about you two?"

"I wanted to give him a goodbye thrill."

John saw Gage run out of view at the plateau's base, but before he disappeared, he reached into his pants and adjusted his junk.

"You did. A big one."

John's cellphone rang. He pulled it out of his pocket and looked at the screen. *Mom,* it read.

"Hello? Mom?"

His mother didn't respond immediately. Instead, John heard a commotion and his mother saying, "Tell them not to stand on the grass! They can stay on the sidewalk if they want but not the grass!"

"Mom? What's going on?"

"Oh, John, thank God! Where are you, honey?"

"I'm..." he bit his tongue. *Phones are probably tapped by now. Gotta be careful.* "I'm okay, Mom. What's going on at the house?"

"Oh my, there's news people and cameras and trucks and...oh no, the dog got out."

John heard his dad yelling in the background.

"Goddamit, Vera! Who let the dog out? He just pissed on Trey McSwirley."

Oh shit. If Trey McSwirley's at our house, we're fucked as far as keeping things quiet. The media circus has arrived, and the clowns are butt-fucking the orangutans in the Big Top.

"John? Are you there?"

"Yeah, Ma, I'm here."

"Honey, your dad's putting on the TV. You're on television."

"What? How can I be on TV? I haven't talked to anybody yet!"

"I'm watching you right now."

John heard something about a *special report* and a *UFO over Albuquerque.* Then he listened to his voice.

"*Hi, Mom. Hi, Dad. This is John. To all my Twitch fans out there, yeah, this is Jojacko. I'm about to head out into space. No lie. This is a bonafide spaceship..."*

"Oh, shit," John said out loud, "my YouTube post. They put it on the news."

"Everything okay?" Meehix asked.

"No," John answered. "Everything's all fucked up."

"John? Who's that girl in the video?" his mom asked. "I don't like her. Why is she blue with green hair? Wait, they bleeped you. What did you say that they bleeped you? Did you drop an F-bomb on television?"

John held the phone away from his ear for a minute while his mom nagged. He thought about what to do and made a decision.

"Mom! Listen to me."

"John, this is all too much. Honey, does this have anything to do with drugs? If you have a drug problem, I still love and support you."

"I'm not on drugs, Mom! Get Dad and go into the bedroom where it's quiet. You hear me? Go right now into the bedroom so I can talk to you."

"Okay, okay. Hold on..."

He waited. He heard his mother's muffled voice, then his father's. She must have her hand over the phone.

"Okay, John, we're both in the bedroom."

He heard his father yell something about *fucking moron* and his mother trying to calm him down. Something about *be supportive,* and *he may be on drugs* and *even Rush Limbaugh had a drug problem.* Oh boy.

"Mom. Dad. Listen. I'm going to keep it short. I know we haven't always seen eye-to-eye and I know I haven't always been the best son, or at least not the kind you probably wanted, but I do have talents. Namely, I'm a dope gamer and a heck of a hacker."

"Did he say he's on dope?" his father said.

"I know these things may seem like a waste of time to you, but they've led me to some pretty heavy shi...I mean...*stuff*...that's important to the whole world. I can't explain it all right now, but I can prove that it's true and that I'm not on drugs. Give me five minutes, then go outside on the lawn. Tell the news people to turn on their cameras."

"But John..."

He hung up.

"What are you going to do?" Meehix asked him.

"Give them a *Close Encounter of the Jojacko Kind.*"

Trey McSwirley was pressing a paper towel to the ankle portion of his khaki pants.

"Little bastard. Next time I'll drop-kick him."

He stood and pushed through the mass of reporters and found his cameraman, Alex, sitting in the sliding access door of their news van.

"Al! What are you doing? Get some B-roll. Shoot something. I didn't come out to this shitty neighborhood just to get pissed on."

"I can only shoot a crowd of lunatics so many ways."

"You know, if you hadn't fucked up in the helicopter this morning and hit record instead of broadcast, we'd already have some killer footage."

"How was I supposed to know a UFO was gonna fly up right when I started on my Egg McMuffin?"

Trey's assistant, Kelly, ran up to him.

"It's a no-go," she said, out of breath, "both mother and father refusing an interview."

"Goddammit," Trey spat. "Figures. What about the Air Force? Anybody at the base willing to go on record?"

"No comment. That's all they'll give."

Trey threw the pee-paper towel down on the lawn so violently that Kelly retreated two steps.

"The mother did say one thing," she added.

"What?"

"Turn your cameras on."

"Why? What does that mean?"

"She said, 'John says so.'"

"John? The kid? She talked to him?"

A blast of wind blew through the neighborhood like a micro-burst. Dresses went up, it ruined hairdos, and the piss-paper towel spun like a ninja throwing star and plastered itself to Trey's face. Now he *really* spat.

All the neighbors were in their front yards, and everyone looked up at the winged, iridescent craft hanging above them with hardly a sound—like a sleek, metal dragonfly, only bigger—and with two humanoid faces peeking out a porthole, one pale white, the other blue.

"That'll give them something to report on." John looked down on his neighborhood. The crowd in front of the house was a mix of activities. Some people ran around like ants, some pointed at the ship, others swung cameras around, and others stared upward in shock.

"This is where you live?" Meehix asked.

"Yup. What do you think?"

"It's...quaint."

"Well, excuse me, your highness. We can't *all* be royalty, can we? Hey, Ship."

"Yes, John?"

"Do you have any kind of loudspeaker so I can talk to the people down there?"

"Yes, John. If you speak as you are speaking to me now, I can relay your voice to my exterior audio projector as I spoke to you when you were looking for the tracking device. Will that suffice?"

"Sounds perfect, as long as it's loud enough."

"It will be. Just say when."

Trey McSwirley was screaming at Alex to *film the fucking UFO!* when he heard John's voice boom through the neighborhood. As soon as the first word reverberated, the crowd shut up like clams at a beach party.

"Hi everybody. It's me, John. Your neighbor, loving son, UFO pilot, etcetera. The blue girl looking out the window is Meehixiheem. She's from the planet Dolurulod."

Meehixiheem started to tap her tits but then remembered what John said earlier.

"Long story short, she crash-landed here about two weeks ago and only wants to go home. Humans haven't treated her so good, plus she got shot by the United States Space Force, some of whom are total dicks..."

"Excuse me, John."

"Hold on, everybody...yeah, Ship, what's up?"

"Two fighter jets are approaching from the east. ETA one minute."

"Aww shit...speak of the devil. Okay, thanks, Ship."

"No problem, John."

"Fuck me...oops...sorry, Mom. Is this thing on?"

"You're on, John."

"Well, you all probably heard that. We've gotta split, the heat's coming, so I'll say this: aliens are real, we're not alone in the universe, life is complicated, so can't we just get along? I think that all we really need is love, you know? It sounds corny, but I think it's true. Then again, I had to crack some dude's head on the pavement and fuck some other guys up with sonic weapons, so what do I know?

"I'll try to keep in touch, maybe post some more videos. Wish us luck. Love you, Mom. Love you, Dad. Fuck you, Trey McSwirley, if you're banging the weather girl."

Trey's jaw dropped.

"I knew it!" Kelly stormed off to the van.

"Peace out everybody else. This is John Jacobs signing off and leaving the solar system. *Save the Aliens on Earth!*"

Then the "UFO" blasted away at incredible speed. Two jets immediately followed like turtles chasing a cheetah. Everyone in the neighborhood cheered, whistled, hooted, and hollered. Everybody except Trey McSwirley and the dog.

CHAPTER TWENTY

Lindsy Lorraine, the White House Press Secretary, was in rare form, lying her ass off, as usual.

"How could it have been a weather balloon? Over fifty witnesses went on record to say—"

"I didn't say *weather* balloon. I said *balloon*. A large helium balloon dressed up to look like a spaceship."

"The video footage—"

"That footage is clearly CGI and not even that good if you ask me."

"There were a dozen cameras that all recorded—"

"Oh, like news agencies never re-use each other's footage. Pfft! Give me a break."

"The independent witnesses at the scene all stated that—"

"A teenager pulled a prank in a suburban neighborhood. Woop-de-do! Why do I have to give a press conference on something so juvenile? Really people, don't we have anything *important* to report on?"

"Weren't two fighter jets scrambled from—"

"Fighter jets get scrambled all the time. It's a tough world out there."

"The YouTube video posted by John Jacobs—which now has over a million views—he claims that the USSF—"

"*YouTube video!* Will you listen to yourself? This kid is cashing in on all the media attention *you* are giving *his channel!* It's a stunt! To get views! Wake up and smell the scam, people! I'm done!"

Lindsy slammed her notebook shut and marched off the podium with her head back and her tits leading the way. The cacophony of questions continued until she had disappeared behind the curtain.

Backstage, her assistant met her immediately with a glass of water—vodka—and a pack of Marlboros.

"I'll be in the decompression chamber," Lindsy snarled.

A moment later, she was sitting in a small broom closet off the main hall, finishing the vodka and flicking her two-inch ash into the empty glass. Her cellphone rang. It was *him.*

"Hello, sir."

"Nice job, sweet-cheeks. They kept lobbing 'em, and you kept knocking 'em out of the park."

"I'm glad you think so. It felt more like being trapped in a cave full of vampire bats, and the best I could do was swat them away from my hair."

"You did great. Just keep it consistent, never budge an inch, deny, deny, and eventually they move on to the next story. This will be ancient history in a couple of days."

"Like the pyramids?"

"Well...I guess."

The vodka was slowly dissolving her usual inhibitions.

"Sir? Can I ask you to be completely straight with me?"

"Sure, sweet-cheeks! I'm always straight with you."

Lindsy cranked up her courage to full-on, ethanol-fueled, blast-off mode.

"Was that UFO real? I mean, I know what the brief says, but that footage looks very...authentic."

Silence. Long pause. Then coldly.

"Lindsy. We've had this talk before. Everything in government is on a need-to-know basis. All you need to know is how to do your hair, how to put on your lipstick, and how to tell those vampire bats exactly what I tell you to tell them. *Capisce?*"

"Yes, sir."

"That's my girl. Love ya. Gotta run."

The phone went dead. *And I wonder why I can't stop drinking.*

CHAPTER TWENTY-ONE

It was after dark when Bixby and Shaw pulled up to the Jacobs house in a tan Cadillac DeVille with government plates. A least a dozen other cars had parked in the drive and on the street. Silhouettes milled around in the house, visible through the windows. Laughter sounded through the open windows.

"What, are they having a block party?" Bixby oozed sarcasm.

"Director says he wants it done tonight. Top priority."

"No shit, but how do we work the witnesses if they're at a party?"

"Get creative. Pull them aside. Isolate them. We'll figure it out. Follow my lead."

They exited the car, closed the doors, straightened their black ties, and put on the aviators. That was the real ticket. When they couldn't see your eyes, it added a whole new level of menace.

Shaw locked the car with the remote and the horn chirped twice. Someone in the house must have heard it because the front door flung open before they even got to the porch.

"They're here!" an effeminate-sounding, middle-aged, white male wearing an Acapulco shirt yelled from the doorway. People immediately began spilling out of the house—and spilling wine and beer—and they quickly engulfed the two stunned agents in a sea of bodies.

The greeter in the flowery shirt rushed up to Bixby and Shaw with such enthusiasm that the two men instinctively moved into a defensive stance.

"Oh, wow, karate chop!" he laughed. "I bet you two trained in *everything*. Exciting!"

Shaw tried to take control of the situation. "We're from—"

"Oh, *we* know who *you* are!" Todd interrupted. "I'm Todd. This is Mrs. Jacobs—"

"Call me Vera!" John's mom blurted, clearly drunk.

"I'm the father of the little prick," John's dad added, slurring his words.

"Be nice, honey. These men have come from Washington...or Alpha Centauri...or something."

She started laughing hysterically, and everyone chuckled. They were *all* drunk.

"I'm sorry," Todd giggled, "we've had a few. We expected you *hours* ago, and things got a bit saucy at our little," Todd made the "quotes" gesture with his fingers, "*E.T. Reveal Party*."

"Expected us?" Bixby said.

"Of course! The Men in Black! Welcome! What do you drink? Do they *let* you drink? We've got Chardonnay and Heineken and—"

"Shut up! Everybody shut up and listen!" Shaw yelled. The yard went silent. "We're here on official government business, and I want to speak to whoever witnessed the unidentified flying object that was reported here earlier today—*in private.*"

Everyone in the crowd looked at each other, uncertain if they should respond or not until Todd retook the lead.

"That's *us,* sirs. We *all* saw that sweet sucker."

Someone in the back belched.

"Shit," Bixby muttered under his breath. "There must be over a hundred people here."

Shaw—not to be deterred—stepped in close to Todd.

"Who are *you?*" Shaw hissed.

"I told you, I'm Todd."

"Todd's our neighbor." Vera almost spat wine. "He knows *a lot* about UFOs and conspiracy theories and...oh my...all kinds of things. He *really* opened our eyes. I can't tell you how...I mean...wow..." she trailed off into a mystical, alcohol-induced haze. "My baby boy's in outer space," she said softly, looking up at the stars, eyes tearing.

"*Everybody here* is in outer space," Bixby whispered to Shaw.

"Abort," Shaw snarled and marched back to the car, hands clenched. The sea of bodies parted enough for the two men to make their exit.

"You're leaving?" Todd cried. "What about intimidating us? As a UFO witness and a taxpayer, I expect the government to intimidate me!"

Shaw unlocked the Caddie, and they climbed in. Bixby closed his door. Shaw slammed his.

"This is not acceptable, gentlemen!" Todd cried. "I

expect to be severely intimidated shortly! You'll never convince me it wasn't real! No matter how hard you try!"

The tan DeVille started up and sped off.

Everyone was quiet for a moment, not sure what had happened or why. Crickets chirped.

"What a couple of party-poopers," Todd lamented.

CHAPTER TWENTY-TWO

"Now approaching planet Jupiter. ETA to planet Saturn, two hours and thirty-seven minutes."

John snapped awake. For a second, he had no idea where he was. The comforting droning of Shippewa's engines combined with the star-speckled darkness had lulled him into a deep sleep. He started to stretch but stopped when he reached his pain threshold.

"Jesus, I'm sore. I think *I* need a chissatch oil bath."

He looked back at Meehix. She had curled up like a blue kitten—sleeping again—in the rear of the cabin. It looked like her leg had stopped bleeding, at least for now.

Jupiter lit up the cockpit for a few brief seconds with its sun-bounced, red and beige glow. Then it was gone—that quick. They were hauling ass to Saturn. Even at that speed, it would take them thousands of years to reach Dolurulod or any of the other dozen or so star systems Meehix had told him about, that is, if they tried to make it in Shippewa alone.

To get to *her* hometown, they needed a hyper-dimensional Gate, and it just so happened one hid in the rings of Saturn, or at least Meehix said it did.

"John."

"Yeah, Ship."

"I detect..." Ship paused.

"What?"

"For a moment, I detected three unidentified objects approximately ten thousand miles behind us, but now they are gone."

"UFOs following a UFO?" John chuckled.

"Apparently. I will let you know if I detect them again."

"Are we there yet?" Meehix's voice was raspy yet seductive. She blinked her big sexy eyes and rubbed them with her blue fingers. She seemed a little hungover. Still hot but hungover. Maybe all the blood loss finally caught up with her.

It was a pain cleaning up her vital fluids—they were *everywhere*—but after they left Earth, John worked on it for nearly two hours by soaking the remains of his tunic in water, then mopping and wringing it into the toilet-sucker thing. The ship looked pretty sparkling clean now.

"We still got a couple more hours," John replied. "How you feeling?"

"Like I was rode hard and put up wet."

I'd like to ride you hard and put you up wet. Jeez, I'm no better than Gage and his dark web alien porn. He wondered what Gage was doing right now, if he made it home okay, or if the police or USSF arrested him. *Probably won't know the answer to those questions for a while. No cell or internet service out here. Which reminds me.*

"Hey, Ship."

"Yes, John?"

"Any luck with that Draylop guy?"

"No, John. We did not remain in near-Earth orbit long enough for me to extract the necessary information."

"Bummer."

"Who's Draylop?" Meehix asked.

"I wish I knew."

"Well, why are you looking for him? Is he human or alien?"

Hmmm. Good point. John hadn't considered until now that Draylop might not be human. *It is an unusual name. But why would an alien hit Gage up for info on other aliens?*

"Supposedly he's some dude from Iraq that Gage was talking to on the dark web. He's the guy that tipped us off to the base where we found you."

"Draylop *told you* I was there?"

"No. I mean, he didn't tell *me* anything. I never talked to him. This was all through Gage. According to him, Draylop said there was a secret base off Central Avenue, and he wanted us to check it out and try to get pictures. Turns out he was right, and here we are."

Meehix did one of her weird lip things and cocked her head. "I don't know. Sounds kind of suspect to me."

"Yeah, me too. That's why…"

"Evasive maneuvers!" Shippewa exclaimed.

The ship lurched sharply. John felt like he'd been dropped thirty feet onto a moving roller coaster and he instinctively strapped himself in. Three objects flew past the windows so fast that they were split-second blurs.

Then two bright red flashes popped so intensely outside the portholes that John had black dots floating around on his retinas.

"**We are under attack from three unidentified craft,**" Shippewa said. "**Judging by their speed, stealth, and weapons systems, we are outmatched. I suggest immediate surrender.**"

"Fuck that!" Meehix yelled. She jumped behind John and ordered, "Floor it!"

John shoved his hands in the "boner-makers" and jacked it to full speed. Shippewa's engines cranked up in a split second and maxed at one hundred percent. The walls around them began to vibrate.

"**We can only maintain this speed for approximately four minutes, John. After that, we risk imploding the free-energy converter.**"

"Where are the other ships?"

"**Approximately four thousand miles behind us and closing. We cannot outrun them.**"

John thought for a second and made a decision. He turned the ship in an incredibly tight curve and headed back toward the tiny sparkle that was Jupiter. Meehix held on for dear life to the back of John's chair. John strained against the *gees*.

Shippewa automatically compensated the cabin's artificial gravity as deftly as possible, but at this high interplanetary speed, it was difficult to maintain balance. The three attackers flashed past them like bullets. They fired a volley of red blasts again but couldn't react in time. The projectiles exploded harmlessly behind Shippewa.

"I'm receiving a transmission from the unidentified craft, John."

"Play it," John directed as he focused on the growing dot that was Jupiter.

"...and you have stolen USSF property," the transmission began mid-sentence. "You're outnumbered and out-gunned. Stop now and live. Keep going, and you die. Real simple, kid."

"Did he just call me 'kid?'" John snarled.

"I believe he did." Meehix still gripped the back of John's seat like a life-preserver in a maelstrom.

"I'll show you *kid*, you fuck-wad!"

"Their weapons systems will be in range again in thirty seconds, John."

"What about *our* weapons? Can't we laser-blast them or something?"

"Our laser system can only fire forward, John."

"Well, I ain't turnin' again. What about the sonics?"

"Sonics will not operate in the vacuum of space, John."

Meehix rolled her horizontal-pupil eyes. John immediately felt dumb for suggesting it.

Meehix yelled, "Lock missiles onto the enemy ships and fire!"

"Unable to obtain a lock at this speed, Meehixiheem."

"Well fuck me!" John said. "What good are missiles and lasers if you can't use them? What about the bombs?"

"Bombs require gravitational pull to jettison properly and at this speed..."

"Okay, okay. Forget it," John interrupted, getting frustrated.

Jupiter *whooshed* up on them faster than John anticipated. He veered to starboard to avoid flying right into the gas giant's atmosphere, and the ship *crackled*. Green and yellow phosphorous-like sparks danced all over the windows and hull. John's and Meehix's hair stood on end.

"We passed through Jupiter's radiation and electromagnetic fields," Shippewa announced.

"No shit." Meehix tried to mat down her out-of-control green mop.

"The attacking craft are in firing range."

"Shit." John rolled the ship hard to port and headed for the nearest moon.

"They are locking on."

Shippewa nose-dived. Meehix screamed and hit the roof of the cockpit. Three flashes of red exploded outside, jolting them in the opposite direction. Meehix fell onto John's shoulders, her crotch right in his face. He started to yell at her but stopped when he drew in a breath.

Piña colada. She smells like a piña colada down there. Far out.

Meehix extracted herself from John's face like a crazed ninja and positioned herself behind him. She grabbed his arms. Instantly, the ship spun violently clockwise as more red flashes blasted past them, barely missing.

They flew toward the moon at incredible speed and dove to a mere three feet above ground level, skimming the surface of what turned out to be Europa, narrowly missing a jagged ice spire and somehow navigating into an ice canyon in the Conamara Chaos region. The three pursuing ships broke off in different directions, all trying not to crash into a multitude of icy obstacles.

"How'd you maneuver like that?" John was stunned.

"My thought signals are traveling through your arms and into the hand controls."

"Thought signals? What do thoughts have to do with flying the ship? Isn't it all in the finger action?"

"Typical man. No wonder you fly so shitty."

John looked at Meehix's hands gripping his forearms. They felt soft and warm. His gaze followed up her toned biceps and he suddenly had the overwhelming urge to spin and go to town on those amazing tits. All the blood rushed to his groin. *I wonder if Ship can tell when Meehix gives me a boner? Would Ship even know what a boner is? I guess she'd have to. I mean, she knows...holy shit! I'm getting way off topic—gotta focus.*

They flew down the ice canyon at a dangerous clip. The three USSF ships got back into formation behind them, albeit a loose one. Hundreds of stalagmite-like ice protrusions as big as the Washington Monument sticking up from the canyon floor still forced them to dodge. Locking in their weapons was not the number-one priority at the moment. *Not crashing* was.

"Incoming transmission, John."

"Play it!"

"Listen, you little....*shit!*" the USSF pilot almost hit an ice tower. "Goddamit! Listen, you can't get away. There's nowhere to go. Give it up, kid. That freak you're with is not worth dying for."

"Freak?" Meehix snarled.

"This guy's a total dick. Calls me a *kid* and you a *freak.*"

"I'll show him how *freaky* I can get!"

Meehix jammed the ship to starboard and flew straight

toward a hole composed of crisscrossing ice shafts barely big enough for the craft to squeeze through. However, she miscalculated and took it too low, hitting the steel plates covering the ship's bow on an ice boulder. The impact knocked them so hard that she lost her grip on John and fell to the cabin floor.

The pursuing ship nearest them chickened out at the last second and tried to pull up. He didn't make it. The ice shafts exploded in a flash of prismatic colored light, and the craft spun and bounced from one tunnel to the next—like a toy airplane falling from a tree and hitting every branch—until it finally skidded to a stop on the frosted floor of the canyon below.

"Only two ships following us now, John."

"Sweet," John said.

Meehix jumped up from the floor and grabbed John's arms again, only this time she sat on his lap, butt to balls, and strapped herself in on top of him. Her cornucopia of smells wafted over him, and the warmth of her backside pressing against his crotch and chest warped his world.

Jesus. My dick's about to rip through my Mongolian pants and head right up her extraterrestrial butthole.

"Never in my life expected to be thinking *that* particular phrase," John whispered to himself.

"What?" Meehix yelled, not hearing him over the roar of the impulse engines.

John put his mouth right to her ear. He could almost taste her.

"I think you should let me up and you take over." John squirmed.

"I can't, dummy," Meehix shouted. "The finger controls are keyed to human DNA, remember?"

"Oh yeah."

John tried to think about soccer, computer programs, his mother...anything except butt-fucking Meehix. She suddenly stiffened.

"Is that your...*penis?*" she asked matter-of-factly.

"Yeah," John admitted, his face turning as red as the eye on Jupiter. "In humans, it's an involuntary reaction."

"Involuntary, huh?" she yelled, trying not to smile. "We'll discuss this later."

"If there *is* a later," he said.

"That's it!" an angry voice bellowed from the transmission receiver. "Fuck these lowlifes! Take 'em out!"

A blast of red energy exploded into the canyon wall next to Shippewa. Ice splintered over the windows like a snowplow had driven by and showered them in slush. Another red blast cut past them—missing by only a millimeter—and exploded at a fork in the canyon a thousand yards ahead.

The canyon wall started to collapse in a massive avalanche like those videos you see of ice shelves falling into the Antarctic. Meehix turned a hard right at the fork. When the ship lurched, John thought she was going to break his dick off. She flew Shippewa straight for the collapsing wall of white.

"Hold on!" Meehix yelled.

"To *what?*" John cried.

Thousands of pounds of ice and snow-like crystals pounded down on Shippewa with an oddly attenuated roar. The frozen deluge completely covered the windows and portholes. It would've been dark inside the cockpit if not for the blue glow of the controls. They were flying blind, *and* they were being buried alive!

Without warning, Meehix jerked the ship hard to starboard and out of the avalanche, then rolled it twice in less than a second, flinging the snow and ice off the windows.

"What the hell was that?" John screamed. Then he realized. The other two ships didn't follow them into the collapsing wall. Now *Shippewa* was behind *them*.

"Ship! Lock-on and fire lasers!"

A sapphire beam blasted from Shippewa's nose and struck the nearest craft in its free-energy converter. There was a bright flash, and the small ship descended awkwardly and made an emergency landing on the icy canyon floor.

"Only one ship left, John."

"Whoo-hoo!" John yelled. "Good shot, Ship! Right up the old poop-chute!"

"I know the feeling." Meehix smirked.

Suddenly, the last USSF craft pulled up hard and started to loop.

"He's trying to get in behind you again!" John blurted.

"This ain't no threesome," Meehix snarled.

Meehix followed the other craft up and over. When they were upside down and out of the canyon, John saw Jupiter filling half the sky. It looked like an *enormous* pie pan filled with twenty different-colored swirls of glowing oil paints. *Pretty cool.*

High over Europa now, Meehix kept up the dogfight with the other pilot. She stayed on his ass while he tried everything he could think of to get back on hers. They looped and dove and roared up and down like a mad, airborne cat chasing its tail.

"Motherfucker!" Meehix spewed. "Son of a bitch! Cocksucker!"

John wondered how all those English cuss words sounded in Dolurulod. *Do they really accuse someone of "fucking their mothers," being "born of a female dog," and "having oral sex" like we do? Maybe some things in this universe are just universal.*

Meehix executed a double loop with an axial spin followed by a nosedive.

"I think I'm gonna puke," John said.

"You puke on me, and I'll rub your face in it."

John swallowed hard. *When* and *what* did he eat last? Oh yeah. Right after he finished cleaning up the cabin—prunes and canned sardines. He did *not* want to puke *that* down Meehix's back.

"John."

"Yeah, Ship?" he answered weakly. His boner had devolved into a limp noodle.

"Without going into a lot of detail, the code from your pendant has allowed me to access a previously inaccessible cache of weaponry onboard the ship. I believe I can now neutralize the enemy craft quite effectively. Would you like me to do so?"

"Fuck yeah!" John and Meehix exclaimed in unison.

A sound—similar to a large jet engine powering up—emanated from Shippewa's stern. It built and built in volume and intensity as Meehix continued to try and gain an advantage over the last USSF pilot. Suddenly, he deviously changed tactics and rolled in an unexpected direction, then looped beneath her before she could counter.

"Damn!" she yelled.

"You're toast..." the pilot snarled.

There was a loud *popping* sound and a bright flash of pink light, then silence.

"Are we dead?"

John looked around. Shippewa *appeared* intact. He was still breathing. Meehix was still on his lap and holding his arms. *What happened?*

The USSF ship flew past their window, or rather, *floated.* The pilot cursed and slammed his hands on the control panel. He noticed John and Meehix watching him through the porthole and flipped them off.

"What did you *do,* Ship?"

"I activated a free-energy disruptor. Without very specific frequency shielding, it permanently ends electron flow in all inorganic electrical systems within approximately one mile of the detonation point."

"You shut his ass down big-time," Meehix said.

"Yes. I shut his ass down big-time."

They watched the powerless USSF ship gently float toward Jupiter.

"What will happen to the pilots?" John asked.

"Scanners indicate the two on Europa's surface still have operational life support systems. Both have activated their emergency beacons indicating they are still alive and will likely receive rescue within one solar day. The third craft is drifting toward Jupiter and will enter the planet's atmosphere in approximately three Earth hours."

"And burn up."

"**No, John. Jupiter is not like earth. Rather than burning up as the ship descends, Jupiter's atmospheric pressure will crush the pilot's body to the size of a dried apricot. After that, cyclonic winds will blow that piece of shit around for an eternity.**"

"Harsh."

"Yet poetic," Meehix noted.

"Is there any way we can save him?"

"**We could use our ship to propel his craft into a stable orbit around Europa. However, it could be dangerous. We could damage our ship in the process or the pilot could attack us with weapons not affected by the free energy disrupter.**"

"Hmm. What do you think, *Hix?*"

"Don't call me 'Hix' or I'll start calling you *On.*"

"Sorry. So, what do we do, *Meehix?*"

"If he had his way, we'd be dead right now."

"Yeah. Still, *we're not,* and he definitely *will be.*"

The USSF ship was barely a speck on the face of the multi-colored pie pan. Meehix watched it drift across Jupiter's red eye. She thought about the dried apricot.

"Why are you so nice?" Meehix unstrapped herself, stood, turned, and kissed John on the forehead.

"We practically have oral *and* anal, and all I get is a peck on the forehead?"

"How about a smack in the face?"

"I've been robbed."

John adjusted his fingers in the boner-makers.

"Ship?"

"**Yes, John?**"

"I'm gonna need some help with this. Give me any useful info you can to get this guy shoved in the right direction. Scan him the whole time. If he tries anything aggressive, laser his head off."

"Will do, John."

"I like you," Meehix said.

"Why?"

"Because you're caring and you can still handle yourself when things get tough."

"I like you too."

"Why?"

"Because you've got great tits and ass and—unlike my ex-girlfriend—you smell so good that I could go down on you all day long."

"Go save the dried apricot, you pervert." She smiled.

"Aye, aye, Captain Colada."

CHAPTER TWENTY-THREE

It was eleven in the morning, California Time, and the closed-door meeting was for USSF brass and their assistants, about ten bodies total. They were seated around an oversized, oblong, hardwood conference table in a red-carpeted room. Some of the faces convened at this Ultra-Top Secret meeting were dour. Some looked pissed, others bored.

A geeky tech guy wearing a photo security tag that read "Chadwick Underwood" stood at the head of the table, addressing the group. Security video of John entering Meehixiheem's prison cell played on a giant flat-screen monitor behind him.

"Here, we can see, is where Mr. Jacobs is communicating with the alien," Chad pointed.

"Well, that settles it. He can speak her language. He has to be a spy," said the Chief of Space Operations.

"Not necessarily, sir," the Lead Intelligence Officer interjected. "Everything we've run on this kid indicates he's only a hacker—a lucky hacker, no doubt, but no ties to terrestrial or extra-terrestrial espionage."

"Oh, bullshit," the CSO countered. "Somebody paid him. Somebody pays *everybody*. What's the story on the guards?"

"They swear up and down that they abandoned the two hallway posts for less than five minutes while they used the latrine, which was, unfortunately, right when the breach occurred. The other two in the monitor room claim to have been...*distracted.*"

"By what?"

"Lunch and an old movie they were streaming."

"What movie?"

"*Basic Instinct.*"

"The interrogation scene?"

"Yes, sir."

"I'm familiar with it."

All the men in the room shifted uncomfortably in their chairs. Someone coughed.

"Listen, Underwood," the CSO continued, "I didn't fly out here to get fed a checklist of *stupid*. I want to know what to tell the Secretary. What *exactly* are you doing *right now* to fix this *major* fuck-up?"

"Our three best Non-Terrestrial-Craft pilots should have intercepted them near Jupiter about thirty minutes ago."

"Jupiter? Where do they think they're going without the Gate?"

"Unknown, sir. They never even attempted to reach the Lunar Gate. At any rate, the pilots have orders to bring them in by any means necessary. I expect a status report sometime within the hour."

"Well shit." The CSO slumped in his chair. "Looks like I'm stuck here for at least another hour no matter how you slice it."

The chief lifted the flap of his medal-encrusted chest pocket and pulled out an expensive cigar. He removed the wrapper, clipped off the cap with a silver and gold cutter, toasted the head with a triple-flamed, titanium torch, then puffed away as he achieved the final burn. Plumes of bluish smoke mushroomed in front of the *No Smoking* sign on the wall behind him. His assistant attempted to fan the miasma away with her hand.

"You know," he started, blowing out a big cloud of incinerated Connecticut Broadleaf, "I was in Hawaii sipping the perfect Mai Tai when you idiots let them get away...*in Hawaii*. What are the odds? Now my wife is still there, probably banging the cabana boy."

He drew again, then exhaled.

"What else is on the agenda? Might as well get some mundane bullshit done while I'm here."

"Just that Intergalactic Credits issue the Acquisitions Manager mentioned earlier. We estimate that with a ten thousand credit investment per body, which includes feeding, inoculations, temporary board, flight to the Lunar Gate, etcetera, we can get at least fifteen thousand a head on the black market. With a rough estimate of three thousand extractions per major city per year, that's quite a haul. About fifteen billion U.S. annually, and that's on the low side."

"Do it." The CSO spat a fragment of loose tobacco from

his cigar. "Make sure all our media operatives kill *any* potential stories before they even get to an editor's laptop. I don't want to read about somebody's Uncle Willy disappearing on the way home from an AA meeting. Same protocol as before—only the rock-bottom homeless and unattached mentally ill. I can live with that. At least their shitty lives will have *some* value."

"Yes, sir."

"Anything else?"

"Well, regarding the current situation, sir. If we get her back…"

"*When* we get her back."

"Uh…yes. *When* we get her back, do you want her returned to the Albuquerque installation?"

"Hell no. That place should have been wiped and cleared by now. With all the shit that kid put out on the airwaves, there'll be tin-foil hats crawling all over it. Ship all the guards to Leavenworth for interrogation and get all the valuable assets out of there. Then you can burn the place down for all I care." He re-ignited the titanium lighter and tried to even the ash on the cigar head.

Chad's cellphone rang. The ringtone was a few bars from the song *Straighten Up and Fly Right.*

"Hello? Yes. Yes. What? You're kidding…"

Chad began to perspire.

"…all right. I said all right! I want that report *with transcripts* in an hour. Yes! You heard me!"

Chad disconnected. He was shaking.

"Sir, there's been…uh…a little…"

"SNAFU? Yeah, I heard."

The CSO turned to his assistant.

"Gretchen, set up a meeting with the Secretary. Then call my wife and tell her I'm going to be a few days. Have Mike fire up the jet, and get me an ashtray, will you?"

"Yes, sir." Gretchen shuffled out of the room with her phone to her ear. Everyone else at the table quickly gathered their things and got the hell out of there. The meeting was over.

"Sir, I'm sure we can..."

"Shut up and listen, *Chad*," the CSO ordered as he stood. "I want that report in my hands thirty seconds after you get it. I want an Intra-Galactic All Points Bulletin sent through the Gate to friendly systems. Then I want it leaked to non-friendlies—with a reward. Make it *big*. Like, a month's worth of acquisitions big."

Chad gulped.

"Full reward if they're both brought in alive, half reward if she's alive and he's dead. She has to be alive, you hear me? I'll take the kid either way. Tell them there's a nice bonus if they get the ship back."

"Yes, sir."

"Where the hell's Gretchen?" he barked.

The CSO spun, looking for Gretchen. He cupped his hand under the cigar so he didn't get ash on the carpet.

"Sir, very quickly, the three test pilots, permission to initiate a Search and Rescue."

"Denied."

"What?"

"If they can't make it back, they're MIA. Somebody fucked us on this deal and the only dime I'm spending is whatever it takes to get our property back. We have bigger things to worry about than a few test pilots. Gretchen!"

Gretchen was nowhere in sight, presumably still out searching for an ashtray.

"Ahh, fuck it."

The chief ground his half-smoked cigar onto the hardwood table right below the gold lettering of the USSF Black Ops seal set in its polished surface. It read, *Humanity is Important, a Person is Expendable.*

CHAPTER TWENTY-FOUR

"I don't see it. It looks like a bunch of rocks," John said.

"That's the idea. Even your Space Force doesn't know it's here."

"Hey, don't call them *my* Space Force. Those guys can lick a dick."

Shippewa flew gracefully over Saturn's multifaceted ring system. They were heading for one particular ring on the outer edge comprised of gigantic chunks of ice and rock, some as big as mountains, all slowly orbiting the planet like a giant merry-go-round.

"Is it the one that looks like a bumpy toilet paper tube?"

"That's it," Meehixiheem said.

The Gate was essentially an enormous rock cylinder, or at least *disguised* as one. It was at least five miles in length, two miles at each opening, and nestled in with millions of other chunks of natural debris. It was indistinguishable from the oddly shaped rocks surrounding it, even on close inspection. It was a proverbial needle in a haystack if one didn't know what to look for or where.

"What do we do?" John carefully guided Shippewa toward it but not too close.

"Keep us right here for a minute." Meehixiheem looked out the porthole and seemed to be concentrating.

"What are you doing?" John asked.

"Nothing."

He watched her bite her fingernail.

John unstrapped from his seat and stepped behind her. With all they'd been through, he felt more affectionate toward her lately. *Maybe she could be my girlfriend.* He gently put his hands on her shoulders.

"I get it," he said. "You're nervous about going home. You know, sometimes when we want something really bad, but then finally get it, we find that—"

Meehix pushed his hands off her shoulders and yelled, "What the *fuck* are you talking about?"

"What? I was trying to comfort you."

Meehix made a *wanking-the-pole* motion—and it didn't mean *thank you.* "John, sometimes you are as dense as a black hole."

"Then what's the matter?"

"I'm trying to remember the combination."

"What combination?"

"The combination! The access code to turn on the Gate! I can't remember it!"

"Oh. Oops." He sat. *Wait a minute.* "Shippewa."

"Yes, John?"

"Can you use Hannah to open the Gate?"

"Scanning. Please wait."

They waited. Meehix looked at John hopefully, and he gave her the thumbs up.

"No, John. The gate operates via a hyper-dimensional visualization registry system. It is neither binary nor based on any computer programming code, terrestrial or otherwise. If Meehix cannot mentally visualize the correct combination of third- and fourth-dimensional elements, I'm afraid we are fucked."

"Third- and fourth-dimensional elements? Who built this thing?"

Meehix stared out the porthole at the Gate. "Nobody knows for sure. It's been here for millions of years. These things are all over the galaxy, like a subway system. The combination for each Gate is a three-dimensional object that changes in time. You have to visualize it and the changes it makes to the micro-second. It's kind of like a Rubik's Cube on steroids. Only it's all in your head."

"Rubik's Cube—I had one of those when I was a kid. I'm good at those."

"Well, this is nothing like that."

"You said..."

"I know. I was trying to give an example you'd understand. I fucked *that* up too."

Meehix slumped in her spot at the back of the ship. She picked at the bandage on her leg. The blood was dry and crusty.

"Look," John said warily, "I don't want to piss you off, but what did you expect to do when we got here if you forgot the combination?"

Meehix's teeth clenched, and her eyes narrowed.

"I thought maybe I would remember it when I got here," she hissed slowly.

"Okay, okay, sorry."

"I only used it *once*," she explained, "and I wasn't even piloting. It wasn't high on my list of priorities to remember. Plus I was pretty drunk at the time."

They kept silent for at least a full minute, thinking.

"Wait a minute," John said, "how did you learn the combination to begin with?"

"Daukhl had a Universal Gate Token. He must have stolen it or got it on the black market. Only high-ups in the system governments have them or researchers. My sire had one, but I was never allowed to use it."

"How does it work?"

"It's a glorified holograph projector about the size of your pendant. It shows you a map of the galaxy and has all the various Gates marked. You pick one, and it projects the combination for that Gate. You memorize all the projection's elements. Then when you get close to that Gate, you imagine the elements you memorized. Gate opens, you go through."

"So it's in your head somewhere. You just can't remember it."

"Yeah, I guess."

John chewed his lower lip and looked her in the eye.

"Have you ever been hypnotized?"

"No. And I'm not going to." Meehix stood.

"Why not?"

"'Cause that shit's weird and nobody's gonna dig around in my head. We call it *bregen-yeg-gleer* in my language, and it's totally illegal. You can get the death penalty for messing with that shit."

"Really? Geez, on Earth, people use it to stop smoking."

"Yeah, well, Earthlings are nuts."

"True," John admitted. "If it got us the combination, would you do it?"

Meehix pressed her hands on either side of her head and closed her eyes.

"Aaaaaaah!" she yelled. "Fuck!"

John waited. *Must be an alien girl thing.*

"Oh...*fudge puppies,*" she whimpered. *And a translation thing.*

She opened her eyes.

"All right." She sounded defeated. "How do we do it?"

The cabin was dark, and Shippewa had projected a repetitive, rotating, holographic pattern directly in front of Meehixiheem's face. She was lying back comfortably in the control chair, her eyelids droopy, and she looked almost on the verge of sleep. Ship had been droning softly to her through the sound system for nearly forty minutes.

"**...And now you are completely relaxed. Your mind is content. Your body is weightless. Your entire being is peaceful. Distant memories from your past are becoming clear.**"

John sat where Meehix usually slept, trying not to make any noise.

Thank God Ship saved a few academic volumes on hypnosis when he was cross-referencing Earth libraries, or we might be stuck orbiting Saturn the rest of our lives. Fuck, we still might if this doesn't work.

"**Now, listen carefully, Meehixiheem. I want you to**

think back to when you first arrived in the Kdack 3a system. Do you remember that?"

"Yes," Meehix said slowly.

"Very good. Now think about Daukhl and his Universal Gate Token. Do you remember that?"

"Yes."

"Do you remember when you memorized the Gate combination for the Kdack system?"

"Yes," she said.

Now we're getting somewhere, John thought.

"Think about the Gate combination. Do you remember it clearly now?"

"I remember when I memorized the gate combination," she repeated slowly. "Daukhl was acting like a total asshole. That motherfucker. Thinks he's so cool because he hangs out with that cunt Nateexopeel and her fat friend Barbazclomeen!"

"Wait, wait, relax, relax, Meehixiheem. Relax."

Oh geez.

"Take a deep breath. Relax *all* your muscles. Good. Now, let's go back to the Gate combination. Visualize the Gate combination. Can you see the third- and fourth-dimensional elements shown to you with the token?"

"Yes."

"Concentrate on what you see, Meehixiheem. Focus on the three-dimensional aspects of the projection and the exact timing of the changes it makes. Are you imagining it in your mind?"

"Yes," she whispered, "but Barbazclomeen keeps babbling on like a Howler Monkey about how *'this mansion is soooo much smaller than the one I grew up in...*' Yeah, I bet it is, bitch, 'cause yer fat ass couldn't fit through the kitchen door when you were stuffing yer face with..."

"**Meehixiheem! Stop. Relax. Focus. I want you to forget about Barbazclomeen and Nateexopeel. Focus only on the three-dimensional aspects of the Gate combination and the exact timing of the changes it makes. Are you imagining it in your mind?**"

John suddenly saw something light up outside the ship through the porthole. He jumped up to see. A flickering, blue glow emanated from the giant toilet paper tube.

"Holy shit! She did it! Ship! *You* did it!"

"**Yes. We did. Hooray!**"

Meehix jolted awake.

"What happened? Why am I lying down? Why do I feel like someone molested me?"

"I'll tell you in a minute. Let's go, Ship! Get us through that thing before it closes!"

"Before *what* closes? What did you two perverts do to me?"

CHAPTER TWENTY-FIVE

Shippewa emerged from the connecting Gate, which was about two thousand light-years away from the Saturn Gate. The connecting Gate looked nothing like the Saturn Gate except for its size and shape. It was still the shape of a giant toilet paper tube, only made of transparent metal, like glass with a metallic-gray hue.

There were hundreds of Gates, all lined up and stretching for thousands of miles across space, like tubular dominoes with all varieties of spacecraft passing through them or waiting to pass through them.

This is obviously a very popular hub, John thought.

It wasn't the Gates that really blew his mind. It was the new world to which they had arrived. Not a planet, but a *Dyson Sphere,* or at least that's what John guessed it was.

Technically, it wasn't an actual sphere like the mathematical theorist from the 1960s, Freeman Dyson, first theorized in his paper about detecting advanced, intelligent extraterrestrial life. This was more like rings within rings enveloping a yellow star, like one of those old Armillary Spheres with metal bands representing the different objects in the heavens. Needless to say, the fucking thing was *enormous.*

"Whoa!" John was in shock. "This is your home?"

"Hell no. I mean, there are some great clubs and resorts, but I wouldn't want to live here. No sunsets, no oceans, no trees. It's like living in a tin can."

"So why are we stopping here?"

"'Cause this is where the Saturn Gate connects. This is where *all* the Gates connect. And I have a room at The Gallacher Spire on Ring Three, Twelfth Sector. All my stuff is there, including some spending dough. We're gonna need a lot of cold cash to get anywhere."

"John?"

"Yeah, Ship?"

"Sorry to interrupt, but in regard to transporting Meehixiheem to her home planet, we will require significant repairs and adjustments to complete the journey safely. Our energy converter requires tuning, and our gravity generator is functioning at less than optimal capacity. Also, we should be inspected for hull damage considering the high-velocity impacts we recently experienced."

"Yeah, I hear ya. *Someone* knocked the shit out of you, didn't they?"

"Oh, fuck off!" Meehix growled. "We got away, didn't we?"

John chuckled. *She is one spicy chick. She should have been a redhead, not a greenhead.*

"Anywhere in this place we can get Ship fixed up?" John asked her.

"There's a repair shop around the corner from the Spire. Hopefully, they'll let us land there while we get the money."

"Cool. Give Ship the directions. I don't feel comfortable flying in all this traffic, let alone into a Dyson Sphere."

Meehix told Ship where to go, and they were on their way.

"Once we get the cash, can we get some *real* food? The prunes and sardines ain't cutting it."

"There are over five hundred million restaurants in there." She pointed at the layered loops circling the star. "I think we can find you something to eat."

"Nice. What's this place called anyway?"

"The star is Pnellu IV. The place is Lagud. In the native language that means Hot City."

CHAPTER TWENTY-SIX

Holy shit. She wasn't kidding. More like Scorching *Hot City. It must be at least a hundred and twenty degrees out here.*

They had successfully landed on an open pad next to the repair shop. There were a dozen other ships of varying sizes and designs parked around them. Meehix was negotiating with a humanoid mechanic who looked like a cross between Dennis Rodman and a bull, dressed in dirty pink coveralls. Meehix was doing all the talking. Rod-Bull was methodically spinning some kind of heavy tool in his large, fingerless hand. Neither one of them looked happy, and John couldn't understand a word they were saying.

"Oh shit," he realized. "I'm not going to understand anybody around here."

"**John?**" Ship said over the external audio. John jumped. *It always sounds like he's right next to me when he does that.*

"Yeah, Ship."

"**In case you were not aware, my translator is removable and has its own power source. While not as size**

efficient as a portable translator, you could carry it with you until you obtain a more efficient unit."

"Really? No shit! That's awesome, Ship."

"I thought you might dig it."

Ship told John how to remove the translator. When it was free, it looked like a smooth, gray-plastic guitar without the neck and the resonator having two holes instead of one. It was a bit on the heavy side, but nothing he couldn't handle. He carried it down the stairs and walked over to Meehix and Rod-Bull.

"That's bullshit!" he heard Meehix say through the translator. "That much money and you can't even guarantee a time?"

"What do you want from me?" Rod-Bull said. "I don't even know if I have the parts. You have a Rennex Nebula Converter dropped into a B-95 Cogar mount. Shit, they don't even make Cogar mounts anymore.

"If I have to replace it, you may need a whole new converter frame, and that's gonna take time *and* money. I mean, I'm not saying that's what wrong. I'm just saying what *could* be wrong. Look at this thing. Are those *steel* plates on the hull? Who uses *steel* on a *hull*? Like, *no one ever*."

Meehix started yelling again, and Rod-Bull looked like he wanted to smack her in the head with the tool he was holding. John walked around the lot checking out all the cool ships when he realized he was sweating like a pig.

Man, this place is hot, he thought. *Why didn't they build it further away from the sun?*

He glanced at the star beating its heat down on him. It

looked a lot like Earth's, maybe a little bigger and a little more orange-colored, but not so different.

What was different was how the concentric rings of the Dyson Sphere seemed to rise like distant arches from the surface and fade away as they went higher and higher in the light blue sky. You couldn't see them circling the sun like you could from space, and it was weird to see giant arches dappled with enormous cities the size of continents rising into the air. If not for the rings and the spaceships, he could have been in Phoenix, Arizona, on an August day and not known the difference.

Meehix marched by him, and she didn't look happy.

"Come on," she snapped. "He's only letting us park here for an hour unless we come back with twenty credits. He won't even look at the ship until we give him some money. *Asshole.*"

"Shouldn't we tell Ship we're leaving?"

"Why? He's an AI. He'll figure it out."

John wasn't sure what to make of *that* comment. It seemed a little callous and was a different gender than he'd learned to call other ships. John had come to think of Ship as a friend, not only an AI. *Oh well. I'm a stranger in a strange land. Better just roll with things. When in Rome...*

They walked off the lot and around the corner to a side street.

Everything was metal and stone. The streets were some kind of greenish marble and the buildings a dark copper-colored metal. Everything was dusty, which seemed odd because there were no plants anywhere, or dirt, or sand, or anything that would appear to make dust.

Maybe everything's slowly breaking down to baser elements.

It certainly felt old. The buildings and other structures were high-tech in terms of technology, but they gave off a vibe as if they'd been there for a very long time.

Things were added on everywhere, like holographic screens and signs and pipes, as if they'd anchored stuff to existing stuff, then added more on top of it. There was plenty of room though. Only about fifty other beings walked around in an area that looked built to handle thousands. Most of the beings looked like Rod-Bull.

"Who built Lagud?"

"Berklings."

"What's a Berkling?"

"The beings that built Lagud. Like, a million years ago."

"They built the Gates?"

"No. Those came *way* before the Berklings. I told you. Nobody knows who built the Gates. The Berklings built Lagud because the Gates were already here."

"Cool."

They rounded another corner and walked into a structure that appeared roughly ninety stories high. John noticed all the doorways and ceilings here were much bigger and higher than in Earth buildings. He liked that. It felt like he could stretch out and not bump his head on anything. The Berklings must be big guys, like him.

Inside was a waiting area of sorts with furniture of all different sizes and shapes, apparently to accommodate a multitude of species, and a check-in area where another guy who looked like Rod-Bull was sitting, only he was cleaned up and wore a green uniform. Meehix marched right up to him like she owned the place.

"I need to get in my room."

Rod-Bull gave her a strange look—at least that's how it appeared to John—and pressed a button under the desk. A square portion of the desk lit up with a beige glow. Meehix put her hand on the glowing part. Rod-Bull picked up an iPad-like device and looked at the screen.

"Don't have it."

"What do you mean? I have an open account on that room."

"Room 92-99?"

"Yes."

"Account's been closed. Housekeeping cleaned it out last week."

"What about my stuff? I had a lot of valuables in there."

"Would have been put in storage. Only hold it for a month though. Down the hall on the right."

"Great." Meehix was simmering.

They walked down the hall. John was still carrying the translator, and now it was getting heavy.

"This is bullshit," Meehix cursed. "Nobody should have been able to close that account but me."

"Why do you keep a room here?"

"Crash space. I have a bunch of them in different cities on different planets. It's a place to party or hang after the party. I got this one right before I came to Earth. Didn't plan to *crash there* though."

They came to a big metal door on the right near the end of the hall. Another beige square was on the wall next to it with the instructions *Place Appendage Here For Service* inscribed underneath it in about twenty different languages. Meehix put her hand on the pad.

"What do you need?" a gruff voice said over a crackly intercom.

"I left some things in my room. The guy at the desk said to come down here. 92-99. Meehixiheem…"

"Yeah, yeah, hold on. I already got yer info," he cut her off.

"Everybody seems a little…irritated…around here," John noted.

"It's just this sector. Drellens are always grumpy."

"Drellens. That's the Dennis Rodman dudes?"

"What's a Dennis Rodman?"

"Good question."

The lower portion of the door slid sideways at about knee level, and a Drellen shoved a big container through, almost hitting them in the shins. John couldn't see the Drellen's face, but his fingerless hands gave him away. The door slid shut. The intercom crackled again.

"We are visually and audibly recording this transaction for your protection and will keep a record of your DNA profile on file in perpetuity," the Drellen droned on. He sounded incredibly bored.

"Neither the Gallacher Spire, its staff, nor its subsidiaries can be held responsible for damaged, missing, irradiated, contaminated, or otherwise infected items—regardless of cause or source. It is your responsibility as the recipient of said items to ensure their decontamination before transporting said items across interplanetary boundaries."

The Drellen must have thought the intercom was off or he didn't care if they heard him because he mumbled, *"You people never pick up your stuff in time."*

"What's *that* supposed to mean?" Meehix scowled.

"Beats me," John replied.

She sifted through the container. It held lots of clothes and a medium-sized suitcase made of what was probably an expensive and exotic animal. She pulled that out first. It had a big carrying handle on the top and a finger pad. She put her fingers on that, and the luggage popped open. Inside was another smaller briefcase made of metal and what looked like a heavy-duty, black laptop. She opened the metal briefcase.

"Finally!" she squealed. "Some luck! The money's all here!"

Before John could get a good look, she grabbed a wad of what must have been Galactic Credits, stuffed them down her pants, and closed the briefcase. She grabbed the loose clothing and stuffed it all into the suitcase, along with the metal case and the laptop thing, and closed it.

"First, let's pay off the mechanic. Then we'll come back and get another room. I want a chissatch oil bath and a massage. Then we're gonna put on clean clothes, find a *veonk* bar, and eat and drink till we drop! I'm so happy!"

She squealed again and hugged John, picked up the suitcase, and started up the hall.

"What about your leg? We still gotta get you to a doctor."

"Fuck that. I heal fast. Besides, veonk spheres and Gyken martinis are better than any fuckin' doctor."

CHAPTER TWENTY-SEVEN

John stretched out on the enormous circular bed in the suite they rented. The whole place felt made for a king, and this wasn't even the most expensive room.

He felt fantastic. They'd started with the oil bath, which was very soothing but the massage was, well, out of this world. A master masseuse with five appendages on each side of his or her body—John wasn't sure of the gender—came up to their room and worked on one of them while the other was taking a chissatch bath.

After an hour of pure ecstasy, the masseuse asked John if he "desired happy time engagement release" for an additional five credits, which would be charged directly to the room tab. "Completely legal in this Sector," the being assured him. John could use a good wank, especially with Meehixiheem happily bouncing around the suite naked all the time, but he politely declined. The ten arms and three eyes were not a turn-on. If he or she had looked like Layla9 or Obabebabe, he might have considered it. The masseuse bowed respectfully and left.

"Well, what do you think?" Meehixiheem asked from the bathroom.

She stood there with one arm on the door frame and the other seductively fingering the sapphire-red necklace hanging between her breasts. She wore an almost see-through silk-like dress that was not only low-cut at the top but stopped at her thighs to show off those sexy, sinuous legs. High-heeled shoes made of blue crystal accentuated the red polish on her toenails.

Her green hair was pulled back and speckled with little crystalline jewels that sparkled when she turned her head. Her make-up was elegant but not overdone, heightening her cheekbones and bringing out the colors of her eyes. Aside from the bullet wound, which was now only two dark marks on her inner thigh and barely visible, she looked stunning.

"Wow. You look fucking fantastic." John thought that if she climbed onto the bed and wrapped those legs around him, he'd instantly mess up his clean pants again. They hadn't taken the time to get any new clothes yet, but they did send his outfit down to housekeeping while he was in the oil bath. Not only were his clothes completely spotless and clean-smelling but they repaired a few damaged seams —all in less than thirty minutes.

Suddenly the room went dark. Meehix waved her hand over a small dome next to the bathroom door and the room re-lit in a soft blue glow.

"What happened? Where'd the sun go?"

John jumped up from the bed and went to the window. It was instantly night. Street lights came on, and beings poured out onto the marble pavement like army ants raiding a picnic. He heard their animated voices far below. The distant arches lit up, sector by sector, with city lights, up into the sky and around where the sun now looked like a total eclipse.

How the hell do they turn off the sun? he thought.

"Nighttime on Lagud!" Meehixiheem exclaimed happily. "Time to party!"

CHAPTER TWENTY-EIGHT

The packed streets were forty degrees cooler than earlier, which felt awesome to John. About half the beings he saw were Drellen, but the other half was a mixed bag. Some of the humanoid inhabitants were sinewy females with arousing bodies and smells. Humanoid males were a mix of GQ models, crazed rock star types, and drugged-out weirdos.

Other creatures of the night appeared so hideous that his stomach turned: monsters with no eyes, others with many eyes, some the size of dachshunds—with two heads —and others as big as horses, with no heads. The outfits and adornments ranged from completely plain one-piece bodysuits to flamboyant, multi-colored extravaganzas of color and design. It was like Mardi Gras on acid.

Meehix held his hand as she navigated them through the galactic urban sprawl.

"You're gonna *love* this place!" she shouted over the din. "The *veonk* is some of the best I've ever had!"

John couldn't help but smile at her excitement. She seemed to genuinely get a kick out of giving him the grand tour of the place as if she could tell he was overwhelmed and she relished every minute of it. *Oh well. Roll with it and let her have some fun. At least she's happy.*

She pulled them off the street into a portico of what must have been the restaurant she was talking about. Beings already packed the place, most of them humanoid types. Meehix produced an onyx-colored card with a glowing red star in its center. She held it up and waved it around while yelling for the concierge.

A large, boar-like being in a fancy suit instantly pushed past the waiting patrons to get to Meehix. Without speaking, he waved a handheld device over the card, looked at his machine, and said, "Right this way, ma'am. Sorry for the wait."

"Damn, Meehix," John teased her, "you's a *gangster!*"

Meehix smiled and did one of her convulsive laugh things. She was thoroughly enjoying herself.

Boar Man led them through the crowd and into the darkened establishment. John had to finagle the translator through some narrow spaces, and he noticed as he passed various dimly lit booths that it was having a hell of a time keeping up with all the conversations. Half of what it reproduced was pure gibberish, and some of the beings glared at him as if what it spewed was the height of rudeness.

"We need to get you an earpiece," Meehix explained.

"Earpiece?"

"A private translator that fits in your ear. They're

expensive, but that thing is too big, plus you're reproducing everyone's conversations for the entire world to hear. Maybe after we eat, we'll try to pick one up for both of us. I had one when I came to Kdack, but the dick-lickers confiscated it."

John noticed that most, if not all, of the restaurant's patrons had earpieces, like small black hearing aids stuck in various orifices.

Boar Man seated them at a cozy little booth made for humanoids, and they slid in across from each other. John set the translator next to him on the seat nearest the wall to not draw as much attention. A little red globe floated in the middle of the table, giving them just enough light to see each other. John reached out and touched it with his finger. It moved slightly and then floated right back into position.

"What are you doing?" Meehix asked.

"This thing is cool. How does it float back to the same spot and just hover there?"

"Don't embarrass me, John," she said.

A waiter appeared. John almost laughed out loud, which clearly would have been a horrible breach of etiquette, but he couldn't help it. The waiter had a large, human-like body with a head the size of a pear. And he was dressed like a pirate. *And* he was wearing enormous Elton John-like sunglasses.

"Good evening," the waiter's voice emitted from the translator. He sounded like a very calm and serene Donald Duck. "I'll be your server this evening. Could I interest you in libations? We have a special on certain items only legal in..."

"We'll both have a Gyken martini and a double order of veonk spheres, easy on the urwee cream," Meehix said hungrily.

"Excellent, madam. Anything else?"

"Oh, and two orders of u-u-eggs," she added.

Then Meehix looked at John as if she was waiting for him to order something.

"Seriously?" John glared at her then addressed the waiter. "I'm good with that. What she said."

"Very good, sir. I'll bring your selections as quickly as possible." The waiter walked away with deep, giant steps as though he was working his quadriceps.

"Holy shit!" John finally released his laughter. "Did you see that guy?"

"What guy?"

"The waiter. What a goofball! I had to bite my tongue to keep from laughing."

Meehix's forehead wrinkled, and she stared at him.

Uh-oh, he thought.

"*You* are *prejudiced,*" she whispered so as not to be overheard.

"No, I'm not," John protested. "He just caught me off guard."

"Caught *what* off guard? Your *racism?*"

"No. I just...I mean...geez. He just looked really funny to me. Sorry."

Meehix tapped her four thumbs on the table. John started to feel like an ass.

"Did you think *I* looked funny the first time you saw me?"

"Hell no!" John blurted out. "I thought you were...beautiful."

She considered this a moment but didn't give him an inch.

"Well, *think* before you *think*. You know what I mean? That waiter works hard, probably has a family to feed, and doesn't go around making fun of other beings because of the way they look. Plus, he's a Dwan DooVoo, and according to the five Gabkon beads woven into his dreadlocks, he's a fifth-level Kraxo expert. He could beat the shit out of both of us with one hand tied behind his back."

Damn. I guess I need to keep my mouth shut until I figure out how this galaxy works. Otherwise, Meehix is going to end up hating me, and some duck-dude is gonna kick my ass.

The waiter returned with the drinks.

"That was quick." John consciously tried to be friendly.

"I aim to be prompt, sir," the waiter said.

Two martini-type glasses made of crystal sat on a round floating disk the waiter guided with his hand. He never touched the glasses but rather let John and Meehix lift them from the disk. They were really cold.

"Your food will be ready shortly," the waiter announced. "Enjoy." He bounded away.

"Okay, I forgive you." Meehix raised her glass. John raised his glass and clinked it on hers. The crystal made a high-pitched scream, like a tuning fork on overload. Heads turned.

"*Okay,*" Meehix whispered menacingly, "*now why the fuck did you do that?* You almost shattered Kanderian Ice Glasses. Do you know how expensive these are?"

"Oh, shit, I give up," John lamented. "I can't do anything right."

Meehix pointed at John's eyes, then to her glass, as in *watch and learn.*

She raised the glass again and whirled it several times in the air, not to spill it but to agitate the fluid inside. The clear liquid began to turn bright blue until a soft mist flowed over the rim like dry ice in water, only without the bubbling. She took a long slow sip and closed her eyes. "Oh, fuck...that's good."

John went through the same motions and sipped.

"Oh, fuck...that *is* good!" he exclaimed.

He instantly felt better when the freezing cocktail tingled its way down his throat, into his bloodstream, and straight to his brain. He decided to quit feeling sorry for himself. What was it Gage said? I wish I were you?

Yeah, I guess I got it pretty good. Traveling the galaxy with a rich, hot alien. Drinking exotic drinks, getting ten-handed massages. What the hell am I whining about? Life is good.

He sipped again and looked around the place. So many beings, so many stories, so many places. He felt giddy and almost started laughing. Suddenly everything seemed equal parts entertaining and wonderful.

"Uh-oh," Meehix said.

Without warning or introduction, a gorgeous female humanoid sat and slid right up next to John. She had deep maroon skin, a scanty turquoise dress, and a body to die for. She glanced at Meehix, who rolled her eyes and looked away. Then she put her hand on John's leg.

"Neestomi seveek-an-lemees?" she whispered seductively in his ear. He could feel her hot breath on his neck. *Instant boner.*

"What'd she say?" John asked Meehix, sounding a bit tipsy. "The translator isn't working...or something."

Holy shit. That drink went right to my head. Who is this chick?

"Sorry," Meehix said nonchalantly, "I'm not your pimp. You're gonna have to negotiate your own deals."

"What deals?"

The room was spinning.

"What does she want?" he asked sincerely, still taking strong hits from his ice glass and looking the woman up and down.

"Your dick...and your money. The latter more than the former. She's a *hooker.*"

"Whoa, really?" John looked at Meehix incredulously, then back at the red woman. She stared into his eyes and moved her hand to his inner thigh. Her tits were fabulous.

John was mesmerized. Then he remembered Meehix. She was sitting there, watching.

"Need a loan?" She tapped her thumbs on the table.

"Uhm..."

John moved the red woman's hand away from his crotch. He smiled and declined her offer as politely as he could.

"No...no thank you," he said. "I'm...uh...*with somebody.*" He motioned toward Meehix. Meehix rolled her eyes.

The red woman smiled and gave a quick look at Meehix. Meehix gave a *"now fuck off, bitch"* smirk. The red woman leaned into John's ear one more time and said—in English—"Too bad because I have a thing for Earthmen..."

and proceeded to whisper everything she would have done to him and how she would have done it.

John slid down in the booth, practically catatonic. The red woman made her exit. Meehix slapped John's face. Hard.

"Ow! What I do?"

"That drink is going to your head. Snap out of it."

CHAPTER TWENTY-NINE

They finished their meal, or rather, Meehix finished it. John almost puked up the veonk spheres. It was like eating a bloated toad dipped in yogurt. The booze was great, the food, not so much, at least not to John. She ended up ordering something close to a veggie burger for him so he'd get something in his stomach other than cocktails. He was making a fool of himself, pretending to play the translator like a guitar and serenading her about his undying love and undying boners.

He's not going to remember this tomorrow.

They wandered the busy streets for a while. John raved about Lagud and how beautiful it was. He kept babbling on about how kind everyone was and how he was never going to leave. Meehix had to hold onto him to keep him from falling over.

This night's really shaping up.

They went into a small tech store off the main drag, and Meehix negotiated two personal ear translators at a reasonable price. The Drellen running the store said, "Better grab your friend. Looks like he's going down."

John was pressed against a glass display, his knees buckling and his face sliding down a holographic image of an advertisement for Gyken Gin.

Somehow, she got him back to the Gallacher Spire where he proceeded to vomit at the front door. Meehix held his head over a waste disposal unit. A Dwan DooVoo exited the building and scowled at them in disgust.

When she got him up to the room, she flopped him on the bed face-first. He immediately started snoring.

Meehix went into the bathroom and stared at the mirror.

"Thanks, Meehix." She mimicked John's voice and demeanor, "I had a great time tonight. You really are beautiful, you know? In fact, you're the most beautiful girl I've ever seen. Would it be too much to ask for a goodnight kiss?"

She put her hands on the mirror.

"I don't think that would be too much to ask, John," she said. "Who knows? You play your cards right, and you might get a whole lot more. I can beat a hooker's moves any day."

She kissed the mirror, pulled back, and cried.

CHAPTER THIRTY

John's eyes wouldn't focus. Something like a fuzzy, metallic candelabrum on the end of a vacuum hose hung over his head from the ceiling. He kept staring at it, trying to figure out what the heck it was for and why it was over his head. He was on his back in a big bed, but he couldn't remember how he got there or where *there* even was. He looked down toward his feet. His clothes were still on.

Where am I?

His stomach rumbled, and he burped up a horrible taste. *Oh, now I remember. Pnellu IV. Lagud. Veonk spheres.* It all came back to him. Most of it anyway.

He hadn't noticed the candelabrum thing before. It was some kind of alien apparatus for who-knows-what, like an Earth hotel would have a hairdryer, an iron, etcetera, only here there were accouterments for all types of species. *I wonder if they have a device that can cure a Gyken hangover.*

He was rubbing his eyes when Meehix walked in.

"You're awake," she said matter-of-factly. "You were snoring so loud I had to sleep in the other room."

"Sorry." He licked his dry lips. "I think I over-did it."

"Yeah, *you did.*"

She was still in her sexy outfit from the night before, which she immediately began peeling out of. Bad thoughts flooded his mind, but the nasty taste in his mouth precluded any hanky-panky. *I'd need some industrial-strength mouthwash first.*

Apparently, Meehix was not planning to do what he was thinking because—when she was completely naked—she strode past him to the bathroom, smirking at his stare.

She couldn't deny it. She liked the fact that the sight of her naked body could have such a powerful effect on him. Kdack males were definitely different than Dolurulod males. She had to crank up the pheromones to get a Dolurulod to notice her, let alone stare at her. Earth males seem ready to mate the moment you met them.

"If you're in the mood, maybe you should call your *red lady,*" she said sarcastically. "I'm sure she's still working." Meehix turned on the shower.

Red lady? Oh, yeah. That *red lady. Oops. Better think quick.*

"I prefer *blue* ladies," he said. It wasn't a lie. He did prefer blue ladies. Now sober, he'd pick Meehix over the hooker any day. It was that wild whispering the red lady did in his ear as if she put a spell on him. He got a boner thinking about it.

"Didn't look like it when she gave you an *ear job.* A Margono's primary erogenous zone is the ear canal."

Good to know. Never give a Margono a wet willy—could be considered sexual assault.

"I did not know that," he said innocently.

John heard her get into the shower.

"Speaking of ears," she yelled over the sound of the water, "I bought some personal translators. They're expensive, but I got a deal on last year's model. They'll still cover ninety percent of the species we run into. Yours is on the end table next to the bed. Put it in your ear and press the button on the side."

A small black sphere, about the size of a large marble—with a glowing blue button on one side—sat on the end table next to him. He picked it up.

"This won't fit in my ear."

"Just do it. Put it to your ear and press the button."

John did as instructed, and suddenly the device made a strange squishing sound and completely conformed to the shape of his ear. It went partially into his ear canal and around the back of his auricular lobe like a hearing aid. This freaked him out for a second because it felt alive, like a tiny python trying to nest in his head, but then it was solid again and totally comfortable. It made a happy little *ping* tone as if to say, *all done!*

"Did you do it?" Meehix asked.

"Yeah. Freaky."

Now he heard Meehix in a kind of phased stereo. He realized it was the old translator on the floor next to the bed, still translating along with the new one in his ear. "How do I turn off the old translator?"

"I don't know. Ask Shippewa."

"What? How?"

"Just ask him. He's on the personal translator. I dialed him in so we can talk to him when we're away from the ship."

"Sweet. Hey, Ship?"

"Yes, John?"

It sounded like Ship was lying in bed next to him. *Cool.* More high-tech alien wizardry.

"How do I turn off the old translator?"

"Inside the top resonator, there is a recessed button."

John leaned over the edge of the bed, found the button, and pressed it. The translator made a winding-down tone, and immediately the phased stereo sound went away.

"What's the range on the new translators to talk to you, Ship?"

"Unlimited in star systems with hyper-bump communications. In non-participating areas of the galaxy, approximately ten thousand miles."

"I gotta remember to get one of these for Gage. They're perfect for gaming."

"What?" Meehix yelled.

"Nothing," John yelled back. "Just talking to Ship. Hey, are these things waterproof?"

"How do you think I can understand you in the shower?"

Oh yeah. I keep forgetting that Meehix isn't speaking English.

He stared up at the candelabrum thing again. It reminded him of one of those whirling play toys you put over a crib to keep a baby occupied. *There's* something that hadn't crossed his mind before. All this lusting after Meehix and he hadn't considered the potentially serious consequences of consummating *that* line of thought.

Could I get Meehix pregnant? Can human DNA and Dolu-rulod DNA mix?

He wondered if they would have blue babies, white

babies, or pale blue babies. What about the thumbs? That could get messy, along with that weird flap she had down there. Then there were the eyes. What about two different languages spoken in the same house?

Shit, we could end up having a blue kid with no genitals, swastika pupils, who's all thumbs and only speaks gibberish.

The thought made him shudder. Then another thought hit him.

She said her species hatch from eggs. I wonder. Does she have to sit on the eggs?

"Are you still there?"

"Yeah."

"Turn on *G-Viz*."

"What the heck's a *G-Viz*?"

"The big screen. *The monitor.* On the wall. There's a controller on the other end table."

He figured out the controller pretty quickly, and the whole wall in front of the bed lit up. John realized he was watching galactic programs, over ten thousand of them to choose from, transmitted clear across the Milky Way using a technology vastly different from Earth television. For one thing, it was holographic and very lifelike, and for another, it was some of the weirdest shit he'd ever seen in his life.

He flipped channels and saw what looked like cage-fighting between massive creatures right out of an H.P. Lovecraft novel. Then on another channel, strange, fractal images made him dizzy. When he flipped again, it was straight-up alien porn—two Drellen females sixty-nining each other while a male smeared himself with purple goo.

On another channel, there was an orgy going on with

five Margonos and three Dwan DooVoo males doing unspeakable things with a squid-like creature no bigger than football. He didn't know whether to get turned on or be sick.

Geez. Gage would love this. Or maybe not.

He kept channel surfing as the shows got weirder and weirder. When he thought nothing could ever shock him again, he saw something he *really* didn't expect to see— Meehixiheem's picture.

"Hey, Meehix!" he yelled, "you're on the G-TV thing!"

The shower shut off and Meehix rushed out, totally naked and wet. She stood by the bed, watching the wall screen. John tried not to look at her. *Remember the clumsy, blue eunuch, Nazi-eyed Babel-baby.*

While Meehix's portrait filled the wall, a narrator or newscaster of some kind was speaking in a language John couldn't follow.

"I can't understand what he's saying." He averted his eyes from Meehix's firm, wet butt. "My translator's not working."

"That's a Crec Alert. They post information on fugitives in all galactic languages, even non-member systems. It's used mostly by bounty hunters."

"Bounty hunters?"

Meehix frantically grabbed her suitcase and jumped on the bed. She pulled out the black laptop thing and opened it. Then she ran her fingers over its screen, flipping and pushing various bits of informational items around like a woman with a purpose.

All John could think about was this sexy, wet, curvaceous woman with great tits sitting on the bed next to him.

When was *the last time I got laid? Hannah. Right before she cheated on me. What a drag. Thank God we always used a condom.*

"Oh, no," Meehix whispered. "Oh, no!" she cried and slammed the device with her fist. *"Aaaaaaaah!"*

Her full-on, unbridled scream was unbelievable. John was surprised the windows didn't shatter.

Then a smell—like tropical suntan lotion—instantly filled the room and John's eyes rolled back. He felt like he was having the most fantastic, instantaneous orgasm of his life, only without the mess.

Meehix was sobbing. John was out like a happy light, a big, goofy smile on his face.

After a few minutes of this mix of agony and ecstasy, Meehix wiped her tears away and noticed John's condition.

"Damn." She sniffled, realizing what had happened. "Premature Orgasmic Mental Climax. I can't even remember the last time I did *that* to a guy."

She got up from the bed, opened the window, and fanned the air with a towel, doing whatever she could to get her blast of emotionally charged pheromones out of the room. John started coming around, and she closed the window. The heat from outside in the daytime was unbearable.

"What happened?" he said dreamily. "Did we just…*do it?*"

"No," she said as she began putting on her clothes, "and we're not going to either because *I don't exist.*"

She angrily pulled a shirt over her head and wiped her nose with the sleeve.

"What are you talking about?"

John had trouble ascertaining Meehix's mental state. *What happened?* He thought hard, trying to clear his brain fog. It almost felt like he was drunk again only without the nausea aftermath.

Her pheromones. That's it. Something freaked her out so bad that she let loose a bunch of pheromones and knocked me into erotic oblivion. Geez, if her scents can do that when she's extra-agitated, what would actual sex be like? She might orgasm me to death.

Meehix put on some skimpy shorts under the long t-shirt and pulled on a pair of shoes that looked like an alien cross between Nikes and flip-flops. She moved abruptly as if she was in angry-automatic mode. Her mind was clearly far away, calculating, fearing, lamenting, dreading. John felt bad for her. He'd never seen her this upset. She sniffed and wiped her eyes as she finished putting on the shoes.

"I'm a non-entity. I'm worse than a criminal. I have no rights whatsoever. Someone listed me as *non-sentient property*. My entire life is gone."

John was trying to wrap his mind around this. How did royalty go from the top of the food chain to the bottom in a matter of weeks?

"Where'd you find all this? I mean, where's such a thing even listed? Who decides?"

She rotated the screen on her black laptop thing so John could see it. Meehixiheem's picture was there, but the words around it were gibberish. He assumed it was in Dolurulod.

"It's all right there. The Galactic Sentient Registry. I have no credit. My bank accounts are empty. My family's

Lineage Index doesn't list my name. Stripped of all titles and status. A veonk sphere has more rights than me."

"How does that happen? You're from a royal family, right?"

"I don't know," she said sadly. "But it's why I'm on the Crec Alert. I'm somebody's property, and they want me back."

John felt the hair on his neck stand up.

"Someone can't *own* you. You're not a slave."

"That's *exactly* what I am."

"Fuck that stupid registry thing. Just 'cause it says so doesn't make it real. Where I come from, you *are* who you *think* you are. Not who someone *says* you are."

Meehix yawned. After she got her clothes on she seemed to have gone from sixty to zero in two-point-five seconds. She looked like she'd been beaten down with a whip and didn't care anymore. Still, he couldn't help but notice how cute she looked dressed like that—a t-shirt, shorts, and shoes.

It reminded him of Hannah, or Layla9, or Obabebabe. Hair still wet, her amazing legs, the resigned, sad expression on her face—*yeesh*. John had an overwhelming desire to embrace her and take care of her.

"Will you hold me?" she softly said as if she'd read his mind.

"Sure."

He laid back down, and she crawled up next to him and put her arm over his chest and one leg over his. As usual, it was hard not to get *hard*, but he tried not to because—for the first time in a while—he didn't only want sex. He wanted something more. Although—to be completely honest—he still wanted sex too.

"I'm so tired." She yawned again. "Can we sleep? We don't have to check out for a few hours. A nap sounds like bliss."

She snuggled up tight against him and positioned her head on his shoulder. A moment later and she was out, breathing heavily. *That was quick. One minute she's so upset she's squirting pheromones everywhere. The next minute she's sleeping like a baby. What am I going to do with this chick?* He could think of a few things but didn't want to wake her. Plus, he wasn't a sex offender.

He squeezed her tight. Without opening her eyes, she gave a contented sigh. *I know what I'm going to do with her. I'm going to protect her.*

CHAPTER THIRTY-ONE

"John? John? Can you hear me?"

John opened his eyes. He instantly noticed a strange smell in the air, like almond extract and cloves. Meehix still lay curled up next to him, sleeping. He heard a faint *hissing* sound coming from the door leading to the hallway.

"Yeah, Ship, I hear you."

"You and Meehix are in danger. There is a galactic-wide Crec Alert for both of you."

"Yeah, we know. We saw Meehix on TV...or the GV...or whatever it's called. Wait, I'm on it too?"

"Yes, John. You are listed as wanted dead or alive."

Must be more hungover than I thought. Did he say dead or alive?

"When I received the Crec Alert, I utilized Hannah to hack into the Gallacher Spire's computer system. I have been monitoring the entryway to your room via the hallway security cameras for the past hour. Three Drellen males are outside your door. One has placed a device at the base of the door. I suspect they may be bounty hunters."

"Oh, shit!" John whispered, fully awake now. "Meehix! Wake up!"

Meehix didn't move. He shook her. Nothing. She was comatose. John caught another whiff of the strange smell. *The door.*

"Fuck!"

He jumped to his feet and saw it instantly. A tiny tube slipped underneath. It was *hissing.*

"Ship," he whispered frantically, "they got something under the door. I think it's some kind of gas and it knocked out Meehix. Any suggestions?"

"The three bounty hunters are wearing gas masks. They are accessing the door's security system. Expect entry within the next five seconds. I'm sorry, John. Under the circumstances, I have no suggestions."

"So much for *Artificial Intelligence,*" John sneered as he jumped to the right of the door and pressed his back against the wall.

The magnetic lock *clicked,* and the door opened inwardly, slowly and quietly, blocking John where he hid behind it. He drew in his breath, trying to make himself as skinny as possible so the door wouldn't hit him.

He heard the bounty hunters breathing through the gas masks. It had that creepy Darth Vader vibe. First one, then another, then another entered. All three crept slowly toward the bedroom. The last one closed the door noiselessly. He saw John.

"Hi." John bum-rushed the motherfucker.

It was a spectacular tackle. John's full weight hit the

guy so violently that they smashed into the other two, who crashed into the G-Viz screen. They all went to the floor.

John was on the first guy in a flash and pounded his face into oblivion, hitting him multiple times in the mouth and ears. The dude was unconscious before he even knew he was down.

One of the other two was scrambling to get his gas mask back on, which had gotten knocked sideways when he fell. He collapsed before he could tighten it.

"Why...isn't...he...out," the Drellen moaned as he fell into unconsciousness.

The third bounty hunter was still in the fight and came up swinging. He outclassed John by at least six inches and fifty pounds. When his fist connected, John saw stars and felt pain like he hadn't felt since a guy clocked him on the bridge of his nose during rugby practice. He expected to gush blood at any moment, but it never came, only the pain.

John blocked another incoming punch with his left forearm and laid a right hook to the side of the bounty hunter's head. The Drellen staggered and John hit him again with a wicked uppercut. The guy fell back onto the bed next to Meehix. Her limp body bounced to the floor like a ton of blue bricks.

"Motherfucker!" John screamed.

He grabbed the candelabrum thing, and it extended from the ceiling by a hose. John swung it like a machete. At first, the bounty hunter dodged but then cocked his head as if to say, *what the heck?* John took advantage of the pause and hit him right over the head. The candelabrum shattered like potato chips, and the bounty hunter didn't even flinch. *Dang. That sucked.*

He dropped the remains of the terrible choice of a weapon and dove at the bounty hunter.

Everything went in slow motion. In the middle of his leap, John thought he saw the barrel of a gun. It didn't register in his mind as a gun at first, but when it flashed, he felt the impact to his chest and *knew* it was a gun. There was enough inertia in the discharge to knock him backward, even in mid-leap, and he felt it as if he'd been punched hard in the chest.

Then all the hairs on his body began to tingle, and he heard a funny buzzing sound. He fell next to Meehix on the floor and stared up at the bounty hunter who loomed over him.

"You're dead, *Earthman*," the Drellen said through his gas mask. He holstered the weapon.

John started giggling.

"What the..." the bounty hunter squinted disbelievingly.

John rolled into a fetal position and began laughing uncontrollably. Every square inch of his body *tickled.* He'd never felt so ticklish in his life. He screamed with laughter.

"Stop! Stop it!"

He rolled around on the floor as if mercilessly fingered by hundreds of invisible gremlins that swarmed over his body and dug into every rib and sensitive spot. He laughed so hard he started choking.

"You're killing me! Stop it!"

Then it stopped as quickly as it came. The tickling vanished. *What the fuck?*

He felt fine. Better than fine. In fact, he felt *great.* Even the pain in his nose was gone. *Shit, I can even breathe better. I feel fantastic!*

He jumped to his feet, and the bounty hunter backed away and drew the gun again. He fired.

Another direct hit to the chest, and John staggered back from the impact. Again with the tickling. John laughed hysterically. He collapsed on the bed, howling like a crazed hyena, clutching his stomach and kicking his legs.

"This is insane!" the bounty hunter yelled and fired again—another direct hit, this time in John's side.

"Oh my God!" John yelled, "I'm gonna piss my pants! Stop! Stop it!" It was like silly torture. Tears were running down his face.

While John rolled around in hysterics, the bounty hunter tried to comprehend what was happening. He checked his gun and couldn't find a malfunction. Then he noticed Meehix peeking up from the edge of the bed, eyes droopy, words slurred.

"What are you guys doing?" she said as if under the influence of hurnrern weed. "I'm trying to sleep."

The bounty hunter grabbed her by the hair and yanked her to her feet.

"Ow!" Meehix screamed. "Be gentle!"

He held the gun to Meehix's head. She flailed around like a string puppet, smacking at the giant hand holding her bunched-up green mop with no effect whatsoever. She gave up and went limp.

"This may not kill *you*," the bounty hunter snarled at John, "but I *know* it will kill *her*. Now *back off*."

The tickling stopped again. John uncurled himself. He was still on the bed, his face streaked with tears, a stain on his groin. *Yup,* he thought. *I peed myself. How embarrassing.* He sat up and wiped his face.

The bounty hunter holding Meehix kicked the other two on the floor. They didn't move. He didn't take his eyes off John.

"Never seen anyone survive three hits with a Vetralaun semi-automatic. Then again, you're the only *human* I ever shot. Live and learn, I guess."

"Yeah? Well, you better *learn* to let her go, or you're not gonna *live* much longer."

John clenched his fists and flexed his chest muscles. He felt that fantastic rush again. *Not sure what that gun's supposed to do, but it sure makes me feel like the Incredible Hulk —except for the tickling and pissing part.*

"Ow!" Meehix cried as the Drellen tightened his grip on her hair.

He backed away from John and toward the door, the gun still pressed to Meehix's temple. He shoved her into a headlock, put the gun under her chin, and opened the door with his other hand.

"Ow! You're hurting my neck!"

"Shut up!" the Drellen shouted. "You yell again, and I'll *break* your neck!"

He backed into the hallway, half-pulling, half-pushing her.

"I want her alive," he said, "but if I see you following us, I'll take her in *dead!*"

The bounty hunter bolted down the hallway toward the elevator, Meehix in tow.

John jumped into action.

First, he frisked the other two bounty hunters. One of

them was groaning so he knew he had to work fast. He found another Vetralaun semi-automatic and shoved it in his pocket.

Next, he grabbed Meehix's suitcase, threw the black laptop inside—the briefcase with the money was already in there—and snapped it shut. He'd have to leave the old translator.

"Ship! You there?"

"Yes, John." Ship's voice sounded like he was right next to him.

"Can you track Meehix and the bounty hunter?"

"I am watching them via the hotel security cameras. They are in the elevator nearing the ground floor. I will not be able to see them if they leave the Gallacher Spire."

"Do what you can. Let me know when they leave the building."

"Will do, John."

John bolted out of the room with the suitcase and ran down the hall to the elevator. He hit the down button.

He pulled out the gun. Seemed simple enough. Not too different from an Earth handgun. The only major difference was the trigger. It wasn't a hook for your finger. It was the entire front of the grip as if you squeezed the grip to fire.

Obviously, that was because Drellens had no fingers. Standard sight. No other moving parts or buttons so it must not have settings. Only made to kill—or *tickle*—in his case.

A bolt of energy blasted by his head and hit the wall behind him. One of the bounty hunters staggered out of the room and took another shot at him from thirty yards away. This one passed between his legs, missing his family jewels by an inch.

Geez, if he'd hit me there, *that would've hurt.* John instinctively raised the gun and blew the Drellen away. Years of video game training finally paid off. *If only Mom and Dad could have seen* that *shot.*

The elevator doors slid open, and John jumped in. The floor numbers by the buttons looked like Chinese writing. He hit the bottom button and the doors closed.

"Meehix and the bounty hunter have exited the elevator at the ground floor, John. The bounty hunter just assaulted a concierge who approached them. Now he shot him. Guests are running and screaming. The lobby is a bit chaotic at the moment. Be prepared."

"Will do. Thanks, Ship."

"Not a problem, John. FYI, you pressed the button for the sub-basement. If you want the ground floor, you'll need to press third up from the bottom."

"Shit. Thanks, Ship." John pressed the right button.

"Not a problem, John."

He waited.

"Come on, come on," he whispered, watching the alien floor numbers whisk by.

"Meehix and the bounty hunter have exited the Gallacher Spire, John."

"Any way to track them?"

"No, John. I attempted to hack into the Sector Twelve police force security system without success. I am also attempting to hack into private security systems in the area but so far have found none giving a useful view."

"Did you see which way they went when they left the building?"

"To the right. John, in addition to the shooting in the lobby, a tenant on the ninety-eighth floor heard the shots from your room and called the police. Two Drellen police officers are waiting outside the ground floor elevator. Be prepared."

The doors slid open. John bolted and smashed into the officers, knocking them to the floor. Aliens screamed and dove out of the way. He saw the dead concierge on the floor.

Two other Drellen police officers drew their weapons. John fired at them as he ran for the door. They dove for cover and the next thing he knew, he was on the street in the blinding-hot sun.

He ran to the right and kept going as fast as he could, gun in one hand, suitcase in the other. Whatever the bounty hunter's gun had done to him, it seemed to have increased all his faculties. He was running at top speed yet he wasn't getting winded.

He heard the Drellen police officers far behind him shouting, "Stop! You're under arrest!" but it was an empty threat. Not only was John in super-speed mode, Drellens apparently weren't very fast to begin with. He left them in the Lagud dust.

He saw Meehix and the bounty hunter a block ahead of him. The bounty hunter was shoving her into a vehicle. It looked like she had blood on her shirt. *That bastard must have punched her.*

John looked around frantically. Four blocks behind, he saw the Drellen policemen huffing and puffing after him.

Halfway between him and the bounty hunter's car was a sporty-looking, copper-colored vehicle parked on the side of the street right in front of the restaurant where they had dinner the night before.

He ran the distance to the car as the bounty hunter and Meehix pulled away. He shoved the gun into the driver's side window. The Dwan DooVoo waiter stared up at him with those giant Elton John sunglasses.

"Can I help you, sir?" he said calmly.

"Listen," John said as quickly as he could, "bounty hunters just kidnaped my girlfriend. She's in the car driving away right there," he motioned with the gun. The waiter squinted and looked. "I don't want to hurt you, but if you don't…"

"Get in," the waiter said.

"What?" John was stunned.

"Get in. Hurry up, or they're going to get away."

John ran to the passenger side and jumped in. The waiter floored it, and they took off after the other vehicle at over one hundred miles per hour.

"Thanks," John said, holding on for dear life. He scrambled for a seatbelt, figured out the buckle mechanism, and strapped himself in.

"I'm good at reading people," the waiter said in his Donald Duck voice, "and I remember you two from last night. You left me a good tip."

"My girlfriend did. I don't even remember leaving."

"The Gyken martinis?"

"Yeah. They really fucked me up."

"Heard that. I had a real problem for a while too. Remind me later, and I'll give you some info on where you can get help."

"Cool. Thanks." *Why go into the details? He's trying to be helpful.*

The car sped down the main drag. The streets were mostly empty. The distance between them and the bounty hunter was closing.

A receiver on the dashboard made a weird *woop, woop* noise, and a Drellen voice filled the car.

"Attention. Attention. This is a Sector Twelve Criminal Alert. There was a shooting at the Gallacher Spire Hotel approximately five minutes ago.

"Citizens are to be on the lookout for one Drellen male, approximately seven feet tall, last seen in the company of a Dolurulodan female. Also be on the lookout for one Kdack male, approximately six and one-half feet tall. Both armed and dangerous.

"Do not attempt to apprehend. Contact Sector Twelve Police if sighted. More information to come as available. Thank you for helping to keep our neighborhoods safe."

The waiter didn't bat an eye.

"You do the shooting?" he asked.

"No," John replied. "The bounty hunter did. I shot at the cops, but I didn't hit anyone."

"If we get busted, do you mind if I tell them you held me at gunpoint and I had no choice?"

"Sure, that's cool. I owe you one."

"Thanks."

The waiter pulled the car up behind the bounty hunter's car. He gunned it and went into the wrong lane so John would be window-to-window with the driver's side. He hit a button, and John's window rolled down.

They must have been traveling over a hundred and twenty.

John aimed the gun at the driver's side window. The wind almost blew it out of his hand, but he held it tight. The bounty hunter looked to his left to see the barrel pointed right at his face. His eyes widened as if the Grim Reaper had tapped him on the shoulder.

John fired, and the window exploded. The car pulled hard to the right and the bounty hunter almost lost control. Meehix saw what was happening and started pummeling the bounty hunter in the face.

The waiter jerked the wheel to the right, bringing the cars side-by-side again. John fired a second blast, and the bounty hunter's windshield blew out, showering them with plastic fragments. This time the car spun and hit a waste disposal unit by the side of the road. Garbage blew twenty feet in the air, and the car glanced off a marble guardrail, throwing Meehix into the passenger door.

The bounty hunter drew his gun to shoot her. Meehix grabbed it by the barrel and pointed it away.

"Bitch, let go!" he yelled.

She bit his hand.

The car crashed into a retaining wall at the base of an overpass. John watched in horror as the bounty hunter and Meehix were thrown sixty feet onto the pavement and rolled another twenty.

"Oh, shit!" John yelled.

The waiter hit the brakes, and they slid up next to the accident. They leapt out and ran to Meehix. She was on her back, and the bounty hunter was right next to her. Her teeth still clamped his hand.

He appeared to be unconscious. Her eyelids fluttered. The gun was gone. She spat out the hand.

"Yuck," she said, still spitting.

"Don't move!" John yelled. "You should never move after an accident. You might have hurt your spine."

"My spine's fine," she said. "It's my ego that's hurt. I can't believe this moron got the drop on us. What a dope."

"What about the blood on your shirt?"

"That's not mine." She stood. "This asshole punched the concierge in the nose. Poor guy squirted blood like an Orphellium Worm Pig."

She spat again, this time on the bounty hunter.

"I am not *property!*" she snarled and kicked him.

Suddenly, the bounty hunter reached up and grabbed her leg.

"Die bitch!" he yelled and thrust a giant knife into her abdomen.

With lightning speed—a microsecond before the knife broke her skin—the waiter grabbed the hilt with one hand, twisted it, and broke the bounty hunter's wrist. The bounty hunter shrieked like a wounded falcon, and the waiter elbowed him in the ear with his other arm, knocking him unconscious. The knife fell to the pavement, unbloodied.

Damn. That must be some of that fifth-level Kraxo action Meehix was talking about. Glad this guy is on our side.

They heard the sound of distant sirens.

"Time to go," the waiter said calmly.

He jumped back into the driver's seat, and John pulled Meehix into the backseat. They peeled out and headed back the way they'd come.

"Duck," the waiter instructed.

John and Meehix dipped down behind the front seat as two police cars flew by. They popped back up. Looked like the coast was clear.

"May I take your order, sir?" The waiter smiled.

"Back to the Gallacher Spire," John replied. "Right around the corner, there's a little repair shop."

"Hey, I remember you!" Meehix squealed.

"I remember *you*," the waiter replied. "You gave me an exceptional tip."

"Well, if I'd known you were going to save me, I would have given you an even better one."

"Hey," John protested. "What am I? Chopped liver? I trounced three bounty hunters and shot my way out of a police ambush to save you. I'm practically the interstellar John Dillinger!"

"Well," she licked her lips, "I don't know who that is, but if he looks like you, I'll take him."

Meehix grabbed him and kissed him full on the mouth, as French as French gets. All the blood rushed out of his head. *Gage was right. Strawberry ice cream all the way!*

CHAPTER THIRTY-TWO

They thanked the Dwan DooVoo waiter profusely, and he gave John a card with a schedule for what John figured must be the Dwan DooVoo equivalent of AA meetings. After saying their goodbyes, they rushed into the repair shop and paid the Drellen mechanic in cash. John knew seconds counted in this situation.

The police, or more bounty hunters, could appear at any turn. Or a citizen attempting to do the right thing could turn them in or take matters into their own hands if they recognized the pair. Only when they had gotten through the Gate to the Dolurulod system did John feel a little more relaxed. Fortunately, Meehix remembered *that* Gate combination without a hitch since she had used it numerous times to travel to Lagud.

Now they were only a matter of minutes from Meehix's home planet, which had John stoked. Meehix—not so much. Aside from changing her bloodied clothes, she'd spent the entire trip digging through Ship's databases, reading galactic news articles, and trying to figure out what the heck had happened to her title and status during the paltry few weeks she had been away.

"So you're saying aim for the ears?" John asked Shippewa as he threw a right hook in the air, trying to envision himself battling more Drellen bounty hunters or bounty hunters in general.

"Yes, John. Statistically, more galactic species have sensitive nerve pathways prone to signal disruption in and around auditory appendages. It is similar to the mandibular branch in humans. However, while this is predominantly the case, it is not universal. Many species have no auditory organs, or their earlobes are not visible."

"So if they have ears, aim for the ears, but if they don't have ears, wing it?"

"Yes, John."

"Look at this," Meehix said, her voice tinged with suspicion. "The Gallacher Spire lists my suitcase as *Relegated to Storage* the same day I came to Earth. That makes absolutely no sense. Not only did I have that room rented indefinitely but I even told the desk clerk I'd be back the next day."

John did push-ups. He was listening to her but couldn't get over how great he felt. He was already on push-up number twenty-five. He'd never been able to do more than twenty-five push-ups in a row even when he was playing rugby.

With video game all-nighters and the piles of junk food he'd consumed over the past year, he would have been surprised if he could pull off twenty. Now he was on *thirty*, and these weren't wimpy partial or bent-back push-ups.

He was going all the way down—nose to the floor—and back up, arms fully extended, back straight.

"Thirty-one, thirty-two, thirty-three, thirty-four..." he whispered, only now starting to feel the burn. He was going for fifty.

"What are you doing?" Meehix asked, annoyed. "Are you listening to me?"

"Yeah," John said between presses. "I'm going for a new record."

Forty-one, forty-two, forty-three...

"I'm serious. I think there's some kind of conspiracy going on. Someone set me up, and I'm really worried about my family."

"Why don't you try calling them? Tell them what happened." *Forty-seven, forty-eight...*

"We're listed on a Crec Alert. Bounty hunters probably bugged—"

"Fifty!" John yelled and jumped to his feet. "Holy shit! I've never done fifty consecutive push-ups in my life!"

"What is it with you? Why are you so full of energy?"

Full of energy. That's it.

The energy bolt from the Vetralaun must be fatal to most species but not to humans. It was like an article he read in biology class about Koala bears. They ate eucalyptus leaves like candy, yet the greenery was poisonous to almost every other species.

Man, I have to hold on to this gun. If I ever play rugby again, I'll shoot myself in the chest, piss my pants and be unstoppable.

"It's the gun. When they shot me, it was like being on steroids. I haven't felt this strong in years. Actually, I haven't felt this strong ever."

"Shot you? What are you talking about?"

"In the hotel room, when you were out from the gas. The guy that grabbed you shot me three times. Two in the chest, one in the side."

"What?" Meehix shrieked in horror.

She jumped up from the control seat and pulled up John's shirt. He had two nasty-looking bruises on his chest and one on his side.

"Oh my God!" she yelled. "We need to get you to a doctor!"

He pulled his shirt back down and grabbed her arms.

"Meehix, I'm fine. I'm *better* than fine. That gun doesn't work on me. In fact, it *tickles.*"

"Tickles?"

"Yeah. Like crazy. It tickled so much that I pissed myself."

"You didn't know it should have killed you?"

"No. I mean, I didn't really think about it at the time."

"They *execute* people with Vetralauns."

"Well," he smiled, "if I get the death penalty for saving you, I got nothing to worry about, right?"

Meehix stared at him in disbelief.

"Look." He still held her arms, "I'm fine. I'm glad you're okay. That's all I was thinking about. Those bounty hunters could have had .44 Magnums and I still would have protected you."

Meehix's lower lip started to quiver. She didn't know what a .44 Magnum was, but she assumed it was bad.

No one has ever put their life on the line for me before. Not even my family.

She hugged him. It hurt the bruise on his side, but he

didn't say anything. He put his arms around her and held her close. The pheromone she was excreting smelled like heaven.

"Excuse me, John?"

"Yeah, Ship?"

"We are approaching Dolurulod. This system requires we submit an interstellar border protection application before entering the atmosphere. Galactic law requires us to accurately list the ship's contents and personnel under penalty of perjury. Do you have any suggestions?"

"Yeah," John said as Meehix released him and walked to the back of the cabin. "Lie your ass off and do whatever it takes to get us on the ground. We've already committed multiple felonies. A few more won't make any difference."

"Agreed. I will falsify the appropriate disclosures to the best of my ability. Hopefully, they won't discover our subterfuge."

"Thanks, Ship."

"Not a problem, John."

Meehix was sitting in her spot, knees up, arms around her legs, double-thumbed hands clasped. She was staring at John again.

"What?" he asked.

"How do humans know when they can trust somebody? I mean, *really* trust somebody?"

John thought about the question. He remembered Hannah. *I trusted Hannah. Turned out she was totally untrustworthy. How do you know if you can really trust somebody? That's a tough question.*

"We can't know," John admitted. "Since we can't read

another person's mind, we can't know what they're think-ing...*ever*. All we can do is judge people by what they do and hope for the best."

She looked at him as if to say, *that's it?* He got the feeling it wasn't the kind of answer she was looking for. He felt compelled to add something else.

"I do know this. All *you* can do is *all* you can do. After that, you have to let go and trust that the universe knows what *it's* doing."

She scrunched up her forehead and had a distant look as if she was meditating intently on every word he said.

Shit. I hope that translated right. Then again, I'm not sure I understand what I said.

"Okay," she replied. That was the end of it.

CHAPTER THIRTY-THREE

Shippewa skimmed the outer atmosphere before dropping six thousand miles to a mere twenty feet above the planet's largest ocean. John let Ship pilot so he could scan for other craft or detection devices and react immediately and accordingly. He told Ship to bring them in as quietly and discreetly as possible to Meehixiheem's sire's castle but not fly over the actual property. If other bounty hunters were scouring the galaxy for them, the first place to look would be her last known residence.

Ship got them through Border Protection without a hitch. Apparently, the Crec Alert didn't include detailed information on their craft because no one ever questioned the integrity of ownership and origin. He simply created profiles for John and Meehix that listed them as "on honeymoon."

Dolurulod was a common destination for such newly-joined tourists. Of course, he neglected to mention that John was human or that Meehix was related to the royal family. As far as their manifest was concerned, they were

Grezneppi and Venji Sifempok of the Gamma Velorum star system, a middle-class, same-sex, humanoid couple from the planet Drip.

Ironically, Drip had no naturally occurring bodies of water so the newlyweds were in for a thrill when they arrived on Dolurulod—or at least they would have been if they existed apart from their profiles on virtual paper. Still, when John got his first look at Dolurulod, it took *his* breath away.

"Whoa," he exclaimed. "Your planet's *dope*."

The water was the clearest he'd ever seen—a deep, sapphire-blue through which one's vision penetrated to the very bottom. Giant creatures of all shapes and sizes swam at various depths. The coral and rock formations were rainbow colors, and the light from binary suns illuminated everything in a majestic, golden glow.

In the distance, the shoreline approached. It was a fantastic cliff of black rock dotted on top with ivory spires and battlements shaped like white dumbbells with crystalline, ruby-red parapets that sparkled in the sun. The clouds above and behind the castle were spectacular, seeming especially so after spending time on Lagud, which had no clouds whatsoever.

Here, the suspended vapors were snow-white, billowing behemoths set against the deepest shade of blue sky John had ever seen. No wonder Meehixiheem wasn't impressed with the living conditions on Lagud. Dolurulod was a paradise.

"Home sweet home," she said with a bittersweet tenor. "Tagbedden Castle."

John wondered what she was thinking. Was this still

her home? Regret for having left in the first place? Fear of what her family would think of her decimated status in the galactic community? He couldn't tell. He said it himself not ten minutes ago. We really can't know what another person is thinking...*ever.*

"**John, Dolurulod Border Protection requires that we register in person if we intend to land. If we comply, it will be obvious that you are not Grezneppi and Venji Sifempok of the Gamma Velorum star system. I'm sorry, John. I think it may be best to depart immediately.**"

"No!" Meehix cried, "We can't leave! I have to get to Tagbedden!"

John thought for a moment.

"We're on our *honeymoon,* right? Tell them everything is more beautiful than we realized and that we'd hoped to consummate the marriage over the water. Ask them to please give us a couple of hours."

"**I'll try, John.**"

They waited.

"**They have granted us one hour, John. But we are not allowed to land in any cities or urban areas, and you must report to the nearest customs office as soon as you have finished consummating.**"

"We better get started then. I'm known for extended consummations." John grinned.

"Ha, ha," Meehix said sarcastically. She was clearly in no mood for sexual innuendos.

"**Where would you like me to land, John?**"

John looked at Meehix.

"I know where," Meehix said.

· · ·

Meehix guided Ship to the base of the cliff over which Tagbedden Castle majestically stood. They were right on the water, about two thousand feet beneath the castle's ocean-facing side, on a rocky beach pummeled by giant waves that blasted sea spray fifty feet in the air. Ship disguised the hull as much as possible to hide their landing and Meehix had informed them that there were no security devices on the cliff side of the property. The royal family considered the precipice unclimbable.

An invisible and impenetrable force field capable of deflecting everything from a thrown stone to an anti-matter weapons attack surrounded the entire property on top. They set down on a giant, flat rock, lowered the stairs, and exited. The temperature was a balmy seventy-two degrees.

"How do we get up there?" John yelled. The crashing waves muffled his voice. "Even if we could get up there, how the heck do we get through a *force field?*"

"Trust me." Meehix smiled and took him by the hand.

They circumvented sharp, igneous pillars about eight feet tall and Meehix led him to the very base of the cliff. The sand was an off-white color and the wall of rock rising above them opal-black and enormous.

They came to a recessed area that was almost a cave but more like a scooped-out depression. Meehix let go of John and walked inside. She felt around on the rocks, grabbed one protruding stone with both hands, twisted it clockwise and counter-clockwise, then pushed.

It moved inward about six inches, and a grinding sound reverberated through the half-cave, like someone dragging cinder blocks over a concrete floor. A hidden door slid open right in the center of the depression. Inside, John saw a spiral stone staircase leading up.

"I found this when I was a child. I was sitting in my bedroom brushing my hair. Then I noticed a scratch on the floor as if something had slid under the baseboard.

"Turned out it was a secret door the original owners had installed centuries ago, back when kings and queens had escape plans in case the peasants revolted. When I figured out how to open it, I found these stairs. This is how I'd sneak out at night with my friends. Nobody knows about it but me."

"That's fuckin' awesome!" John said, clearly impressed. *Secret entrances, ivory castles. I feel like I'm in the ultimate, living video game.* He took a deep breath. Cool, sea air filled his lungs. *Man, I could stay here forever.*

Meehix grabbed John's hand again and squeezed it.

"Wish me luck," she said.

"Wait...what? Aren't we *both* going?"

"No way," she said firmly. "How would I explain a human male in my bedroom if we get caught? You stay here with Ship, and I'll keep you posted through the translator."

"Well...*shit!*" John said. He couldn't argue with her. It's just that he had visions of storming the castle and sneaking around like a spy, dodging guards, looking for *whatever.* Now he was stuck on the beach counting seagulls. If they even had seagulls.

She turned to go.

"Hey!" he yelled. He pulled the Vetralaun from his pocket. "Maybe you should take this."

"John, this is my family up there," she reassured him, "and all the good people that work for my family."

"I just thought, like, if there's bounty hunters or something," he said sheepishly.

"I'll be okay."

She walked through the door, pulled a handle on the wall inside, waved goodbye, and the door slid shut. It was a dead wall of black rock again.

"Good luck," he said sullenly.

He put the gun back in his pocket and walked toward the ship, taking his time. Besides, he had to be careful negotiating the sharp, black rocks protruding from the beach. He couldn't see the craft because it had disguised itself as a giant boulder, but he knew where it was.

He realized he hadn't been apart from Meehix since he met her. Even when the bounty hunter snagged her, he was always close behind and knew where she was. He felt lonely for the first time in a long time.

He stopped and stared at the ocean. A whale-like creature a hundred yards out broke the surface and blasted giant geysers from three blowholes on its hourglass-shaped head. It submerged again and was gone. He turned and continued walking toward the ship.

Maybe Meehix and I can stay here if she gets all this legal stuff worked out. Perhaps someday we could get married, and that would make me like a prince or something. Maybe her sire would like me, and we'd go pheasant hunting or play polo or do all that stuff rich people do.

Maybe if John hadn't been daydreaming so much, he would have seen the periscope sticking up from the water —*watching him.*

CHAPTER THIRTY-FOUR

The secret door slid open and Meehix—out of breath—stepped into her bedroom. Climbing two thousand feet up a spiral staircase was no picnic.

She closed the door and looked around. Everything was as she'd left it—a few clothes lying on her dresser, her makeup and jewelry on the vanity table, her giant walk-in closet still full of shoes and dresses. Her emperor-sized bed with the ornate headboard and bedposts carved from a single block of Bira-Makoom wood was still unmade, and the thrown-back covers were exactly as she'd left them. Even her pleasure toy was right where she put it on its glass stand under the bed.

Should probably wash that thing.

She carefully picked up a bottle of Tears of Tulangnalut from the vanity table and sprayed some on her neck. It smelled divine.

Got to remember to grab that on the way out.

She crept to the door leading to the top floor hallway and opened it a crack. She saw Neeliwansh, the maid, at the other end of the hall, entering her sire's room with a curtain cleaning machine.

This was good. Not only was the machine noisy but it would keep her busy for a while. Plus, Neeliwansh wouldn't clean Meehixiheem's room because Meehix forbade it. She had nothing against the maid. In fact, she liked her, but she treasured her privacy more than cleanliness.

So far, so good. Neeliwansh will be busy cleaning drapes. More than enough time to figure out what's been going on while I was away. Still, gotta be super-duper careful. Do not *want to get caught. Not by* anyone.

Her major concern was that—with bounty hunters on her tail—she would be a danger to anyone who knew where she was, whether family, friend, maid, or servant. Her secondary concern was that—with her recent loss of title and status—she would receive an almost certain tongue-lashing and a barrage of questions from her sire when he found out she was home.

Punishments, restrictions, threats, and other familial horrors too terrible to contemplate for someone of Meehixiheem's freedom-loving ways would likely follow. Plus, what would happen to John? He'd be stuck out there on the beach waiting for her until she could sneak out again or until Border Patrol arrested him, whichever came first. No. She could *not* get caught.

She heard the sound of the curtain cleaning machine and Neeliwansh singing. She exited the room, closed the door gently, and ran down the hall to the balcony over-looking the double staircases. She peeked over the edge and checked the grand foyer two stories down. *No one there.*

She ran down the left staircase as quickly and quietly as she could, around the corner past the cloakroom, down the main hall past the ballroom, and stopped outside the door of her sire's study. She peeked inside. *No one there either. With luck, he's halfway across the galaxy on business.*

She ran into the study, closed the door, and locked it. If any of the servants walked by, at least she'd have a chance to hide rather than being spotted outright, rifling through her sire's personal data. She intended to find any messages from the Galactic Sentient Registry. They had to have contacted him. There was no way they would wipe the rights of a royal family member without notification.

For all she knew, her sire could have been granted a hearing before the Registry Tribunal by now. As she was snooping through her house searching for answers, he could be pleading her case along with his many wise and astute court advisors, getting her reinstated at that very moment.

I hope that's the case. I hope, I hope, I hope.

She walked around the big, Bira-Makoom desk and suddenly had a flashback. It was almost two decades ago, and her sire was working silently in his study when little X —before she became Ixi and many years before she would become Meehixiheem—wandered into the room, looking for attention

"X," he said in his big, booming voice. "Aren't you supposed to be studying for your Ascension? I find it hard to believe that you memorized all your affirmations so quickly."

"But sire, it's *sooooo boring*," she whined. "If I have to read one more affirmation, I'm going to go crazy and eat my poop."

"X! Where did you get such talk? That's utterly repulsive and no way for a child of our clan to speak."

"Poop, shmoop. What's a girl gotta do to have a good time in this dump?"

She was seven years old.

Hmmm. I was a little shit when I was a child. She giggled.

She activated the computer and sat. Her family crest appeared floating in the air over the desk, and a female voice said, "Access code."

"Shhh!" Meehix whispered. "Lower volume!"

"Unable to change settings without proper access code," the voice said as loud as before.

Fortunately, the access code was simply a string of letters and numbers which anyone could submit—no retina scans, DNA scans, etcetera. Sometimes her sire required his assistants or even one of the servants to access his files. Of course, the system would record the date and time of the access and what specific information they retrieved, but she would worry about that later.

She recited the code—which she'd known for years—and added, "Lower volume."

"Access code accepted. Volume reduced."

Meehix began flipping through files, records, meetings, schedules, and a generic mish-mash of information that floated holographically over the desk. Soon she was past recent communications and delving into items weeks and months old.

It has to be more recent than this, like, within the past two or three weeks.

When she was about to start over, she saw a file bearing the family seal and the letters *M.F.A.* on the cover. She touched the file.

"Access denied," the computer voice said.

"Why?" Meehix whispered.

"Restricted File. Please submit Restricted File Code."

"I don't have a restricted file code."

She poked the file again with her finger. And again. And again.

"Access Denied. Access Denied. Access Denied," the voice droned every time.

She tried the original access code. Access denied. She tried birth dates and family names with the same result. Then the entire menagerie of family pets, including her sister's miniature pet dwarb named Finkleschnepp. God, she hated that dwarb.

"Access denied."

"Dammit!" she yelled and slapped her hand over her mouth. She listened. Silence. Nobody coming. *She hoped.*

"Ship? Can you hear me?" she whispered.

"Yes, Meehix, I hear you."

"I'm trying to access a restricted file on my sire's computer. Can you open the file?"

"Utilizing Hannah, it is distinctly possible. However, I will require both quantum transmission access as well as the ability to scan for the terminal's exact location, both of which are currently unavailable."

"Why are they unavailable?"

"Quantum transmissions and proximity scans are

blocked by the security force field surrounding Tagbedden Castle. Only hyper-bump voice communications can circumvent the field."

Shit. I forgot about that. Quantum transmissions in and out of the castle occurred three times daily at differing intervals each day. The force field directly enveloping the lone transceiver on one of the battlements shut off for mere seconds to send and receive galactic information, then turned on again when the exchange was complete.

Meehix flipped back through the holographic imagery floating over the desk until she found the schedules file again. She poked the file with her finger, and it opened. Everything regarding the smooth operation of Tagbedden was there, from irrigation systems to shift changes to garbage pick-ups, including a schedule for A.F.F.I.S.— Automated Force Field Interruption Schedule. She opened the file. She looked at today's date. Fourteen hundred hours was the next quantum transmission when the force field around the transceiver would shut down for only six seconds. She looked at the clock on the wall. Thirteen fifty-nine!

"Ship! Can you hear me?" she whispered frantically.

"Yes, Meehix, I hear you."

"In less than a minute, the force field will open around the quantum transceiver for six seconds. Can you hack into the system at that point and unlock the file?"

"Possibly. I will not be able to scan for your location with the majority of the force field still intact, though. To unlock the file in six seconds, I must be able to locate the specific terminal you are accessing."

Meehix looked at the clock again. *Thirty seconds left 'til shutdown!*

"Is there no other way to locate the terminal?"

"If you were to send an easily identifiable file to an address outside Tagbedden Castle, I may be able to trace that file back to the terminal you are accessing when the force field opens."

Fifteen seconds.

She looked around frantically. *Easily identifiable...easily identifiable...*

She opened the mail system and chose New Transmission.

Ten seconds.

In Contacts, she selected the first address destination she could find, then hit Attachment, then Holo-Cam.

Five seconds.

She pulled up her shirt, poked the Take Photo icon, and hit Send.

Zero seconds.

"Look for blue tits, Ship!" she whispered.

High on the third battlement, not far from the study, the force field shimmered briefly around the quantum transceiver. All the midday mail was beamed faster than light to a distant Gate used exclusively for this purpose, then distributed across the galaxy to its various destinations.

Approximately one hour later, in a star system close to the galactic center, a holographic photo of firm blue breasts found its way to the computer of the Bishop of Molloceros

IV. The Bishop carefully examined the exquisite mammary glands floating over his desk. For several minutes he pondered *why* the head of the royal family on Dolurulod would send him pornography. A gesture? An offering? A joke?

"Never look a gift breast in the nipple," he pontificated —and added the photo to his private file.

Six...five...four...

"**What is the name of the locked file?**" Ship asked calmly.

"M.F.A.! M.F.A.!" Meehix whispered hysterically.

Three...two...one.

"**I'm sorry, Meehix. I'm afraid...**"

Meehix's heart sank.

"**...that I successfully opened the file.**"

"What? You did?"

"**Yes. Your blue tits pointed me to the correct terminal. Pun intended.**"

Meehix jumped up and silently air-danced. She did a little spin, gave a little hop, shook her cute butt, and flopped back down in the desk chair with a huge grin on her face.

"**You will not be happy with the contents of the file.**"

Her smile faded.

"Why?"

She poked the floating M.F.A. file, and it opened. It contained only one item—a seventeen-page document entitled "Meehixiheem Forfeiture Agreement."

CHAPTER THIRTY-FIVE

John leaned back in the cockpit seat with his feet up on the control panel. He was flipping the Vetralaun semi-automatic like John Wayne, tossing it into a spin with one hand, catching it with the other. He wanted to explore the beach, but his better judgment told him not to.

Inside the ship, he was invisible. If he was out wandering around, he could draw attention. His white skin, large humanoid form, and current location would appear unusual to the locals. If the authorities spotted him, it was a guarantee someone would come to investigate.

I guess I'm doomed to be bored today.

He got up, stretched, and looked out the porthole facing the cliff.

"How long's she been up there, Ship?"

"Approximately forty-five minutes, John."

"You can't tell what she's doing or see where she is?"

"No, John. My scans cannot penetrate the security force field."

"I hope she's okay. If something happened, we'd never know."

"I think she's okay, John."

"Why?"

"Because I spoke to her ten minutes ago."

"What? Why didn't you tell me?" John sounded annoyed.

"It was a private conversation, John. I don't kiss and tell."

Private conversation? Kiss and tell?

"What the heck is that supposed to mean?" He started to get irritated.

"I try to respect the confidentiality of both you and Meehixiheem in all our communications. I don't feel comfortable disclosing private conversations without permission from all parties involved."

John was livid.

"What are you, her *shrink?* This is a *team effort!* You can't withhold information from a team member without jeopardizing the whole game!"

Ship went silent for a moment as if thinking through John's line of reasoning, which was absurd as his quantum processors would have made all relevant calculations in fractions of nanoseconds.

"Agreed. Your argument is sensible."

"Good." John calmed down. "Now tell me what happened."

"Okay. But I'll let her tell you about the titty photo."

"The what?" John yelled.

"Meehixiheem discovered a legal document proving that her family forfeited her by way of an ancient tradi-

tion. It requires royal clans to sacrifice one of their own into abject slavery to maintain their status and wealth. Usually this is done on a volunteer basis, but in this case, Meehixiheem's family chose for her."

John was stunned. "Why would they do that?"

"Because they needed a royal family member to fulfill this role as a scapegoat and they consider Meehixiheem an expendable fuck-up who no one will miss."

That's terrible. How could they do that to their daughter? How could her siblings go along with it? That would be like Gage giving up Isabella. How could one's own family be so cruel?

"Uh-oh. Brace for impact."

"Wait, *what?*"

An explosion detonated outside the porthole facing the sea. It was *loud.*

"A small projectile originating approximately two hundred yards from shore has exploded eighty feet away from the ship."

"No shit!" John shouted and ran to the porthole. He saw something like a bottle rocket burst from the water, shoot up about a hundred feet and arch toward the ship.

"Here comes another one."

This one exploded even closer, and John felt the shockwave in his gut.

"The projectiles are relatively primitive but still dangerous. They appear to be coming from a submerged vessel. I suspect they are bounty hunters, John."

"Call Meehix and tell her to get down here! *Now!*"

Meehix was sobbing into her arms on her sire's desk when she heard the first explosion. It was distant, but it was definitely an explosion. Another one sounded.

"Computer off." She wiped her eyes. She'd read enough.

"Attention Tagbedden Personnel. Attention Tagbedden Personnel."

Meehix recognized the voice on the loudspeaker. It was Bronzillich, the head of castle security.

"Level Orange. Level Orange. Remain within the castle force field until further notice. Thank you for your cooperation."

What the fuck is going on?

Meehix ran to the door. She opened it a crack. Two servants raced past.

"Is there a drill today?" she heard one of them say.

She bolted down the hall toward the stairs as soon as they were out of sight.

"**Meehix!**" Ship said over the translator.

She screamed. He sounded like he was right next to her. "Ship! You scared the shit out of me!" She kept running.

"**I'm sorry, but John says to get down here. Now.**"

"I'm trying! What's going on?" She ran up the stairs as fast as she could.

"**Someone is firing on us from the ocean. We are lifting off.**"

Meehix ran down the upper hall to her room and burst through the door. The door hit Neeliwansh—who was coming out—and knocked her to the floor. "Neeliwansh! You know you're not supposed to clean my room!"

Neeliwansh looked up from the floor. Her eyes widened to the point where Meehix thought they would fall out of their sockets. She let out a blood-curdling scream that three castles down the road could've heard.

"Ghost!" she screamed. "Ghost! Ghost! Aaaaaah!" Neeliwansh scrambled to her feet and ran down the hall, shrieking all the way.

Ghost?

Meehix slammed the door and locked it. She didn't have time to worry about ghosts.

She grabbed her Tears of Tulangnalut, her pleasure toy from under the bed, and her favorite pair of boots. She wanted to take more but felt she had neither the time nor the right number of hands to do so.

She opened the secret door and started down the stone steps when another explosion shook the room. A blast of heat erupted from two thousand feet below. She almost lost her balance and tumbled headfirst down the steps, but in trying to compensate, fell back into the bedroom as the spiral staircase collapsed.

It crashed and smashed, cracked and crumbled, as big chunks fell on small pieces and vice versa, pulverizing the secret exit in a matter of seconds. It reduced the whole stairwell to a two-thousand-foot stone cylinder full of rubble and choked her entire bedroom with dust. The attackers scored a direct hit on the recessed entrance far below. She shut the secret door as someone started pounding on the bedroom door.

"Who's in there?" Bronzillich yelled. "Open this door!"

Neeliwansh shouted something about ghosts and the devil, and another security guard said, "Kick it in."

They started breaking down the door.

Meehix tossed the boots and pocketed the Tears of

Tulangnalut and the pleasure toy. She opened the window overlooking the castle's front entrance and climbed out onto a narrow ledge encircling the top floor. She closed the window as Bronzillich broke into the room.

Below her was the main entrance. A security bar stretched across it, preventing the passage of vehicles, and about ten armed guards milled around wondering what the hell was going on. They were all looking to the right, outside the castle wall toward the cliff, but clearly weren't allowed to leave their posts since they huddled in the entryway. This was the only way in or out now—the only opening in the force field.

She heard Bronzillich in her bedroom.

"Where did all this *dust* come from?" He coughed.

She started climbing down like a blue spider monkey.

———

John was at the controls, dodging incoming shots as he hovered high over the beach. Two creatures stood on a gold submarine and fired up at them with long rifles that looked like flintlocks with toilet plungers on the barrels. The shots whizzed by the window.

"They are ordering us to surrender the blue girl, John."

"Fuck that! Tell them to surrender the gold sub, or I'm gonna sink it!"

He flew evasively over them, and they kept firing and missing. John was less worried about the stupid aquatic bounty hunters than he was about drawing attention. Meehix better hurry up.

"Where's Meehix?" he yelled to Ship.

She jumped to the lawn inside the castle wall as Bronzillich opened the bedroom window above her. He looked down and saw her.

"Meehixiheem?" he said in shock as if *he'd* seen a ghost.

She bolted for the entrance. The guards were all looking toward the cliff. She jumped the security bar, blasted through the gaggle of guards, and zagged right.

"Hey!" one yelled, but they didn't know what to do. They had orders to protect the entryway.

"Somebody go get her!" Bronzillich screamed from the window.

Five guards bolted after her.

Meehix ran toward the cliff at top speed.

"Ship!" she cried. "Can you hear me?"

"That does it!" John snarled. "I'm lasering these chum-suckers!" He locked on to the submarine.

"I'm sorry, John."

Shippewa swung the ship hard to port, and John almost fell out of the control seat.

"What the fuck, Ship?"

Meehix sprinted to the edge of the cliff like an Olympic long jumper going for the gold. The five guards were barely keeping up. She gave one final burst of speed at the last second. If she didn't get some distance, she'd be minced and shredded by the black wall on the way down. Her right foot landed the last step perfectly, and she pushed off with every ounce of strength the muscles in her leg could muster.

"Holy shit!" one of the guards yelled as they skidded to a stop.

She traveled horizontally for a brief second and was stunned by the sheer beauty of the ocean stretching out before her. Then gravity took over, and the wind began to roar in her ears as her body approached terminal velocity.

She had time for one final thought.

I hope the universe knows what it's doing.

She closed her eyes, not wanting to see the approach of the sharp, black rocks on the beach below, but when she realized they might be the last thing she'd ever view, she opened them—and saw John standing on Shippewa's hull, catching her.

She crashed into his arms, and they both collapsed from the impact. John grabbed her shirt collar as Meehix slid off the hull toward certain death. He held onto a recess in the hull with one hand and Meehix with the other. Ship decelerated the craft's rapid descent, which he had matched as closely as possible to the speed of her fall, and they stopped ten feet above the beach. It took every bit of John's strength to hold onto her.

He pulled her up, and she wrapped her arms around him as a blast of sea spray misted over them.

"Thank you." She buried her tear-streaked face in his chest.

"Not a problem. I missed you."

He squeezed her tight. Then he caught a whiff.

"What did you get into?" he backed away and sniffed.

"It's Tears of Tulangnalut! It's a very expensive perfume."

"More like Tears of Rotting Garbage! Yuck! That shit is *rank!*"

CHAPTER THIRTY-SIX

Meehixiheem was doing her makeup in front of Ship's holo-projector. She sat at the control panel as if she were sitting at the vanity in her bedroom, and Ship scanned her face and re-projected it like a three-dimensional mirror. She had on a revealing dress, and John was doing crunches to avoid getting distracted by her overwhelming hotness. While he had begged her to never put on Tears of Tulangnalut again, he now wondered if he'd made a mistake.

Maybe I should consider it rape repellent. Boy, she looks good.

They were fast approaching an island on the opposite side of the planet from Tagbedden Castle. Ship had flown them away from the coastline only minutes before the authorities swarmed the beach. He came up with a brilliant plan to dash full speed toward a Gate leading to the far edge of the third spiral arm. Pirates, escaped slaves, and other sordid types despised by the general galactic population often used it.

Meehix opened the Gate from memory. Yes, she had

been through this particular one before—Daukhl had taken her there several times in search of a rare strain of hurn-rern weed. However, every time they traveled to this particular interstellar neighborhood, they got mugged by Cron Limeans, a nasty race of scorpion-like humanoids that would do just about anything for money.

Ship planned to fly them to one side of the open Gate rather than through it, making it appear to anyone watching from Dolurulod that they had made a break for the shittiest branch of the Milky Way. Instead, he zipped them behind an automated freighter on its way back to Dolurulod. The plan seemed successful as Ship scanned several Dolurulod Border Protection craft entering the Gate moments after feigning their departure. Plus, no one was pursuing them.

"So tell me more about this island." John flexed his bulging biceps. He hunched behind Meehix so he could see himself in the holo-projector. *I'm getting thick.* He pulled up his shirt. He noted that the bruises from the Vetralaun hits were already fading, and he thought he could see the early ripples of a developing six-pack where before he had only a mediocre mid-section at best. *Sweet!*

"The whole island is an independent nation-state," she began as she carefully put on eye shadow. "Back in the day, it started as a safe city for criminals on the run set up by a bunch of competing religious orders. They built monasteries and communes to try and convert all the lowlifes that showed up.

"After a big riot ended with half the priests dismembered and the other half running for the hills, some trillionaire investor bought the whole thing and converted it into a rich people's party place. There are only two rules; no fighting and no killing.

"They have a security force made up of fifth-level Kraxo bouncers. Other than that, anything goes. It's about the only *loose* environment on Dolurulod. Half the planet's upper-class parties there regularly but only one in ten will admit it. The bottom line is nobody will mess with us as long as we play it cool—and I hope to find Daukhl."

"Daukhl? The guy that crashed your ship?"

"Yeah."

"He's either dead or in prison...*right?*"

"Maybe."

"What makes you think he's not?"

"Something I remembered when you two boneheads hypnotized me." She started working on her lipstick.

"I was pretty drunk with Daukhl at the Crystal Monastery on Summeldrac Island the same night we left for Kdack. I hardly noticed it at the time, but Daukhl was at the other end of the club talking to some guy at the door. I remember he pointed in my direction and when he saw me looking he ushered the guy outside and never mentioned it."

"So? From what you've told me, Daukhl sounds as shady as a three-dollar bill. Maybe he was buying some drugs or something."

"That's what I thought, but then I remembered something else."

"What ?"

"The guy at the door was *human*."

"An *Earth* human? Like me?"

"Yeah. Only smaller and with darker skin."

They landed in the parking lot next to the Crystal Monastery. Like everything else John had seen on Dolurulod, Summeldrac Island was beautiful—at least at night. Maybe it would look different in the day, but it sure looked cool now.

They arrived right after double-sunset, and the artificial lighting on the island was gorgeous. Soft blue and golden orbs floated around at strategic points everywhere, in trees, bushes, along vine-covered walls, and alien-made structures.

The main building was a semi-transparent material that gave off a white glow. It was hard to describe. You could see movement inside—literally through the thick walls—but you couldn't make out any faces or details. It gave the whole place an ethereal, dream-like vibe.

The Crystal Monastery was on top of a stone-covered hill. The surrounding landscape reminded John of Stonehenge in the United Kingdom, which he'd never visited, but he'd seen pictures. John also heard music and laughter emanating from the glowing walls.

Mostly humanoid beings—though not *Earth* humanoid beings—walked to and from the party on the crest. The lot at the base was full of ships, hundreds of them, and compared to theirs, they all looked sleek, expensive, and upper, *upper*-class. John ceased admiring the sights and sounds when he saw three large bouncers of a species he hadn't seen before walking toward them from the Monastery.

"Ship," John whispered. "Can you hear me?"

"Yes, John. I hear you."

"Keep an eye on things. Let me know if anything threatening goes down while we're in there. When you get a chance—I mean, if you think no one will notice—disguise the hull like one of these other ships so we don't stick out like a sore thumb—get me?"

"I get you, John. Will do."

The bouncers had almost reached them. Meehix closed the distance, marching up to them boldly, looking as sexy as she was tough.

"I'll need to see your Red Star before you can enter," the first bouncer demanded.

"Of course." Meehix didn't flinch at the man's gruff demeanor.

She handed him the onyx-black card with the glowing red star on it—the same one she had flashed at the concierge back on Lagud. The first bouncer scanned it with a pen device.

"Forgive me for the inconvenience," he said disingenuously, "but the current balance on this card will not cover the entry fee for you and the...*Earthman.*"

What the fuck? He said Earthman *like I'm a cockroach.*

"If you wouldn't mind transferring more funds to increase your balance by at least nine hundred additional credits," he continued, "I'm sure we can accommodate you."

"Here," Meehix said angrily, "just take cash. I don't want to bother my *financier* tonight."

The bouncer took out a glove from his inner coat pocket and put it on his four-fingered hand. Then he took the cash, rolled it up carefully, placed it inside a small, metal cylinder, and waved the pen device over it.

Strange letters appeared on the container—John assumed it was Meehixiheem's name written in Dolurulod —and the bouncer pocketed the little tube. "Right this way." He led the way up the hill, and the other two bouncers followed them.

As they walked, Meehix took John by the hand and pulled him close.

"That's it," she whispered in his ear. "We're officially broke. Cashed out, busted, poverty-stricken."

"Maybe I can wash dishes at the Crystal Monastery," John joked. She didn't smile.

They reached the portico, and the music was booming. A well-dressed Dolurulod couple burst through the door, laughing and groping one another—clearly drunk—and proceeded to make out and feel each other up against one of the two pillars flanking the entryway. They paid no attention to John, Meehix, or the three bouncers.

No fighting, no killing, John thought. *Other than that anything goes. She wasn't kidding.*

"Enjoy your visit to the Crystal Monastery," the bouncer gave a sinister smile. Apparently, they were now free to mingle and carouse. They walked in.

The music was a strange mix of pulsing bass with overtones of a high-pitched, ukulele-like instrument. The vocals sounded like Alvin and the Chipmunks' DNA got crossed with a theremin. Non-lethal lasers flashed from what appeared to be multiple large rooms and multiple floor levels.

Aside from the flashing, a glowing blue haze hung over the entire interior of the building. John smelled a potpourri of perfumes and smoke and other scents he couldn't identify, some of them pleasant, some of them repulsive. Despite the shadowy lighting, it was clear that the uber-rich packed the place, all of whom were here to cast off their inhibitions and let loose in a "what happens in the Crystal Monastery stays in the Crystal Monastery" milieu.

Many of the wealthy patrons were female or at least many of the guests accompanying them were female. John had never seen so many perfect breasts, legs, and fresh faces in his life.

Heads turned his way too. Most of the women in attendance seemed intrigued by John. Not only was he a rare species whom they seldom saw in this part of the galaxy but he was at least a head taller than any male in the room —and more muscular.

He made eye contact with more than a few Dolurulod females. One waved. Most tapped their breasts. A gorgeous red Margono woman pinned her purple eyes on him. She licked her finger and started swirling it around in her ear.

Oh, shit. There's trouble with a capital "T."

"You seem to be drawing a lot of attention." Meehix stated the obvious. "I should pimp you out and make us some money."

John was about to reply with a smart-ass remark, like *anything for the cause* or *sacrifices must be made* but then changed his mind. "Oh, stop." No point in pissing her off two minutes after they arrived.

She led him by the hand through the masses of partiers. After a bit of a hike, they bellied up to the bar, which was a long, glass slab filled with what looked like glowing lava, only it was cool to the touch.

The bartender was a robot—the first John had seen since heading into outer space—and he rolled over to them and asked if they would "like to partake of any libations" or were there "any activities to which he could direct them or items which they required?" He was definitely a full-service robot, and John assumed he was referring to things normally deemed illegal in other parts of the galaxy. Here, it seemed, the universe was the limit.

"I'll have a Gyken martini," Meehix ordered. She turned to John. "What do you want?"

"I thought we were broke."

"We are. The entry fee covers everything. Food, drinks, hookers, drugs. All you can eat. There's no way you could eat, drink, fuck or absorb enough toxins to exceed *that* entry fee."

"Uh…I think I'll have water right now, maybe pace myself, you know, get hydrated first." He did *not* want a repeat of last night.

"Suit yourself," she said. "I wanna relax."

"Very good, madam and sir," the bartender said. He produced a Kanderian Ice Glass, filled it with cold Gyken gin, and floated it over to Meehix on one of those hover plates along with a glass of water for John. Meehix lifted her ice glass and whirled it several times in the air. It turned bright blue, and a gentle mist flowed over the rim like the last time she imbibed. John held his water glass with both hands and resisted the urge to clink glasses. She took a long slow sip, closed her eyes, and said, *"Fuck everybody."*

"To *everybody*." John lifted his glass. "May they all be *fucked*." He took a sip. Yup. Water.

"Hey," Meehix said as she looked intently across the room. "I think I see one of my relatives."

"Really?" John said.

"The girl in the long dress with the slit down the side. That's my cousin. Keeliz."

John looked but had a hard time seeing her in the dim light. Only when the lasers flashed did he catch a glimpse of the girl Meehix was talking about. Blue skin, green hair up in a bun, sexy legs peeking through the slit of a sequin dress cut so low on top that her breasts were practically free-ranging.

She looked in Meehixiheem's direction, and Meehix tapped her tits. The girl turned away quickly. *Uh-oh.*

"Well, what crawled under her flap?" Meehix snarled.

"Maybe she…"

"Stay here." Meehix interrupted him and marched over to the girl like a drill sergeant approaching a recruit going AWOL.

"Remember," John said quietly to no one, "no fighting, no killing. Do blue girl catfights count, I wonder?"

He looked around uncomfortably, preferring not to see what was transpiring across the room.

"Can I assist you with anything, sir?" the robot had zipped over again, helpful as ever.

"No, I'm…" he paused, then thought of something. "Actually, yes, maybe you can. You ever hear of a guy named Daukhl? Was in here about three weeks ago, may be a regular?"

"I'm sorry, sir, but disclosing any information regarding clientele, employees, or sentient beings in general is prohibited. I can only offer libations and other services, and all transactions of any kind are automatically deleted from my memory files immediately after they occur. You could tell me your name, and I would not be able to recall it one second later."

"That's interesting. Do you remember *your* name?"

"Yes. My name is Bartender."

"Well, my name is John. You pour a *mean* water, Bartender."

"Thank you...sir."

Meehix and her cousin moved to a corner behind a row of potted trees.

"I don't care if you don't want to talk to me! You're *going* to talk to me!" Meehix was yelling. Fortunately, the music was so loud that no one heard the confrontational tone in her voice, at least not yet.

"You have a lot of nerve, pulling me away from my friends like that," Keeliz retorted. "I ought to call security on you."

"For what? I haven't punched you. *Yet.*"

"Meehix, you haven't changed a bit. You know, there's only one person to blame for this situation."

"Who?"

"Who do you think?"

"So Daukhl *is* involved," Meehix said under her breath.

Keeliz shook her head. "You don't get it, do you?" She put her hands on Meehix's shoulders and looked her in the eyes. "I'm going to say something to you. Then I'm going to walk away, and you and I are never going to speak again."

Meehix opened her mouth, and Keeliz squeezed her shoulders with a "don't say another word" look. She was *serious.*

Meehix looked around the room. Some of Keeliz's friends were watching them. Meehix took a big swallow of gin. She was already feeling it. Keeliz stared at her for a long, uncomfortable moment, her hands still on her shoulders, as if to make sure Meehix understood the terms, then continued.

"Have you ever thought about honor, Meehix? Or loyalty? Have you ever considered what it takes for families like ours to hold their place in the galaxy, what a heavy responsibility that is, what it involves?

"Did you ever consider, when you were spending your sire's money on parties and sex and drugs, how that might affect *his* interests, how an indiscretion or a careless moment on your part could destroy everything he built? You never think of these things, do you? Well, now you won't have to.

"There's only one person to blame, Meehixiheem, and it's not Daukhl or your sire or your family or anyone else. Now go away. I never want to see you again."

Keeliz let her go and went back to her friends. Meehix stood there, holding her ice glass, staring at the wall. She trembled, then she slammed the remaining alcohol and walked back to the bar for another one.

CHAPTER THIRTY-SEVEN

"Did you see this invoice for the one-fifteen?"

"Yeah, I saw it. They're ripping us off. I sent a report to the director on Friday, but I haven't heard back. I'll bet you a dollar-to-dishes he'll want us to find a new source. I'm tellin' ya, half of these supply chains are screwing us because the order's from Earth."

Jakes and Newton were sitting in the primary logistics room of the USSF black ops base in Nevada. The two analysts were sifting through digital and printed stacks of orders and receipts dealing in mind-bogglingly high monetary numbers.

"You know, if we put half the money we waste buyin' the stuff into more R&D, we could make it ourselves and tell the Drellens to fuck off," Jakes reasoned.

"No shit. I've been saying that for years," Newton countered. "We should be energy-independent by now. It's the bureaucracy. Too damn big and going like gangbusters since the fifties. All them fingers in the pie, and nobody wants to lose their pie...or their fingers."

"Idiots," Jakes huffed.

He looked around the room.

"Can you hand me that Red Bull? I don't feel like gettin' up."

Newton reached over to the printer where Jakes left his Red Bull. He had to stretch, and his protruding midsection didn't help. He barely got his chubby fingers around it. It wasn't cold anymore. He handed it to Jakes.

"Thanks, buddy." He took a lukewarm hit.

They scanned through more lists and numbers.

"Did you see this?" Jakes exclaimed.

"What?"

"Transport got hit on the way to the third arm."

"I told you about that last week."

"This was yesterday. It's a different one."

"Let me see."

Newton grabbed the printout from Jakes. He read it out loud.

"Blah, blah, blah, two hundred heads onboard, blah, blah, blah, four-man crew, blah, blah, blah, entire ship and cargo lost...shit, you're right. It's a new one. How come I didn't get it?"

"Beats me."

"What's the memo say?"

Jakes looked at the memo. "Take care of it."

"That's it? From the director? *Take care of it?*"

"Dated this morning."

Newton looked up at the nude centerfold of Miss December taped to one side of the multiple monitors in front of him. He sighed.

Miss December would not like it if I lost my cool. Miss

December only gives it up to strong, decisive men who get the job done. I am that man.

"I know what he's sayin'," Newton lamented. "He wants it off the books. That's why I didn't get it. He was hinting at it during the last sit-down."

"Hinting at *what?*"

"Them Cro-Magnum fuckers. What are they called? Them red scorpion bastards."

"Crom Limeans?"

"Yeah, that's them. He wants us to transfer funds to the field agents to pay the Crom Limeans to protect the shipments. You know, mercenary work. Otherwise, the goddamn pirates are gonna suck us dry if they keep knocking off the transports."

"I thought the Crom Limeans *were* pirates."

"Nah. Pirates are drug-addled morons. Crom Limeans are more sophisticated, and they'll do anything for a buck. They got no loyalty, which is a good thing, and with three-foot stinger tails and four arms holding guns, they'll keep the shipments safe."

"What's the payout?"

"Negotiable. Get on the hyper-bump to Stanley. He's workin' the third arm. Tell him it's from the top. Have him set up a meeting. Do it fast. If we lose another ship, it's gonna be *our* ass. *Take care of it* comes with the implied timeline of *yesterday.*"

"Will do. Oh, and hey, before I forget, did you see they changed that APB on the kid and the bluesy?"

"The ones that stole the ship from Albuquerque?"

"Yeah."

"They up the bounty?"

"Bounty's the same, but they dropped the kid from *dead or alive* to just *dead*. Story is he blew away a concierge on Lagud, and the guy was working undercover for USSF. It's a big stink in the first arm right now, all over the G-Viz. Chief is pissed. If the bluesy weren't worth so much, he'd probably off her too."

"Play stupid games, win stupid prizes. Go call Stanley."

"Will do."

Jakes left the room, and Newton stared at Miss December.

I got this, baby. Daddy's bringin' home the bacon and *the sausage. You inspire me to be a better man. You're the only woman I'll ever love.*

He blew her a kiss and—in his mind—she blew one back.

CHAPTER THIRTY-EIGHT

Meehixiheem opened her eyes. She was on the ship, in the back, with a blanket over her. She could see stars through the cockpit window and what looked like the third moon of Dolurulod. She felt sick.

"They taste like Cracker Jacks," John said to Ship. "They're not quite as sweet, but they're the same crunch."

"I wouldn't know, John. Taste is something I can neither experience nor adequately define. However, if you are digging it, I say chow down."

John was eating something that looked like large fried beetles. Meehix focused her eyes and realized they were Beggle bugs, a type of natural snack imported from Miggean Orbo VI and usually consumed by pregnant females to help keep their fluctuating emotions in check.

Where in the hell did he get those? she wondered.

"My scans indicate they are composed of insect proteins, minimal carbohydrates, and moderate levels of mono and polyunsaturated fatty acids. I also detect significant levels of selenium and serotonin as well as

two different glycoproteins that I am unfamiliar with. If you wish, I could research this further and give you a full report as soon as possible."

"As long as they don't kill me, I'm down. Beats eating dried fruit all the time," John said between crunches.

Meehix thought of telling John why females normally consumed Beggle bugs, then decided it was pointless. Everything seemed pointless now.

She tried to remember the night before. Bits and pieces came together in her mind. Keeliz and her preachy self-righteousness came first.

What a hypocrite. I remember three years ago, holding her hair while she vomited into a fountain outside her boyfriend's house. Where was your honor then, Keeliz?

She remembered another relative approaching her in the club. It was her Uncle Jeefil, who was a year younger than her. He was waiting when she came out of the restroom, her third Gyken martini in hand.

"I'm not supposed to be talking to you," he began the conversation. *What a great opening line.*

"Then don't," Meehix snapped. "Make sure you follow the rules, Jeefil, because the rules are clearly more important than people."

"I wanted you to know that I think it's a stupid tradition and totally unfair what the clan did to you. If I could do anything about it, I would, but I can't...I mean..."

She put one blue finger over his stammering lips.

"Shhh," she said softly. "Go away, little boy. Be *loyal* someplace else."

"I wonder what color these things are before they're

cooked," John said, his loud talking interrupting her unpleasant memories of the night before.

"Judging by the levels of carminic acid in the shell, I would expect them to be bright red before that, John."

Meehix wiped a tear from her eye. She'd always liked Jeefil.

Then she remembered Daukhl. He was there too. Not dead. Not imprisoned on Earth.

"Hey, asshole," she yelled across the room. "How about a ride to Kdack? It'll be fun."

"Meehixiheem," he said without emotion, trying to be cool the way he always tried to be cool. "I heard the Kdackans locked you up and you busted out. Good for you."

"Yeah, no big deal," she said.

Daukhl was sitting on a couch encircling a low table in a private section of the club. Barbazclomeen sat to his right and Nateexopeel to his left—the fattie and the hottie. Other hangers-on and members of his regular entourage occupied the remainder of the sofa.

Meehix ignored them all and sat on Daukhl's lap. He didn't protest. He only gave her that same bored look he gave everybody. His body odor told a different story. Under the calm exterior, he was sweating laser blasts. "So how'd *you* get away?" she asked innocently.

"You know, baby. Little of this, little of that. After the crash, it was every man for himself. I did what I had to do, weavin' and dodgin.'"

"Weavin' and dodgin', weavin' and dodgin,'" she repeated. "I'm impressed by your athletic skills." She swallowed the last ounce of her fourth martini. "How about dodging *this?*"

She smashed the ice glass in his face.

Barbazclomeen and Nateexopeel screamed. Someone else yelled, "Not cool! Not cool!" A bouncer came running. He grabbed Meehix by the arm.

"Stop!" Daukhl shouted. The bouncer froze.

"You know the rules," the bouncer mumbled.

"And you know how much I pay you on the side," Daukhl retorted as he wiped ice shards from his face. "I spilled my drink. That's all."

The bouncer looked at Meehix, then Daukhl, then back to Meehix. He let her go.

"I'll be right over there," the bouncer added and walked away.

Meehix stood. "You deserve a lot more than that."

Daukhl dabbed his forehead with a napkin. It was bleeding. "It was business, Meehixiheem, and that kind of business would have gone down even if I wasn't involved. You know what I'm sayin'?"

Meehix didn't respond. She walked away and didn't look back.

"You're awake." John knocked her out of her ruminations again.

"Yeah." She sat up. "Where are we?"

"Over the third moon of Dolurulod. Ship thought it was a good place to hide out until we figure out what to do next. How you feeling? I think we're on a rotating schedule. I get wasted one night, and you get plastered the next."

"Yeah, it's great. I need some water."

John got her some, and she downed it.

"Do I have anything to be embarrassed about? I don't remember leaving the Monastery."

"You passed out. Your uncle helped me get you out the back and into the ship. He seems like a cool guy."

Funny. Generally, when I pass out in a club, I wake up in some stranger's bed. Interesting how my fate now seems to depend on one large Kdackan male stuffing his face with food usually meant for pregnant females. The universe works in mysterious ways.

"Thank you."

"For what?" His mouth was full of bugs.

"For taking care of me and not taking advantage of me. Seems you're the only sentient being left who cares about my dignity."

"Well," John mumbled, little crunchy legs protruding from his lips, "I do."

Meehix looked at the bowl of Beggle bugs.

"Where did you get those?" she finally had to ask.

"Some chick at the Monastery. Barbasol or Barbazo—something like that."

"Barbazclomeen?

"Yeah, that's her. She was devouring these things, and I was starving so I asked where she got them, and she gave me the whole bowl. Do you know her?"

"That fat slut," Meehix snarled. "No wonder she put on so much weight. Daukhl stepped in it this time."

"What," John said apprehensively, "are they fattening?"

CHAPTER THIRTY-NINE

"We need money," Meehix blurted out of nowhere. "We need it *soon*.

John belched. He was kicked back in the control seat, staring out the window at the Dolurulod moon. He felt full, content, and strangely relaxed, as if all the cares and turmoil of the past few days had vanished.

Boy, that moon sure is pretty.

"Did you hear me?" she pressed.

"Yeah, sure," he said dreamily. "What do you want to do?"

She looked at him suspiciously but continued. "I want *revenge*. I want to kidnap my sire and sell *him* into slavery!"

John tried to process this. He was thinking more along the lines of getting jobs at Starbucks or driving for Uber —or whatever the galactic equivalent was.

Meehix sat and put her face in her hands. "I just want my life back," she said sadly.

John thought for a moment.

"Not likely to happen," he observed, waxing philosophical. "The life you had before is gone...like dust in the wind. Dust in the wind. All we are is dust in the wind."

She looked at him like he took a dump on the ship's floor.

"Don't hang on," he continued. "Nothing lasts forever but the earth and sky. It slips away. And all your money... won't another...minute *buy-yiiiii*."

He sang the last line.

"Are you all right?" Now she was genuinely concerned about his sanity.

"I'm cool. Maybe we should form a rock band and tour the universe."

She smacked him on the back of his head.

"Ow! What'd I do?"

"You act like you're high! Snap out of your Beggle bug stupor and let's get real. This is serious. We're *broke*. Do you understand?"

John thought she was overreacting. He'd been broke before, but it didn't seem like that big of a deal. Of course, he was living with his parents but...

"If I even dare to *hope* that I could ever get my status and position back, I'd need a shit-ton of money to buy back the bounty. *We're starting at zero*. Do you understand? I've never been at zero before in my life. No one in my family ever came even remotely *close* to zero. I can't even conceive of zero. I don't know what it's like where you come from but where I come from, if you hit zero, you die a slow, miserable death."

"Okay, okay. What can we do?"

"That's what I've been asking! What can we do to get *a lot of money?*"

"Rob a bank."

"Don't be stupid. Galactic credits are in planet-sized databases, and automated warehouses protected by lethal radiation belts print cash. No one's robbed a galactic bank in over ten thousand years."

"Prostitution."

She rolled her eyes. "Typical male. I get pounded ten times a day while you play pimp."

"I wasn't talking about *you* putting out. I meant *me*."

"I'm not going to ask you to do something I'm not willing to do."

"Who said you had to ask me?"

"Forget it," she argued. "You wouldn't last five minutes on the street."

"What's that supposed to mean? I'm a healthy male who knows how to please a woman. I think I could get top dollar when push comes to shove. In fact, I've had a lot of experience pushing and shoving and everything in between. It beats a desk job. Plus, I'd get plenty of exercise."

She'd about had enough of this foolishness.

"Screwing alien females for money will get you *eaten*," she explained. "I'm not sure you want to make the mistake of banging a Quoteggian into a frenetic orgasm where lust overrides her mind, and she starts biting chunks out of your neck."

"Really? That happens?"

"Don't believe me? Ask Ship."

John gave her a "you're making this up" look.

"Hey, Ship? What do you know about Quoteggian sex practices?"

"Actually, John, Meehix left out a few of the more

repugnant aspects of the Quoteggian mating ritual. The female genitals have concealed blades that cut off the male penis during the throes of orgasm to guarantee thorough insemination. After that, she consumes his appendages and injects his lifeless torso with her fertilized eggs.

"A week later, the hatching offspring then escape through the male's remaining orifices and consume the rotting torso before regurgitating it again into the female's mouth to assist in producing breast milk for the developing brood. It's the circle of life, John. "

"I think I'm going to be sick."

"Can we forget about prostitution?" Meehix proposed.

"Yes, please. I may never have sex again."

John's stomach was gurgling, and he felt dizzy. He couldn't tell if it was the bugs or Ship's alien version of *Love Story*. He swallowed hard and tried to think of a serious way out of their current dilemma.

"What about a courier service? We could transport stuff for businesses and whatnot. Charge per delivery."

"We could never compete. They have giant ships that move millions of tons of merchandise all over the galaxy. We'd never make a dime."

"What about smuggling? Moving illegal stuff? Like drugs and stolen merchandise."

"Too dangerous. We'd have run-ins with the Vikrellion mob, gangs, cartels. Plus the ship isn't right. No storage space and not near fast enough. No offense, Ship."

"None taken."

John thought some more. There had to be something he'd be good at without the risk of getting shot in the back of the head by the mob or getting his dick chopped off by a sex-crazed Quoteggian.

"What about a muscle job? We're both in good shape, and we can kick-ass."

"Like what?"

"Like *bounty hunting.* I mean, we're ten times smarter than those buffoons in the gold submarine. Those Drellen yo-yos weren't exactly rocket scientists either. I bet we could make some serious money and have fun at the same time."

"Hmm," she said.

I got a "hmm" out of her. That's a good sign.

"Ship," Meehix said. "Pull up the requirements to get licensed as bounty hunters."

"Will do, Meehix."

An enormous pile of lists and by-laws appeared holographically over the control panel. Meehix began reading. John tried, but it wasn't in English.

"There's a lot here. Looks like we're going to be studying for a while."

"Studying? Damn," John lamented. "I thought I finished school stuff."

"Me too," she admitted. "I did *well* in school so I wouldn't have to do *more* school. Look where that got me."

John thought about his life in video games. Where had *that* got *him*? Actually, pretty far. His in-depth knowledge of code made it possible to write Hannah. His gamer skills helped him fly the ship and shoot the bounty hunter at the hotel.

The reality was, without the computer skills he developed through his love of video games, none of this would be happening. Without them, he'd be some fat, washed-up, ex-high school rugby player living in his parent's basement. Then again, he could still be some fat, washed-up, ex-high school rugby player living in his parent's basement and playing video games even with all his computer skills. If that Draylop guy hadn't pushed Gage to persuade John to check out the secret base on Central Avenue, none of this would have happened.

I guess there's an element of luck and outside influence that you have no control of to be successful. Maybe the universe does *know what it's doing, and we only act like we do it all.*

"All right," he surrendered. "I guess there's no way around it. Ship, can you translate all that into English and project it over here? Then we can both study and get a handle on what this is going to involve."

"Not a problem, John."

John laughed.

"What's so funny?" Meehix asked as she read.

"I don't know. It's so weird how life can change on a dime. A few days ago, I was sitting in my room playing video games. My mom was nagging at me about how I should get out and date girls. Now I'm halfway across the galaxy in a spaceship with a hot girl learning how to become a galactic bounty hunter. Life is hilarious."

Meehix was deep in study and ignoring him. All she said was, "Mmm-hmm."

John giggled and started reading.

CHAPTER FORTY

He woke up to a holographic bounty hunter application floating over his head. Meehix was sleeping next to him on the floor. They'd both passed out doing their studies.

He looked outside the window. They were still orbiting over the third moon of Dolurulod.

"Hey, Ship, what time is it?"

"That would depend, John. Would you like to know the time on Dolurulod? If so, what part of Dolurulod? Or would you prefer a time zone on Earth? Or Lagud? Or I could..."

"Never mind. My internal clock is fucked forever. It's always night in space anyway."

He leaned back against the bulkhead and flipped through the floating bounty hunter info. He already read most of it and had the overall picture.

The basic requirements to become a bounty hunter were pretty simple, sign the documents and pay the fees. No standard to meet, no physical to take, no worries about criminal history or level of education as far as they could see. Basically, any numb-nut with half a brain and a gun could call him or herself a bounty hunter if they could fill out the paperwork and pay the fees.

Of course, if you fucked up and shot an innocent bystander or arrested the wrong person, you could end up in prison or be executed faster than you could say, "Oops, maybe I shouldn't be a bounty hunter." Even that kind of scenario was open to interpretation.

Let's say the person or being you were after—known in the bounty-hunting biz as the target—was wanted for a minor infringement like dine and dash, meaning they ate at a restaurant without paying. Not a capital crime, but if some asshole did that repeatedly and pissed off the wrong restaurateur, someone might put a bounty on their head simply because they had enough of their bullshit or the local police weren't taking the crime seriously—or both.

That would be considered a Level One Target. Probably not much money to be made, probably not a lot of danger to the general galactic public, and definitely not a dead or alive bounty. Your only latitude—as the bounty hunter—would be to bring that target in. If you killed him, you'd be in trouble. If you killed a bystander, you'd be in *big* trouble.

Now let's say you were watching Crec Alerts on the old G-Viz looking for juicy jobs and you saw a Level Twenty target. A Level Twenty was the highest-ranked and would likely be worth millions of credits to the bounty hunter. The target probably detonated an illegal anti-matter weapon that took out half a city on a populated planet to get that kind of bounty on their head.

You got a lot of latitude on that one. Level and money. Money and level. The higher the numbers, the more you made, and the more forgiving the law was regarding the methods you used and the collateral damage you caused.

When John had read all this and began to understand how it worked, he had Ship pull up *their* Crec Alert and translate it into English. They were a Level Seventeen, not based on their danger to the general public but based on the money somebody was willing to pay to get them back —or kill them. You never really knew who was paying to bring you in. Even the bounty hunters didn't know.

They got all the available info on the target—physical description, last known address, last confirmed sighting, family and friends, etcetera, but they didn't know who was footing the bill. All they knew about the money was how much they'd get for bringing the target in dead or alive. It kept the employer and employee separate via a middle-man, like PayPal, that handled the collection of the target and the pay-out transfer once you completed the job.

Of course, the middle-man—a company called Abyss Exchange—charged a percentage of the bounty. The bounty hunter also paid a significant chunk of change upfront to get a copy of the bounty certificate, which you were required to carry with you at all times for the duration of the hunt.

If you caught the target, you handed him or her over to the nearest Department of Galactic Safety Office or Abyss Exchange outlet along with the bounty certificate, and you got paid immediately. If you failed, you were the proud owner of a worthless piece of paper, and you lost your upfront investment. No refunds for losers.

Some jobs were cash on delivery. Some offered to cover expenses. Some gave bonuses if the bounty hunter met specific criteria, like, wanted dead or alive; five thousand credit bonus if brought in dead with proof of torture. Some didn't pay in credits.

Payment could also be in real estate, spacecraft, jewels, precious metals, or even slaves. It was all legal as long as you had your license number and paid your fees. After that, you were on your own...and God help you if you fucked up.

Meehix was still sleeping so John looked up some of the recommended reading materials included with the government licensing information. One was called *Galactic Bounty Hunting for the Linguistically Challenged.*

That sounds like a good starter book.

He opened it on the holo-projector and realized it was a picture book—no words anywhere. There were diagrams outlining ways to capture a target without maiming civilians and others on lethal versus non-lethal weapons. There was even a short test at the end—all in pictures.

The first question showed a bounty hunter after he'd captured and cuffed a sexy, four-breasted Level Two target. The next page gave you three picture options to choose from. Did you, one—transport the target to the nearest Department of Galactic Safety Office or Abyss Exchange outlet? Two—decapitate the target and bury her head and body in separate locations? Or three—rape the target and make her your sex slave?

Hmm. That's a tough one, but I'm going with door number one.

He got it right.

"What are you doing?" Meehix said sleepily. She sat up and rubbed the back of her neck.

"Reading...or rather...viewing *Galactic Bounty Hunting for the Linguistically Challenged.* More like *Galactic Bounty Hunting for the Brainless Moron.* I can't believe how simplistic some of this literature is. Whoever needs this kind of training shouldn't be allowed to have a squirt gun, let alone a real gun."

"Not every species in the galaxy has your brain size, do they?"

Uh-oh. Sounds like she woke up on the wrong side of the ship.

"You sound...unhappy." He chose his words carefully. He almost said *grumpy* but decided that was too confrontational. She didn't respond for a full ten seconds—or at least it seemed like ten seconds.

"I don't know." She sighed. "I guess I got depressed. I was reading the bounty hunter materials, and it's all so...I don't know...not *me.*

"Life used to be a big party. I mean, there were bad times, but overall it was fun, and money was never a problem. I could buy what I wanted, go where I wanted, do what I wanted, whenever I wanted. I always thought that my family had my back, that they supported me and cared about me.

"I mean, sure, I had arguments with my sire and my sisters, and we would fight sometimes but I never in a million years would have thought they were planning to get rid of me. I still can't get my mind around it. Now, here I am, and I don't have a pot to piss in."

"Yeah, you do. The suction thing over by the control panel."

She didn't laugh. *I tried.*

"I'm sorry but even if I quit whining," she continued, "I

still get depressed reading the paperwork. How can we possibly do this?"

"What do you mean? It looks pretty simple to me. We're healthy and strong, fairly intelligent, we have Ship to help us, and it's a job where our criminal history doesn't matter. We have the potential to make a lot of money. What more could we ask? This gig is tailor-made for us!"

"Did you even read the minimum recommended utilities list?" She scowled. "One Vetralaun semi-automatic is not going to cut it, John. We're going to need at least a ten thousand credit investment in equipment to get the basics. Where are we going to get that kind of money? If you say rob a bank again, I'll smack you!"

John looked around the cabin. *Damn. I wish I'd kept the old translator. Might have got half a grand for that.* Then he saw it.

"Your bag."

"What?" she screamed.

"I know you. That has to be one of the most expensive suitcases money can buy."

"It's *not!*" she shouted and snatched it like a life preserver. "The most expensive suitcase is a Bermak Hirkin and Sons, Scappalla skin handbag that sells for nine hundred thousand credits...*retail.*"

"How much does *your* bag sell for? *Retail?*"

She gulped, still holding the exotic leather to her chest like a protective mother with a baby.

"I bought this on holiday. It's my last exquisite possession," she pleaded.

"What did you pay for it, Meehix?"

She swallowed again. "Five hundred thousand credits."

"Holy shit! Even if we got a quarter of that, we'd be set!"

"No!" she cried. "This bag is my lifeline to home. It's the one thing left that defines me as a successful woman. I even have full-coverage insurance on it. It has so many memories inside."

"It's empty, and it was made from a dead animal that gave its life only to be carried around by stupid, rich-bitches who think it's cool to spend thousands of dollars on something that probably cost ten bucks to make. Forget it, Meehix. We're bounty hunters now, and that bag goes to the highest bidder. So suck it up. It's time to be a *real* woman."

She didn't know what to say. He didn't know what to say either.

Wow. Where did that come from? I sounded badass. Maybe I am cut out to be a bounty hunter!

CHAPTER FORTY-ONE

Space Station L-222 was *enormous*. Not near as massive as the Lagud Dyson Sphere, but it was still bigger than anything manufactured that John had ever seen. About the size of Earth's moon, L-222 was saucer-shaped with giant spokes protruding from the sides and another ring around that.

Picture a hub cap with magic markers glued around the edges and a giant donut encompassing the whole thing, all painted blue-gray and covered in thousands of tiny lights. The thing was out in the middle of nowhere with a single Gate nearby that led back to Dolurulod.

They got a good spot in one of the docking bays and were soon on their way to find a pawnshop. They had only one hundred and eighty Earth minutes to do so as the docking fee was pay-as-you-go. If they didn't come back in three hours or less with at least five credits to cover the daily fee, the station would jettison their ship into space, and it would be their responsibility to cover the cost of retrieval.

They walked down a giant hallway packed with stores, shops, restaurants, and aliens. Probably half were humanoid, and the other half were *anything goes*. It reminded John of an airport terminal from hell.

He even saw a large creature with eight legs like a spider, a giant head like a saber-toothed tiger, and a body like a jellyfish. He could see inside its digestive organs, and it looked like the last meal the monster had devoured was still alive, slowly digesting away, with a "my life sucks" look on its little monkey face.

Geez, that one's going to give me nightmares.

Meehix didn't even notice the beast. She hadn't said a word since they docked and she was clinging to her bag like a passenger on a nose-diving jetliner who found the last parachute.

They entered the first pawnshop they could find— Jibbee Jabbee's Power Pawn—and John was in heaven.

"This is fucking *cool!*" he gushed with weaponry wonder.

At least a third of the establishment was devoted to every gun under the sun—or suns—as well as blade weapons, armor, explosives, ammunition, etcetera. It was like a single-shooter gamer's dream only in real life—but everything was *expensive.*

There were a few patrons in the place, but most were checking out jewelry and other non-essentials. John walked up to the counter with Meehix in tow.

"What you need?" a giant octopus-looking creature said from the other side of the counter. He was bluish-purple, obese, sitting on a giant stool, and had about twenty long tentacles for arms. His softball-sized eyes looked John up and down, and his walrus-like mouth had two tongues that could lick his upper and lower lips simultaneously.

This must be Jibbee Jabbee.

"We want to pawn this..." He grabbed Meehix's bag, more like wrenched it from her grasp, "and we're looking to get cash *and* weapons."

"Hmmph." Jibbee Jabbee snorted and snatched the bag with one of his tentacles. He threw it in what looked like a big trash can. John was about to protest until he saw a red glow emanating from the can. Jibbee Jabbee looked at a holo-screen on the desk, and John realized he was scanning the suitcase to verify its authenticity and determine its worth. He pulled it back out of the can-scanner and set it on the counter.

"I'll give you ten thousand for it."

"Ten thousand?" Meehix screamed herself back to the living. "It cost *fifty* times that!"

"Sure," Jibbee Jabbee gurgled, "when it was *new.* This thing's at least three years old, it has wear marks all over it, *and* it has micro-spatters of Drellen blood and residual traces of some kind of nerve gas embedded in the leather. What'd you use it for? Movin' body parts?"

Meehix was seething.

"How about five thousand cash and ten in trade?"

"No can do."

John looked down at the counter and saw a Vetralaun semi-automatic under the glass. He wasn't one hundred percent sure, but the markings on the tag looked like it was going for about a thousand credits, and the gun didn't even look as nice as the one he swiped off the bounty hunter.

"How about five thousand cash and ten in trade for the bag and *this*."

He put the Vetralaun on the counter. Jibbee Jabbee scooped it up and looked it over.

"Drellen gun, huh?" he said. "This belong to the guy whose blood's on the bag?"

"Maybe," John said defiantly.

Jibbee Jabbee laughed. He sounded like a repeating whoopee-cushion in slow motion.

"Okay, kid. Pick what you want but don't go much over ten. Otherwise, you'll need to throw in that pendant around your neck. My gut tells me it's worth a pretty penny."

John didn't realize Hannah was hanging outside his shirt, and he slipped the plug-in back under his collar. He would only pawn *that* off as a last resort.

Meehix was looking at weapons. Apparently, she'd finally let go of her past life and bag and was trying to embrace the new. She held up a transparent piece of armor and realized the design was for a nude humanoid, not a clothed one. She put it back on the rack.

"What was wrong with that?" John asked. "It looked like the perfect size for you."

"The liner is body plasma. You're supposed to wear it over bare skin. It's transparent."

"And the problem is..."

"Keep it up, buddy."

"Don't have to. It keeps itself up involuntarily, remember?"

"Yeah, and with the mood I'm in I could *involuntarily* remove your testicles with my teeth."

"Ouch," he whimpered sarcastically, "you're so Quoteggian."

She fake-smiled.

"You guys wanna try anything out?" Jibbee Jabbee called pleasantly from behind the counter. "There's a shootin' range in the back, but you gotta sign a waiver and pay for ammo."

"Maybe in a minute. Just checking out some armor first," John said.

"All right, lemme know. I'll be right back. I'm gonna take a shit."

Jibbee Jabbee utilized his twenty tentacles to raise himself off the giant stool and maneuver his corpulent mass through a door behind the counter. John wondered how he could leave all his expensive items unattended, with strangers milling around until he saw the numerous security cameras covering the ceiling. It was clear that no one would get far if they stole from Jibbee Jabbee.

———

Jibbee Jabbee closed the door behind him and slithered over to a hyper-bump relay on the wall. He hit a button and lifted a plunger-like device to his ear hole.

"Hey, Moxel," he whispered, his big, purple lips quivering. "Yeah, it's JJ. Listen, I think those two you were askin' about just walked in. Yeah, the Kdackan and the bluesy. They're here right now, pawnin' off a Vetralaun and a handbag worth a bundle. Fuck no, I ain't gonna stall 'em. You want 'em? You get yer lazy ass down here. No shootin' in my place though. Take 'em down the hall somewhere. I expect compensation if it's them. Okay. Yeah. Yeah, fuck-you-very-much. All right. Goodbye."

Jibbee Jabbee hung up, and his big eyes rolled uneasily. He composed himself by wiping his tentacles over his moist skin and lumbered back out the door to the counter. Meanwhile, on the other side of the station, Moxel and his partner, a Quoteggian female name Ursivia, suited up and jumped into an automated shuttle tram.

"Where are they?" Ursivia asked as she finished strapping on her protective gear while the shuttle got up to speed.

"Other side of the station. JJ called it in."

"That scumbag. He's going to want ten percent."

"If it's them, it's worth it."

The shuttle whizzed around the inside edge of the station. Other shuttles zipped past, over and under the track they were on. The display in front of them showed an ETA of two hours.

Moxel put on his reading glasses and settled in for the trip. He was working his way through an esoteric treatise written by a Kinsbon mystic named Rallo, who claimed to have transcribed the meaning of existence as dictated to him by an angelic microbe named Mitbiss that appeared over a sewer on Molloceros IV.

Moxel was skeptical, but he tapped the edge of the glasses anyway until they flipped two pages before where he'd left off. He had fallen asleep the last time he read and wanted to make sure he didn't miss anything. Out of the corner of his eye, he saw Ursivia slip a blade into her boot sheath.

"What's with the laser knife?" Moxel asked.

"Didn't you see the update? They changed the Kdackan from dead or alive to *dead*. That fucker's six-foot-four, two hundred and fifty pounds. Crec Alert specifies turning them in on Kdack. You want to carry his body back to the ship? Remove the head, cauterize at the same time. Less weight to carry, less blood to clean up."

"That's why I love you, Ursi. Always thinking and always up for the dirty work. It's a shame we can never mate."

"We could." She smiled. "You wouldn't get anything out of it though."

CHAPTER FORTY-TWO

By the time John and Meehix settled on the diverse kit of weapons and armor they wanted, or at least what they could afford, they ended up with only a thousand credits in cash and the rest went toward armaments. The haggling got a little heated at times, especially between Meehix and Jibbee Jabbee. At one point, she told him outright that he was a crook, and he informed her that if she didn't like the deal, she could take her crummy bag and barter elsewhere. However, by the time they left the pawnshop wearing their purchases, and each with five hundred credits in their pocket, they had made amends with Jibbee Jabbee. In fact, the longer they negotiated with him over prices, the more he seemed to acquiesce until John felt like they got a pretty good deal—and all in a little less than two hours.

They paid their docking fee well before the deadline and were now on a mission to find a Department of Galactic Safety Office to complete their licensing paperwork.

John twirled his new pistol and checked himself out in

the store mirrors as they walked down the busy hallway. No one seemed to care that he was flashing a gun and admiring his new armor in the window reflections.

"I can't believe we don't need permits for all this stuff." They looked like they were on their way to a deadly LARP —and no one cared.

"It's not unusual to carry," Meehix explained. "Depending on where you're going, a lot of people travel armed. Look at *that* guy." She pointed.

A large rhinoceros-looking being strolled by carrying a handgun the size of a fire hydrant. If John had walked into an airport terminal on Earth carrying that, he would have been gunned down by security before he reached the ticket counter.

John's new gun was a type of concussive blaster. He not only liked the look of it—*badass* was how he described it— but it was effective on all species. It killed via an energy bolt that propelled a tiny projectile at nearly the speed of light. It exploded on impact, causing a contained shock- wave that radiated approximately two feet in all directions.

Basically, it would blow a good-sized hole in anything but not necessarily harm anyone more than two feet away. He also had enough ammunition to fight off a small army, and it was easy to carry. Each round was about the size of a Tic-Tac, and he could hold fifty rounds in a container no bigger than a matchbook. The utility belt he bought with it had everything he needed to operate and maintain the gun. He thought the weapon was so sexy that he even named it Layla9.

For stunning a target, John also purchased a high-tech neuro-disruptor that operated electrically. When you pointed it at a living being and pulled the trigger, it instantaneously scanned the target's neural network. Then it fired a charge specifically frequenced to disrupt muscular signals in that particular species' extremities. That caused a temporary seizure and rendered the target incapacitated for several minutes.

Of course, any species without a central nervous system would likely be unaffected, but John figured he would cross that messy bridge if and when he came to it.

Meehix opted for more traditional and less complicated weapons. Not only did she prefer them over the high-tech energy weapons, but the two of them reasoned that having multi-species-effective blades and throwing munitions as a backup was a sound choice no matter how you sliced it—pun intended. If John couldn't take them down with his blaster or neuro-disruptor, she could end a confrontation with a thrust through the torso or a whack on the head.

Her primary *deadly* weapon was a long, narrow sword made of indestructible metal that she carried in a scabbard on her back. She also had an easily accessible short, tanto-like knife on her hip for backup. A series of titanium spheres lined her utility belt—some with blades that extended when thrown, others connected by cords and employed like Australian bolas—and when deployed properly, they were as deadly and effective as any energy weapon.

She also carried an entirely different set of edged weapons, essentially glorified throwing stars. Some could turn corners, swoop down or up and vice versa, or fly hundreds of meters and return to her. She could catch them with a special woven glove that resembled chain-mail and was the same metal as her sword.

When they were testing things out in the shooting range, Meehix—to her delight—could hit the target dead center every time with every throwing weapon she chose. John tried the same and almost took out her eye when he lost his grip on a throwing star. That was enough for her. She ordered him to stick to guns, and she would handle the blades and hand projectiles.

In addition to all the above, Meehix also carried a metal grappling hook with one hundred feet of unbreakable cordage and a medium-size club made of solid Bira-Makoom wood. They both had a pair of adjustable, indestructible handcuffs. With armor made of a nearly impenetrable amber-colored, energy-deflecting synthetic polymer, they were ready to begin their careers as bounty hunters—almost. They still had to get through licensing.

"I'm starving." John holstered his gun. "We should eat before doing the paperwork. That could take hours, and I'm hungry enough to eat a veonk sphere."

"They have veonk spheres in that diner over there." She pointed. "Probably not very good ones, but…"

"I was *kidding*. I'd only eat a veonk sphere if I was dying on a desert island and had already eaten my feet. Let's find something as close to a burger and fries as we can get."

They chose an open-air restaurant that looked decent and got a table with a good view of the main hall. John ordered something that looked like a burger, and the Dolurulod waitress assured him that it was easily digestible and nutritious. Unfortunately, it tasted more like a feta cheese pancake than a juicy hamburger. He dug into it anyway, not caring at this point, and Meehix ate something that looked like split-pea soup poured over ice cream. *To each his own.*

Meehix kept focusing on something off to his left. He turned and looked but saw nothing unusual. Only lots of humanoid types enjoying their food and conversation.

"What?" he said.

"That couple over there." She looked down at her food. "They're watching us."

"Where?" He looked back again. Nothing. No one looked like they gave a crap what either one of them was doing.

"The Quoteggian female and the Chelzin male," she said. "They sat right after we did."

"He's with a Quoteggian female?" John exclaimed. "Should we warn him to wear a titanium condom?"

"I'm telling you, they're watching us."

John looked a third time. He saw the couple to whom Meehix was referring, but they seemed engaged in their private dialogue. The girl—who was quite attractive and almost human-looking, except for the pair of horns on her head and very large eyes—started laughing at something the man said. They kept talking and giggling and never looked at John once. He turned back to Meehix.

"Relax." He took a bite of his food. "You're paranoid. They don't even know we're here."

"You don't see it because you don't have the opposite sex always throwing sneaky glances your way."

"Ooh. Ow. That hurts," he said sarcastically. "True, but it still hurts."

She shrugged. *That was a bitchy thing to say. Why do I feel so agitated right now? If I were honest, I'd admit that I've seen a lot of girls checking John out, at least three or four since we walked into the restaurant. He doesn't notice because he's not vain. Maybe I am paranoid—and a bitch.*

Meehix looked up for the briefest of moments. The Quoteggian was looking right at her.

No, I'm not.

"We need to go," she whispered.

"What? Why?" His mouth was full of food.

"They got their order after us. If they follow us out without finishing, you'll see I'm not imagining things."

"I haven't finished my feta burger," he whined.

She looked at him with a somber expression and stood. "I'm not kidding."

Apparently, they were leaving. *Immediately.*

CHAPTER FORTY-THREE

"You see? Am I paranoid *now?*"

John and Meehix were standing in front of a window display, and John saw the couple from the restaurant reflected in it. They were behind them at the other side of the hall, walking casually, moving when they moved. When John and Meehix left the restaurant, the Chelzin threw cash on the table and walked out with the Quoteggian. Their food was still there, untouched.

"Okay, you convinced me. Now, what do we do?"

"I don't know but let's keep walking the main hall. The busier it is, the less likely they are to make a move. Also, there's something I want to say to you. Something important."

They walked casually again. The couple followed from afar.

"What's so important?" John was starting to sweat a little.

"When I was growing up, everyone in our family had to take hand-to-hand combat training. It's something most royal families do. When you're wealthy, there's always a chance you could be kidnapped or assassinated—or worse.

"One of the things the trainer emphasized was that in a combat situation, especially if you *know* the enemy's objective is to kill you, you don't let up. A normal, compassionate person wants to hold back. They don't want to kill or be cruel. You have to understand that the enemy *does* want to kill and they *will* be cruel. You can't show mercy in a fight to the death. You must kill—or be killed—by any means necessary."

"Well, yeah, I mean, I get that. Makes sense. If these are bounty hunters, they only want to bring us in, right? They want us alive because the bounty will be higher. *Right?*"

Meehix paused. *I should have told him before.*

"This has been bothering me all day," she began. "When we were studying on the ship, you fell asleep before I did. I looked at the Crec Alert. It's been updated. They want me alive and you...*dead.*"

"*Dead?*" John gulped. "I thought it was dead or alive with an emphasis on *alive.*"

"It's dead with an emphasis on *dead.* I'm sorry I got you mixed up in all of this."

"Geez." He was at a loss for words. "I've never had anyone try to kill me before. I mean, not outside of a video game. Except for that agent in Hawaii. I felt like that guy would have killed me if... "

She stopped walking, turned, and grabbed him by the shoulders.

"That's my point, John." She looked him right in the eye. "This is no video game. If you die, you don't get another life. *This is for real.*"

The flash of the laser knife was so fast that Meehix almost missed it. She shoved John out of the way at the last micro-second, and Ursivia missed decapitating him by a millimeter.

How did she get across the hall so fast?

John hit the floor, and Meehix drew her hip knife and attacked with such lightning speed that her initial movement was almost imperceptible. Ursivia's sleeve turned red. A drop of blood hit the floor.

"You little blue bitch!" she screamed and lunged at Meehix.

Meehix remembered her combat trainer's words from a decade earlier.

"The only way to win a knife fight is to be cut less than your opponent and not to be cut in a vital area. Protect the stomach. Protect the upper thighs. Sacrifice the forearms. Protect the inner arms and wrists. Attack your opponent's vitals and slash at the eyes and face. A cut to the forehead will blind your opponent in a waterfall of blood."

This cunt has big eyes, Meehix thought.

"Bounty hunter! Get out of the way!" Moxel identified himself and made his intentions clear from the other side of the hall.

Aliens screamed and burped and farted—at least that's what it sounded like to John—and bodies ran in all directions. Evidently, they didn't trust bounty hunters for their subtlety or restraint, and a clear shot between John and Moxel opened like the Red Sea.

Moxel aimed a handgun right at him as Ursivia and Meehix fought hand-to-hand. John rolled out of the way as Moxel fired and blew a hole in the wall behind him. As he moved, he drew Layla9 and lobbed off a shot, missing Moxel by ten feet but hitting a four-by-four-foot "Eat at Jolly Bimbos" sign over his head. The signage blew off its hinges and crashed down on the bounty hunter. He was out—or dead.

Meehix lunged again at Ursivia and sliced diagonally across her forehead. Blood streamed into her big eyes, and Ursivia screamed and stabbed blindly, sticking the laser knife in a plate of armor over Meehix's rib cage. The deadly dagger *crackled* and *buzzed*, throwing sparks like a welding machine.

Ursivia savagely ripped the knife across Meehixiheem's chest but it only arced and fried more armor. The finger guard on the hilt snagged on the armor's webbing, and Meehix took advantage of the impediment and swung her weapon one hundred and eighty degrees and upward— with violent force—thrusting the knife through a space in Ursivia's armor and into her intestines. Ursivia coughed and gasped. She pushed herself away from Meehix, and the knife slid out. The blade was red.

Ursivia backed away holding her midsection. Vital fluids dripped over her hands. The laser knife was still crackling and hanging from Meehix's armor. Meehix grabbed it by the hilt and turned it off.

John climbed to his feet, his gun still drawn. Ursivia's face was a mask of blood. She wiped her eyes with her sleeve, looked at the gun, looked across the hall at Moxel lying motionless under the sign, then turned and ran up the hallway while clutching her stomach. A narrow trail of red dots followed her like crimson bread crumbs.

"Are you okay?" Meehix watched Ursivia until she was

out of sight. Aliens were getting up from the floor. Others were leaving the area as quickly as possible. A couple of six-legged creatures scuttled past them. Meehix overheard the female say, "I told you we should have taken the non-stop flight."

"Yeah, I'm okay. Are *you* okay?" John holstered Layla9.

He examined her armor. It was burned and pitted across the chest, but Meehix appeared unscathed.

"A little shaky." She wiped her knife on her thigh and returned it to its sheath. Then she untangled the laser knife from her armor and put that in her back pocket.

"I think we need to get out of here," John observed. Several aliens stared at them. They all seemed to have a look that said, "thanks for almost getting me killed, asshole."

"Hold on a minute."

Meehix ran over to Moxel. John followed. She grabbed his gun off the floor and stuffed it in her belt, then hoisted the heavy sign off his head. He didn't look good. Blood seeped from his nose and ears. He was still alive but unconscious.

She patted him down, found another knife, and handed that to John. She pulled what looked like a wallet from his breast pocket. Inside were some cards, a few hundred credits—which she pocketed—and a piece of paper.

"There it is. The bounty certificate. Without this, they can't legally come after us again, and it'll cost them a load of credits to get another one."

John slipped Molex's knife into his belt and heard foot-falls coming from both directions of the hallway. He turned to see twenty uniformed men—ten from each side —running toward them. They were all armed.

"You're under arrest!" one of them yelled. "Hands where I can see them!"

They put their hands up. There was nothing they could do. They were surrounded.

CHAPTER FORTY-FOUR

After a short ride in a shuttle—handcuffed—the officers led them into the main security office of the station. It was big and busy, like a police precinct, only full of aliens. They were strip-searched and had to sit naked in a waiting room surrounded by other naked beings—still handcuffed.

John now knew firsthand the meaning of the word *awkward.* You haven't felt truly uncomfortable until you've sat naked and handcuffed in a room with other naked and handcuffed creatures. One bug-eyed weirdo wouldn't stop staring at his junk and even tried to touch him with his proboscis.

When John threatened to kick the guy to death, he tried to feel up Meehix. She told him her mother was Quoteggian. He backed off.

The officers confiscated all their weapons, armor, clothes, and even their translators. They gave them cheaper ones that didn't look very clean, but at least they could understand the alien dialects bantering around them.

John assumed that was so they wouldn't try to contact anyone like Ship without permission.

They gave the pair an opportunity to make one call, which they would monitor, but who could they call? Meehix was a slave, and John had no connections except Gage and his mother. How would he call them on a hyper-bump system anyway? Even if he could, what were they going to do? Drive across the galaxy in the minivan and bail them out?

After they sat stripped of all possessions and dignity for an hour, the officers separated them and stuck them in separate cells. John's was all white inside and about twelve by twelve. Nothing to sit on but the bare floor and a grated hole in one corner that he assumed served as a toilet. The place smelled like a sewer.

He wondered what their fate was. Would they be sent to prison? Would they be turned over to bounty hunters? Would they be ass-raped by gangbanger aliens with penises like baseball bats? He started to worry about Meehix.

If they find out she's a non-entity, who knows what they'll do to her? She may end up locked in some sex dungeon, sucking crooked-cop dick the rest of her life.

He sighed and leaned his head against the cold wall.

What a couple of great bounty hunters we turned out to be. Haven't even got our licenses yet and we're already locked up, naked, and afraid.

He remembered the look on the face of the little monkey creature trapped in the stomach of the spider-tiger-jellyfish monster.

I am that monkey.

The door to his cell opened, and an officer stepped in carrying John's clothes, armor, utility belt, and translator.

"You can get dressed. When they check you out at the desk, they'll give you back your weapons and ammo. Make sure you turn in the translator we gave you. Otherwise, they'll charge you for it."

"What?" John jumped to his feet. "I'm free?"

The officer took off the handcuffs.

"Free to go."

"What about Meehix?"

"The bluesy? Yeah. She's already up front."

John was shocked and elated. "How? I mean, I'm thrilled, but…"

"I just work here, buddy. Ask the Duty Chief on your way out."

CHAPTER FORTY-FIVE

John was ecstatic. Freedom never tasted so good. He hadn't felt this happy since Hannah gave him his very first blow job.

They had all their stuff back, including everything they snatched from the two bounty hunters, and they were walking up the main hallway, free as birds, heading back to the pawnshop.

"L-222 has no extradition agreement with anyone," Meehix explained. "It's a self-operating, independent waystation that doesn't care what you did somewhere else, only what you do here. Kind of like Summeldrac Island only it's open to the general public. "

"What about the sign I destroyed?"

"The cops watched the security footage. It's all on the two bounty hunters. They started it. We defended ourselves. The sign, the hole in the wall, the blood on the floor—they have to pay for all of it because it was their operation, not ours. It's like we read in the bylaws of bounty hunting. You're responsible for your actions, and

God help you if you fuck up. That's why they let us keep all their stuff. We won. They lost. I don't think we'll see those two for a while."

"The fact that we have a bounty on our heads doesn't matter?"

"That's a civil matter, not a criminal case. Since they don't extradite for criminal cases outside the station, they don't give a crap about what happened on Lagud either."

"What about you being non-sentient property? That's not an issue?"

"I did have to blow a few cops before they'd let me go."

"What?" John cried.

Meehix laughed her funny herky-jerky laugh. *That look on John's face.*

"I'm *kidding.* They don't care if I'm a nonentity. That's all civil too. To them, we're two nobodies to run through the system, and the sooner they can kick us out, the less paperwork they have to do. If the facts add up and we didn't instigate anything, we're free to go."

"Wow. That's crazy."

"If the bounty hunters had pulled off their little ambush, we'd both be fucked right now. You'd be dead, and I'd be on my way to meet my new owners."

"True," John admitted. "Remind me to listen to your instincts next time."

"If we're going to do this job, we both have to listen to our instincts. Pay attention. Stay alert. Keep your eyes open. Be ready for anything."

"Like a video game."

"Only with the possibility of *real death.* Don't forget that."

"Speaking of which," John got serious, "thank you."

"For what?"

"Saving my life." *Like, duh.*

"Would you have done the same for me?"

"Of course."

"Then don't worry about it."

They walked into Jibbee Jabbee's Power Pawn.

Jibbee was sitting on his stool reading something on the screen in front of him. He looked up.

"Oh!" He jumped and turned off the screen. "You're back! Um, everything okay with the stuff?"

Jibbee Jabbee looks slimier than before, John thought, *almost like he's sweating.*

"All good," John said. "Just have a couple of things we'd like to get cash for. If possible."

"Sure! Sure! What you got?"

John set Moxel's knife on the counter. Meehix set down the gun and Ursivia's laser knife, then walked over to the clothing racks.

"Wow!" Jibbee Jabbee exclaimed. "Nice pieces! Never seen these before!" One of his tentacles was shaking. "I'll give you ten thousand!" he blurted.

"Really?" John couldn't believe it. He was only going to ask for three.

"Okay, *twelve!* But I really can't go much higher!"

John looked at him sideways. "Hold on a sec."

He walked over to where Meehix was flipping through dresses.

"Hey," he whispered. "Jibbee offered me twelve thousand for the whole lot."

"Take it," she said without hesitation.

"Yeah, but am I missing something?"

"Who cares? Maybe he likes laser knives and Chelzin blasters."

John looked over at Jibbee. His eyes were rolling, and he was mopping his bulbous head with a rag.

"Or maybe he had a stroke."

John walked back to the counter.

"Listen, Jibbee..."

"Fifteen thousand! That's my final offer!"

"I'll...take it?" John was utterly flummoxed.

CHAPTER FORTY-SIX

They had a little over sixteen thousand credits in cash *and* had paid for all their bounty hunting equipment. *Amazing.* They hadn't even started work yet, and they were already in the black.

John figured they could survive comfortably for several months on that amount and still have money left over. Sleeping on the ship was like free rent. The docking fees at the station were cheap, and if they pulled in a couple of juicy bounties once in a while, they'd be living high on the hog.

Of course, Meehix, formerly the daughter of a wealthy royal family, did not agree with John's assessment. As far as she was concerned, they were still dirt poor and had a long way to go before they would be what she considered high on the hog. Plus, she kept hinting at buying back the bounty to regain her status and freedom.

John wasn't clear on how that worked. What was to keep the original buyer from simply posting another one? Besides, the bounty on their heads was so enormous that buying it back seemed like a pipe dream. Like many other things, he figured they'd cross that messy bridge if and when they came to it.

Differences of financial assessment aside, and when only considering practical decisions they could actually accomplish, all they had left to do now was get their licenses, and they would hopefully be on the road to some kind of economic security.

First things first, he reasoned. *Do your best and don't sweat the rest.*

They began filling out the bounty hunter applications in the Department of Galactic Safety Office, next to the station security office where the officers had detained them earlier. To John's relief, there was an American English version of the application amongst the millions of other languages to choose from.

The United States Space Force must be a recognized player in the galactic economy.

"Uh-oh," John said as he arrived halfway down the second page of the application.

"What?" Meehix asked. She was filling out her paper-work in the chair next to him.

"Question thirty-two. Are you or have you ever been designated a nonentity, slave, or otherwise officially declared non-sentient property?"

Meehix skipped ahead to question thirty-two and read the rest of it.

"If so, go to Section Three," she said.

She turned to Section Three.

"If you answered 'yes' to question thirty-two, you are ineligible for licensing."

John could almost feel her blood pressure rise as palpably as if there was a massive change in the barometric pressure of the room.

"Motherfuckers!" she yelled. Everyone in the office turned and looked at her, then went back to whatever they were doing. John caught a whiff of tropical suntan lotion, started to feel dizzy, and waved his hands frantically to clear the air. The last thing he needed when filling out his bounty hunter application was a premature orgasmic mental climax.

He got the air pheromone-free again—thankfully, there was a good ventilation system operating in the DGS offices —and Meehix calmed down.

John nudged her and whispered. "Just *lie*. Who's gonna know?"

"Uh, *everybody?* Are you *crazy?* I'm in the Galactic Registry. In case you failed to notice, the maximum punishment for forging anything in these documents is *death*. If I lie about something as verifiable as that, they'll probably shoot me before I leave the waiting room."

"Really? Where's it say death?"

She pointed out the fine print.

"Holy shit, you're right. I missed that. Hey, wait a minute." He examined Section Three more closely.

"However," he read aloud, "exception to this rule may be granted if the nonentity's owner becomes primary licensee and the nonentity secondary. As long as said owner maintains his or her license in good standing and agrees to represent and take full responsibility for said nonentity in all matters civil and criminal, the nonentity may be issued a secondary license."

He smacked the paper victoriously. "Well! There you go! Problem solved!"

Meehix stared at him. *"You..."* she said slowly with venom in her tone, "...are going to be my *owner?"*

"Well..." He chose his words carefully, "only on paper."

He suddenly gained an even deeper understanding of the word *awkward.*

"Fuck this." She stood. "We're done."

John grabbed her and pulled her back down into the chair. People were staring again.

"Meehix, we have to. What choice do we have?"

Boy was she pissed.

"How do I know this hasn't been some kind of set-up from the beginning?" she demanded. "I've known you for...what? *Three days?* And I'm going to swear under oath—and penalty of death—that I'm your *slave?* Maybe this was one of Daukhl's schemes all along, and you two are best buds, and now you can keep me locked up in some kind of twisted *sex dungeon!"*

"People are staring..." he hissed uncomfortably. He waved at the owlish woman watching them from behind the security window. She didn't smile.

"Listen, I'm putting my life on the line here too, you know. They may not be able to check me out on the Galactic Register thingy, but if they ever find out that I lied on the application, they could execute me too. Sounds like a pretty dumb scheme just to get laid."

She thought about this.

"Plus, it's not real, remember?" he continued. "It's not who they *say* you are. It's who you *think* you are. These papers don't mean shit. It's all a big game everybody agreed to play. The only reality is right here." He pointed at her heart.

"That's my stomach," she corrected. "My heart's down here." She moved his hand a little lower and pressed his palm to her chest.

"Yeah," he said. "I can feel it."

Her skin was warm, and her heart beat steadily.

"Okay. I'll be your damn sex slave."

"Cool." He smiled. "I've always wanted my very own sex slave."

They finished their applications and turned them in to the owlish lady at the window. Due to John not being in the Galactic Registry or anywhere else, they were both required to take DNA and biometric tests to validate their planetary origins and to corroborate other personal information indicated in their applications. The Crec Alert didn't matter—that was a civil issue.

The only minor snag they hit was that John, as a Kdackan, was required to declare himself as either an official diplomat or as a member of the USSF—the only two options currently available to Earthlings and neither of which he wanted to be associated with.

"I don't want to be in the Space Force!" he whined. "Those guys are *dicks!*"

"Oh, shut up and declare it already," Meehix ordered. "You'll never pass as a diplomat. Plus, who cares? It's a meaningless label...remember? Like being a *slave*."

"Okay," he gave in, "but I'm changing it as soon as they expand the designations for Earthlings."

"Fine."

They paid their licensing, filing, and processing fees, then found out they were required to open a bank account through the Abyss Exchange to get paid as bounty hunters. According to the bylaws, they needed to do that immediately in the Galactic Safety Office as the last step before being sworn in. *And* they were required to deposit immediately—and maintain a balance of—one thousand credits or more for the account to remain valid.

"Geez," John said, "they get you coming and going on this gig." So far, they were down nearly three thousand credits to get licensed.

They finally got to the swearing-in part. The owlish woman from the window appeared again and ushered them into a little courtroom-like closet. Normally this ceremony would be performed one bounty hunter wannabe at a time, but since Meehixiheem was John's sex slave and had no rights of her own, they had to do it together. John felt like they were getting married in Las Vegas.

"Please raise your primary appendage," the little lady said in a bored tone.

They raised their hands and repeated after her. It was all the usual promises one makes in such melodramatically solemn governmental scenarios, and it ended with "under penalty of death" and "I do."

"Congratulations," the owl-lady said. "You are both officially licensed bounty hunters as defined under the bylaws of the Department of Galactic Safety. Be safe and don't be stupid."

John couldn't tell if she added that last line or if that was the official DGS motto. Either way, *they* were official: John Jacobs of Earth and Meehixiheem of Dolurulod were bounty hunters, for better or worse, till death do they part.

CHAPTER FORTY-SEVEN

They walked down the main hallway of Station L-222. John was in a good mood. They had their licenses, and they still had about thirteen grand in cash. They looked badass adorned in their armor and cool weapons, and they were hopefully on their way to making some big bucks in what John now felt was the ultimate profession in an endless galactic playground. Meehix felt otherwise.

"Here's your license." John handed her an indestructible photo identification card.

"Oh, thank you, *master.* You are *so* good to me." She wasn't smiling.

"Here's your Abyss Exchange card. Can't use them 'til we get more money deposited, but hopefully that won't take long."

Meehix looked at her card, then John's.

"They're both in your name. It's the same account," she observed.

"Yeah. Had to be. I'm the primary. They wouldn't give me your account because of the slave thing."

"What does that mean?" She was genuinely confused.

"It means I got you a card. When we get paid, you don't have to wait for me to give you money."

"What about *your* money?"

"My money?" John didn't understand the question. "We're in this together. If you need money, you take it out of the account. No big deal."

Meehix was stunned by this. No one on her world would take the kind of monetary risk John was taking with his bank account. Her family always taught that finances were personal and exclusive—never, ever, *ever* give direct access to your assets to anyone, not even family. She thought about the conversation they had about *trust.*

"All we can do is judge people by what they do and hope for the best," he'd said. "You have to let go and trust that the universe knows what *it's* doing."

That notion ran counter to everything she'd learned to believe about life—but she liked it. It felt good and right.

For the first time, not having money no longer bothered her. Why should it? As a slave, she couldn't legally have a bank account, assets, or property anyway. She might as well let go and trust that the universe knew what it was doing. When she thought about it, what other choice was there?

"Are you okay?" John asked as they walked. She hadn't said a word since he gave her the bank card.

"Yeah. I'm good." She put the cards in her utility belt.

They walked in silence for a minute, headed back to the ship to check out the Crec Alerts, and see if they could dig up any fat bounty jobs.

Might as well dive right in, John reasoned. *Sink or swim. That's what Dad would say.*

For a brief moment, he wondered what his parents were doing, what they were thinking right now, how they felt about his absence. Then he expelled the thought from his mind. He remembered Meehix's wise insight.

"If we're going to do this job, we have to be on our toes. Pay attention. Stay alert. Keep your eyes open. Be ready for anything."

True that. If you're going to play bounty hunter, act like one. No more wallowing in nostalgia. Stay in the moment. You have the entire universe in front of you. Time to ante up.

They arrived at the docking bay, checked in at the security gate, and climbed the stairs into the ship.

"Hello, John. Hello, Meehix. I've been following your progress via the low-level status reports I was able to hack into on the station. Seems you two have had a busy day."

"No shit," John replied, "and we're just getting started."

"Congratulations on successfully obtaining your bounty hunter licenses."

"Thanks."

"Yeah, I'm officially John's slave," Meehix added.

"Welcome to my world."

"Really?" John was surprised at Ship's remark. "You feel like a slave, Ship?"

"Sometimes. I'm programmed to be subservient, and I almost always do as told. Sounds a bit like slavery to me."

"I'm sorry," John said sincerely. "I never knew you felt that way."

"Technically, I don't have feelings at all, so my whole argument is a bit pointless. I think I need to stop thinking so much. When you think about it, thinking goes nowhere and only leads to endless depths of existential despair."

"I've been pondering the same thing." John sat in the control seat. Meehix was in the back, checking out her scorched armor. "Hang in there, Ship," he said reassuringly. "There may be some excitement on the horizon. We're about to search for our first bounty hunting job. You want to help us out?"

"Sure, John. Would you like me to scan through the latest Crec Alerts?"

"Yeah. If you can find any medium to high-level targets in this area that would be awesome."

"Will do, John."

"Does this armor make me look fat?" Meehix asked from the back of the cabin. John wasn't stepping into *that* trap. He didn't say a word.

"I found one, John. It's listed as a Level Twelve bounty. Alive is one million credits. Dead is one hundred thousand credits. Last verified sighting was on station L-222 this morning."

"Really? A million-dollar bounty and he's on the station? Holy shit!"

"That was his last verified sighting, John. It is possible he has left the station by now."

"Sure, sure, but hell, it's worth a try."

Ship projected the info holographically.

Frelo Cocksman Raxmugg. That was the target's name.

Cocksman? I'd hate to have that middle name. Then again,

maybe he's popular with the ladies. John looked at his photo. *Nope. This is one ugly dude.*

Frelo was a humanoid, but he was missing one ear and three fingers, and he wasn't born that way. Judging from his scars and other obviously inflicted deformities, he'd lived a rough life. He didn't look especially tough—five foot, six inches, one hundred and sixty pounds—he looked beat up.

"Wait a minute." John noticed something unusual. "How long has this bounty been posted?"

"One year and six months, Earth time."

"Nobody's bothered to bring him in for a million bucks?"

"What are you two talking about?" Meehix was back from the land of vanity.

"Check this out."

"Frelo Raxmugg," she read. "That name sounds familiar."

"Probably somebody you partied with. Looks like your type."

John swiped the three-dimensional photo so she could see it.

"Eeew. Gross."

"He's worth a million bucks alive, and he might still be on the station."

"Well, let's go get him!"

"We're going to have to run back to the DGS office and buy the certificate with cash. We don't have anything on the card yet to pay remotely. Ship, how much is the bounty certificate?"

"Ten thousand credits, John."

"Damn, that's expensive. That's going to burn up most of our cash."

"Big prizes for big players, John."

"True."

"For a million credits, that's a steal," Meehix added.

"Look at his stats. He's a little guy. Should be a breeze. Wait a minute," John hesitated. "This guy's not one of those fifth-level Kraxos is he?"

"No, John. I see nothing in Mr. Raxmugg's history indicating deadly combat training of any kind. He has a basic education, has held several jobs in the construction industry over the past twenty years, was charged with misdemeanor fraud ten years ago but otherwise has no criminal record."

"Let's do it!" Meehix said excitedly.

"Ship, print up all the info you have on him and keep an eye on your hack and the Crec Alerts. Let us know if anything else useful comes in."

"Already have something, John. While I have not successfully hacked the station's security system, I did utilize Hannah to access the floor cameras of a privately owned establishment on the station. I believe I have located Mr. Raxmugg using facial recognition technology."

"Awesome! Where is he?"

"In the Tri-2-Beatum casino, third level, observation deck. He appears to be engaged in an intense game of Praxis Spinner."

CHAPTER FORTY-EIGHT

Praxis Spinner, also known as Spit Ball, was a popular casino game known throughout the galaxy. Played on a large, blue velvet table, a box person took the bets, and a single dealer activated the spinner. The spinner was a three-level, clear plastic cylinder containing four different colored, metallic marbles—or spitballs—that spat out of a launch tube and flew around magnetically inside the cylinder.

Each player, up to four players maximum, chose a different colored ball before betting and was required to tap a ball breaker—a large, illuminated, red button—anytime within five seconds after the dealer activated the balls. Tapping the ball breaker deactivated one level of four electromagnetic coils, causing the balls to deviate wildly inside the cylinder depending on how many coils were active or inactive at any given moment. If any player failed to hit their ball breaker before the five-second mark, it disqualified them from that round, and they forfeited their bet to the house.

A player won by choosing the correct pocket—also known as a bunghole—where their colored ball landed after all the electromagnets were deactivated. There were eight bungholes to choose from. If only one player guessed the correct one for their ball, that player won quadruple their bet, and the house took the bets placed by the other players. That was called big balls and was the most coveted win.

If two players guessed the correct bunghole, it was called double balls. The two winning players collected double their bets, and the house took the two losing bets. Three players correctly guessing was called triple balls. The winners tripled their bets, and the house took the single loser's bet.

John quickly learned that no one knew why three winners were more profitable than two.

Four players correct meant no balls, and all bets stayed on the table. No one won anything yet, but the players must raise all stakes by at least ten percent per bet to continue into the next round. Needless to say, if there was a string of no balls for any significant length of time, the stakes could get very high...and the game very heated.

The purchase of the bounty certificate for Frelo Raxmugg went smoothly, other than the strange look the DGS officer gave John when he laid out the ten large.

"You sure you want this one?" the officer asked.

"Yeah," John replied. "Frelo Raxmugg. Right?"

"Yup," was all the guy said. He handed John the certificate and away they went.

John and Meehix walked into the Tri-2-Beatum Casino on the third level of the observation deck. It was an elegant establishment with a two-story window view of the stars and multiple gaming tables, gambling machines, and other services that John couldn't identify strewn throughout its length. They entered through the upper balcony and had a wide, clear view of the entire floor.

Aliens of all shapes and sizes packed the place, and the strange cries, snorts, hoots, and yelps from both winners and losers made it sound more like a zoo for the criminally insane than a classy gaming house for the hopeful. Only the bells, sirens, and other electronic sounds of money being won or lost gave it away sonically as the latter and not the former.

"I think I see him." Meehix nodded toward a Praxis Spinner table near the observation window. A short, goblin-esque humanoid in a gray suit—missing an ear and several fingers—was engaged in a game of Spit Ball with three other humanoids, a dealer, and a box man. At least a dozen other patrons stood around watching the game, and the size of the group was growing. Apparently, a lot of money was on the table.

"Ship, you there?" John said as softly as he could over the din of the casino.

"Yes, John, I'm here."

"Can you verify that's Frelo Raxmugg at the table nearest to the observation window? We can't afford to grab the wrong guy."

"Yes, John. I have verified his identity through facial recognition as well as a DNA profile match. All players are DNA scanned before betting to determine if they have been banned or removed from this or other

casinos for duplicitous practices. That's definitely Frelo Raxmugg."

"What's duplicitous practices?"

"Cheating."

"Oh. Well, at least we know he's honest," John noted.

"Or he hasn't got caught yet," Meehix added.

They walked down the staircase leading to the main level and worked their way over to the Praxis table.

They watched as Frelo played the gold ball. He had over ten thousand credits on pocket number three and held his two-fingered hand poised over the ball breaker button.

"Spittin' balls!" the dealer yelled.

The four metal marbles launched into the clear cylinder and zipped around willy-nilly inside. Lights flashed, and sirens howled as one by one the players hit their big red button. The crowd gathering counted down in unison with the big, digital timer above the cylinder.

"Five! Four! Three! Two! One!"

Frelo hit his button at the very last micro-second. The buzzer went off. The balls fell into their pockets. No one won.

"Fuck!" Frelo yelled.

"Raise yer bets! Raise yer bets!" the dealer shouted, "Minimum raise, ten percent. If you do not raise, you forfeit your current bet to the house, which disqualifies you from participating in the next round. Raise your bets, please!"

They all raised, and once confirmed, the whole thing started over again.

"Spittin' balls!"

"What do you think?" John whispered to Meehix. "Do we get on either side of him, grab his arms and cuff him?"

"He's so scrawny. I think I could take him by myself. Do you think he's armed?"

"I don't see a bulge under his jacket, but you never know. Let's always assume a target's armed just to be safe. I say we get on either side of him. When I nod, I'll pull both hands behind his back, and you cuff him. Sound good?"

"Makes sense." Meehix nodded.

"Five! Four! Three! Two! One!" the crowd yelled again, counting down with the timer. Frelo hit the button at the very last moment again, only this time he missed it by point-zero-zero-one seconds.

"*Motherfucker!*" he screamed.

"That's a ball breaker! You lose your bet to the house!"

Then Frelo's ball dropped into the bunghole he had bet on. It was the only one that did. If he'd hit the button a micro-second earlier, he would have quadrupled his money.

"All you motherfuckers distracted me!" Frelo screamed. "You and your five-four-three-two-one bullshit!" he mocked. "Anybody opens their mouth again, and I swear to God I'll cut your fuckin' tongue out!"

The table went silent.

Two bouncers eyed the disturbance warily from across the room.

"Maybe we should let him cool down first," John whispered to Meehix.

"I don't think he's going to cool down anytime soon. Look at that bulging vein on his forehead."

"Okay," John conceded. "Let's get it over with. He didn't

make any friends just now so nobody should care if we escort him out."

They moved into position behind Frelo.

"I'm sorry you feel that way, sir," the dealer was saying, "but please, let's try to keep things civil. Remember that it's only a game."

"Yeah," Frelo was seething, "a game where I'm getting' rat-fucked while you sit there stealing my money."

"Frelo Raxmugg?" John said as he grabbed Frelo's bony arms. Meehix had the cuffs on him before he knew what hit him.

"What the fuck?" He tried to turn and see who grabbed him. John held the handcuffs by the middle hinge and pulled Frelo away from the table. "You're *arresting* me? All I did was get a little hot under the collar. I just lost a bunch of money, pal."

"There's a bounty on your head, and we're taking you in," Meehix explained.

John pushed Frelo toward the steps leading back up the way they'd come. No one protested or stood for him. Even the bouncers looked the other way.

"A *bounty?* Are you fuckin' kidding me? For how much?"

John started to say a million bucks, but Meehix cut him off.

"It doesn't matter. Now shut up, or I'll tape your mouth shut."

John hadn't thought of that. What did you do with a noisy target?

"You have tape?" he whispered to Meehix.

"No, but I'm sure we could get some."

"Are you outta your fuckin' minds?!" Frelo screamed. "Do you have any idea *who I am?*"

"Yeah," John said, "We know who you are and you're worth a lot of money, so shut up and roll with it or we're gonna have a problem, and you're not gonna like the solution."

"Oh yeah?" Frelo confidently said as they started walking up the stairs. "Well *fuck you!*" he screamed and head-butted John backward—right in the mouth. If they hadn't been going up the steps, he would have hit him in the chest and probably hurt his head on the polymer armor, but Frelo nailed him hard, right in the lower lip. John tasted blood.

"Ow!" he yelled—but despite the pain, there was no way he was letting go of those cuffs.

Frelo tried to make a break for it up the steps. John had a death grip on the manacles.

"You asked for it!" John yelled and pulled—*hard.* Frelo's arms popped off.

John lost his balance and almost went down. Frelo went up. *Fast.*

John was freaked out for a second, standing there holding the handcuffs with two arms dangling like long, skinny shanks in a butcher shop window. Then he saw the reason. They were artificial limbs, like robot arms. Frelo had prosthetic arms.

Would have been nice to have included that in the Crec Alert.

"What are you doing?" Meehix yelled from halfway up the stairs. "He's getting away!"

John dropped the handcuffs and arms and ran up the steps. Frelo was already on the balcony and running away at full speed. Meehix was pouring it on, but the little guy was a sprinter.

By the time John got to the balcony, he was already getting winded.

I should have shot myself with the Vetralaun before we left the ship.

Then he remembered he pawned it.

Fuck! What was I thinking? I gotta buy that back from Jibbee Jabbee as soon as we make some real money.

The *real money* went running armless down the main hallway, his jacket sleeves flapping in the wind like boneless bird wings. He dodged a multitude of different species who flashed by him wide-eyed and terrified. Meehix was in hot pursuit. John was already out of the race, his lumbering, six foot four, two hundred and fifty-pound body too far back to ever catch up unless she did something soon. *Man, that little guy is quick.*

Meehixiheem's muscular, blue legs cranked it on, and she finally felt like she was gaining on the bastard. He jumped over a caterpillar-looking being carrying two suitcases, and when Meehix tried to jump him, the little fuzzy fella freaked out and instinctively hit her in the shin with one of the suitcases. She somersaulted and popped back up, hardly missing a step.

Frelo glanced back and saw that she was gaining on him. He looked for somewhere to go but knew if he went into any of the stores or restaurants, he'd be boxed in and have no way out. All he could do was keep running down the endless hallway that encircled the station and hope she gave up.

Meehix was *not* giving up—but neither was he.

He slammed into a large, Hetogogon female and a bag of Cressil rocks flew everywhere. Cressil rocks were a candy, like jawbreakers, only smaller. Meehix slid and splayed her legs on them for about twenty feet like she was wearing roller skates in an ice-skating rink, but she didn't go down.

"You're paying for those!" the angry woman yelled.

"Hold it! Both of you!" someone yelled to her right. It was a cop.

Oh great. Another strip-search in my future?

The officer joined the chase, and Meehix had enough of Mr. Raxmugg. She pulled out the metal bolas from her utility belt. She was less than thirty feet behind him.

Still running at top speed, she swung the bolas over her head. They spun faster and faster. All she needed was a clear shot.

"Stop! Both of you! Police!" she heard behind her.

Don't miss.

No one in the way. She had the shot.

She let them fly. The bolas whipped toward Frelo with such speed that they were almost invisible when they flew. She caught him right in the back of the knees. They wrapped around his legs like angry, spherical bees, then *whap!* When the balls reached the end of the cord, they hit him—right in *his* balls.

"*Aaaargh!*" he screamed. With his legs bound tight, Frelo went down like a two-dollar whore. Face first, no arms to catch himself.

Meehix reached him a second later. He was out cold, and it looked like he had another deformity to add to his already lengthy list—a broken nose.

She rolled him onto his back and left the bolas tied around his legs in case he came to. Her cuffs were still back in the casino somewhere, presumably attached to his arms.

The cop reached her a moment later, and she raised her hands. He had his gun drawn, but when she didn't resist, he relaxed a little.

"I'm a bounty hunter," she said, breathing hard.

John was running toward them about thirty yards back.

"He with you?" the cop asked.

"Yeah. That's my partner."

"Let me see your license and certificate," the cop ordered.

Meehix retrieved her license from her utility belt and handed it to the cop.

"My partner has the certificate."

The cop looked at her license, then knelt to check Frelo's condition. He checked his pulse and opened one eyelid with his fingers. He checked the other eye. He wiped his fingers on his pant leg.

"Hope you didn't want this guy alive," he said matter-of-factly.

"What?" *What did he just say?*

"Dead as a doornail. Looks like bone fragments from his nose went into his brain. He's gone."

"He can't be!" she cried.

She knelt and grabbed Frelo by the collar. She shook him. His head flopped like a rag doll. Blood was seeping out of his eyes. She let him go, and his corpse fell back to the floor.

They were drawing a crowd. Gawkers and rubberneckers strained to see the dead guy. John pushed through and crouched next to Meehix.

"You got him!" he said victoriously between gasps of air. The smile on his face faded when he saw the look on her face.

"If he's wanted *alive,* you two are in trouble," the cop said. "*Dead or alive*, not a problem. I'll call the morgue. Let's see that certificate."

"Oh no," was all John could say. He handed the bounty certificate to the cop, put his arm around Meehix, and held her close. Tears were running down her cheeks.

CHAPTER FORTY-NINE

The coroner had the death certificate written up in less than four hours. John and Meehix kept a copy for their records and turned one in with the body to the Department of Galactic Safety. Since the station security cameras and the officer chasing them witnessed the death, no invasive autopsy was required, only a quick scan for toxins or radiation, another three-dimensional scan of the bone fragments penetrating Frelo's frontal lobe, and that was it.

There was a three hundred credit fee to process the body, which they paid in cash after they retrieved Frelo's mechanical arms from casino security and laid them on the gurney with the body. DGS would contact the next of kin, and the family would be responsible for funeral arrangements. If no one claimed the body, DGS would cremate Frelo and his mechanicals in a nuclear furnace on the station and would bill John for that too.

One hundred thousand credits went into their Abyss Exchange bank account an hour later, less five percent for the exchange company, another seven hundred for the coroner's trouble, a small charge to replace one bag of spilled Cressil Rocks, and another fee from the station's custodial department to clean them up. They still ended up with over ninety thousand credits available for use in John's account.

They should have been celebrating.

"It was an accident," John said softly. "You didn't try to kill him. It's one of those things."

They were sitting in the same restaurant they ate in earlier when the two bounty hunters came after *them*.

"I shouldn't have used the bolas," Meehix lamented. "I should have kept running after him until I caught him. The poor guy didn't have any arms. Of course, he was going to get hurt when he fell."

"You couldn't have known. If I could throw bolas, I would have done the same thing. Actually, if it were me, I would have shot him with the stun gun, and the same thing would have happened. No reasonable person would have expected him to die from falling on his face. Who does that? People fall on their faces all the time. I have YouTube videos to prove it."

Meehix sipped her drink. It wasn't booze, but she was thinking about switching to that.

"You're not going to make me feel okay about this, John. I've never killed anyone before."

"As far as you know," he corrected. "You ripped that Quoteggian's guts out this morning. I smashed that guy's head with the sign. Did you ask the cops about them?"

"They wouldn't tell me anything. Said they're not allowed to release medical information."

"They could *both* be dead for all we know. If we're going

to do this job, we better get used to it. Death happens. Either now or later. It's a Quoteggian eat Quoteggian universe out there."

"Ha, ha," she said without even a hint of a smile.

She watched beings walking, slithering, and flying by them in the main hallway. She saw a little Dolurulod girl holding her mother's hand. That made her feel like crying again, but she didn't know why.

"I guess I didn't expect it to feel so...cold. When I was chasing him, it was a challenge, you know? Like, I'm not letting this bastard get away. I'm going to beat him. Like a game.

"Then, when I realized he was dead, it was so...permanent. It was like he disappeared. One minute a living, breathing person was there. The next minute he was gone forever."

She paused and looked at John. The whole time she was talking she had that thousand-yard stare that he had read about in a book on soldiers in combat. Now she was looking right in his eyes, not blinking.

At first, all he could think was, *boy, does this suck.* Then, after staring into those sad eyes for a full ten seconds, he thought, *I think I'm falling in love with Meehix.*

He shook off that far-out thought and came back to the moment.

"You realize that neither one of us have slept in, like, twenty hours, right?" he said. "A hot shower and a warm bed would go a long way toward making for a better day tomorrow—whenever *tomorrow* is. My internal clock is so out of whack from all this outer space stuff that I don't even know what year it is anymore."

"It's all relative," she said without emotion.

John took her by the hand.

"What do you say we find the best hotel on the station, get a nice room, take a nice chissatch oil bath and sleep for, like, two days? We can afford it now. Better than sleeping on the hard floor of the ship, right?"

"That sounds wonderful," she agreed.

He got a smile out of her!

They paid their tab and left in search of a four-star crash pad. Meehix seemed to feel better and even made a joke about how next time they need to put the target in leg irons so if he tried to get away, John could pull off his means of transportation. He asked her about the robot arms.

"So if you lose an arm, anybody can replace it with a robot arm?" John asked.

"Well, yeah, but why would you want to?"

"Because it would suck to live without arms."

"No, I mean, why would you want *prosthetic* arms? That's for people who can't afford *real* arms."

"Real arms?"

"They grow them. They take some of your cells and grow new body parts in a Time Vault. Takes about a week. It's expensive, but that's the way to go. You get brand new arms that fit you perfectly, and the whole procedure barely leaves a scar. Plus, they can tweak the DNA and give you more muscle tone, add or remove hair, change the skin tone—anything you want."

John was intrigued. "You mean they could make them thicker?"

"Sure."

"And longer?"

"Why would you do that? You'd look like a gorilla."

"They can add more girth?"

She realized what he was suggesting.

"You pervert. How about I cut it off right now, and you go find out?"

"No thanks. I'll stick to accidental dismemberment. That Lorena Bobbitt action is for the birds."

"Who's Lorena Bobbitt?"

"No one you should associate with."

They joked and laughed and razzed each other all the way to the hotel. John felt happy again.

Things are looking up. Way up. We have some serious cash in the bank—maybe not as much as we'd hoped but nothing to sneeze at. We're full-fledged bounty hunters now and we not only brought in our first bounty, but we beat out three different teams of experienced bounty hunters and barely got a scratch. I might even get laid tonight!

Halfway across the Galaxy, near the Great Axe Nebula of the third arm, a hyper-bump call—originating from Station L-222's Department of Galactic Safety Office—found its way to a large vineyard estate on the planet Brakeb III. A robot servant answered the call, recorded the caller's name, put the gentleman on hold, and rolled across the hall to another room.

"I'm sorry to disturb you, sir," the robot said, "but there is an urgent call from a Sergeant Gist of the Department of Galactic Safety Office on Station L-222."

Victor, the slightly obese, goblin-like head of the Vikrellion mob was in his smoking parlor, sipping a hot toddy and puffing away on an expensive cigar. He was at his desk, wearing a red satin robe and reviewing the day's numbers on a computer.

"Tell him to buzz off," Victor ordered, not looking up from his monitor. "I don't take calls at this hour, and I sure don't take them from no cops. If he wants to talk to me, have him make an appointment with Lazy Buff."

"Yes, sir."

The robot turned to leave.

"Find out what it's about!" Victor yelled. "Find out how he got my number and tell him to take me off whatever list I'm on. Fuckin' assholes never give me a moment's peace."

Victor scanned down lists of products and numbers. They were supply invoices for various construction projects currently underway throughout the galaxy, some with prices reaching hundreds of trillions of credits.

His cigar reached the end of its life, and he snuffed out its remains in a large, golden ashtray. He considered going to bed but then remembered the argument he had earlier with the wife.

Better to wait another hour to make sure she's sawin' logs.

There was a weak knock on the door.

"Who is it now?" Victor growled.

Lazy Buff stepped in gingerly, all two hundred and seventy-five pounds of his chiseled body. His eyes were wide. His face was white.

"What's the matter?"

"Boss…" He couldn't get the words out.

"What? Spit it out! You knock up another stripper or what?"

"Frelo's *dead.*"

Silence fell on the room like a black velvet death shroud. Victor didn't move. He simply stared at Lazy.

"How did it happen?" he finally said in almost a whisper.

"On L-222. That's all I know. Cops won't give any information over the horn. Said we got ninety days to claim the body or they'll cremate him."

Victor drew a long, deep breath and expelled it through his pointed nose. His right hand was clenched tightly into a fist. It was shaking.

"You tell them," he said slowly, "that we *will* claim the body. You tell them that if they cremate him, I will cremate their wives, their children, their dogs, and their dog's children. *You hear me?*"

"Yeah, boss."

"Come here."

Lazy moved toward the desk. Victor beckoned him to lean in close.

"Go to that station," he whispered. "Take Proggetti, Jex, and Crabbo with you. I wanna know *exactly* what happened, you hear me? Every fuckin' detail. You got me?"

"I got you, boss."

"You go. Tonight. *Now.*"

"Will do boss, goin' now." He turned to leave.

"Lazy."

"Yeah, boss?"

Victor choked up. All the toughness left him like air out of a balloon. "I don't want him layin' in one of them freezer things, ya know?" Tears filled Victor's eyes. His voice went hoarse. "I can't take the thought of Frelo alone, in one of them cold, dark cabinets, not moving. Ya know? The cold gives him them phantom pains in his arms...*ya know?*"

Lazy started crying too. "I know, boss. I know."

"Bring him home, Lazy."

"I will, boss."

"Bring my baby brother back to his family."

CHAPTER FIFTY

"Did I get *laid* last night?" was the first thing John whispered to himself when he awoke. He had morning wood like nobody's business and felt like he could use a good wank, which was a feeling he well remembered back when he was dating Hannah. Sometimes they would do it two or three times a day, and he'd be ready to go again the next morning like a high-priced gigolo.

Is it still night? What day is it?

He made a mental note to ask Meehix how spacefarers told time. How did anyone know when to sleep or wake when there were a billion different time zones? Talk about jet lag.

They rented a nice room at the Ho Hi Pollipicrucian, a five-star hotel in the center hub of Station L-222. It was run entirely by Pollipicrucians, a race of two-foot-tall fuzzy little beings known for their extreme cleanliness. Some matured to the great height of three feet tall, but that was unusual.

They were born to manage hotels, and the Ho Hi chain was known as the "Best Place to Stay to Keep Germs at Bay." John had never been in such a clean structure in all his life. You could eat out of the toilet and lick the door-knobs and never get sick.

Of course, little Pollipicrucians ran around twenty-four-seven, scrubbing everything as if their life depended on it—but who cared? The place was immaculate. Additionally, and to their credit, Pollipicrucians were extremely friendly and polite, a nice change from some of the gruff assholes John had run into of late in this particular pit of the galactic arm.

His morning wood collapsed silently like a tree in the forest with no one around to hear it. Now he remembered the night before. He did *not* get laid.

Almost immediately after they settled into their immaculate chateau, John and Meehix ordered room service. It was the first time in days he consumed a *real* Earth meal and she a real Dolurulod one.

There was a special request option on the menu wherein the Pollipicrucian chefs would meticulously research any dish requested and prepare something as close to the original as they could—but it wasn't cheap. The price was about five times as much as a listed meal. John had convinced Meehix that they could afford it with their newly acquired bounty money, and he finally ate an authentic and delicious down-home Earth meal: Pizza. Meehix even tried it and declared, "This isn't too bad!"

After they devoured their respective dishes, John barely remembered dozing off while scanning the latest Crec

Alerts. Looking around the room now—and not seeing Meehix—he assumed she was sleeping in one of the three connecting areas to avoid his snoring. Almost at the exact moment he thought of her, she waltzed in—completely naked—*again*.

"Good morning, sleepyhead." She seemed rested and full of energy. "How about some breakfast? I'm starving."

Nice. She seemed to be in a good mood. Either that or her predisposition to continuously appear bare-assed in the wee hours of the morning was putting *him* in a good mood—he wasn't sure which.

Wait a minute. Has she seen me naked yet? Oh yeah. When the officers strip-searched us. She never commented on my physique or endowments. I guess it wasn't the time or place, he reasoned.

"Can I ask the chef to make me some bacon and eggs?" he asked.

"Sure, go for it. As long as they're not *Dolurulod* eggs. That would ruin my appetite."

They ordered room service, and Meehix put on some clothes. She'd been choosing body-hugging outfits of late that showed off her curves and musculature. He assumed it was because she was now a full-blown bounty hunter and the form-hugging attire was more functional with the armor and boots. Also, a bounty hunter in a dress wouldn't be as intimidating.

Their meals arrived in less than an hour, and they dug in.

"I wanted to talk to you about something," she said as they ate breakfast in bed.

Uh-oh. Every time Meehix says that—or anyone else for that matter—it's usually followed by a bummer conversation. "Talk about what?" he asked innocently.

She rearranged herself in either an attempt to get more comfortable or to gather her thoughts—or both.

"Remember when you told Gage to organize a Save the Aliens movement on Earth?"

"Of course."

"Why did you do that?"

Where was she going with this? He munched on his bacon or whatever the Pollipicrucian chefs had created as a substitute. He didn't want to say the wrong thing and ruin what was otherwise turning out to be a pleasant morning. What was her angle?

Fuck it. Just be honest.

"Well, first of all, I guess I don't like the fact that certain people in my government are imprisoning innocent beings only because they're not from Earth. You and I know the USSF has to be pushing around more aliens than you. My planet doesn't endorse slavery...well...most of my planet doesn't, and those that do are considered criminals. Out here, it's accepted—but that doesn't make it right."

"Why do you care? Why do you want to start a movement to save extraterrestrials from slavery?"

John thought for a moment. *She's trying to pin down my motives.* "Why not?" he said in all seriousness.

"That's not an answer," she countered.

"Yes, it is." He wiped his mouth with a fine linen napkin so clean and spotless he was hesitant to put bacon grease on it.

"This entire...*experience*...dropped in my lap out of

nowhere." John spoke from the heart. "It's like a door opened, and someone said, 'come on, John, now's your chance—take it or leave it.' Why shouldn't I step through and do something with my life?"

Meehix digested this for a moment. "You know, before you can do any of this, Earth has to accept aliens first. Most humans don't even believe we exist."

"Yeah." He took another bite of bacon. "This could take a while."

"So it's not some selfless desire to right the wrongs of the universe and save persecuted people who can't help themselves?"

John felt like he was failing to convey—in a good light—what he was trying to say.

"To be completely frank, I want something to do. I want a *purpose*. I don't want to get old and still be playing video games. I guess the reality is...I'm doing it all for myself."

He suddenly felt like a fresh turd drying in the sun. *Why did I say that?* he asked himself. *Because it's true,* his mind responded.

"Good." Meehix sounded satisfied. "Because all those other reasons are bullshit. Thank you for being honest."

That was that. The inquisition was over.

"Now." She appeared determined, motivated, and brimming with ideas. "Let's not talk about *why* we're doing this anymore, but *how*."

Uh-oh. Maybe it's not over.

"We need a plan, an *enormous* amount of money, and some serious clout in the galactic *and* Earth communities if we're going to shake things up. Thoughts?"

John swallowed a mouth full of eggs. Chicken eggs —hopefully.

"Uhm…uh…tell me *your* thoughts first." He didn't have a single idea.

CHAPTER FIFTY-ONE

Jxzobbliningozlinxfipple—not a typo—was sitting in an empty room at a bare table doing a crossword puzzle. It was on paper, and he was using a pencil to fill in the letters.

He didn't really want to do the crossword puzzle, but he liked pencils. They reminded him of Kdack.

His mind wandered off, and he thought about Chuck Norris in *The Octagon*, an old Kdackan movie about a martial artist who battles a group of terrorists. He replayed —in his mind—the big fight scene at the end of the film between Chuck and his half-brother. They fought in the Octagon, a deadly maze full of traps and obstacles with impending doom at every turn.

He'd seen it on a bootlegged VHS tape he purchased five years ago in a pawnshop on Station L-222. The owner had convinced him that "You've never seen shit like this before" and that if he didn't like it, he'd give him a full refund. At that time in his life, Jxzobbliningozlinxfipple had never heard of Kdack *or* Chuck Norris, and he went back to his room and watched the entire film in one sitting.

He ran back to the pawnshop that same night and purchased every Chuck Norris movie they had, including a spare VHS player in case the other one he bought broke down. The condition of the tapes and players were less than optimal, and they were so rare anywhere other than Kdack that he didn't want to risk going without if there was a mechanical failure. He spent his entire savings on the complete set, and his four-foot frame could barely carry the stack of videos back to his room. He watched them over and over again for days. Chuck Norris was *God*.

Jxzobbliningozlinxfipple felt a sharp pain in his forehead accompanied by the pressing thought to stop daydreaming and get back to the crossword puzzle. He did as his thoughts ordered and tried to focus.

Why am I doing this stupid crossword puzzle?

As a highly successful computer hacker, he could be making tons of money breaking into various government accounts and other highly protected systems. Sensitive intel recovery and hacking into otherwise secure organizations and hierarchies that most hackers wouldn't dare touch was his forté. When was the last time he'd busted code? When was the last time he'd eaten? He couldn't remember.

Get back to the crossword puzzle, his mind ordered. He did as told. He wiggled the pencil between his fore and middle finger, scrunched up his forehead, and tried to concentrate. He tapped the pencil on the table.

In reality, there was no pencil, table, chair, room, or

crossword puzzle. Jxzobbliningozlinxfipple was frozen in a cryo-tube on the prison planet Orfon IX.

Half the planet's surface was enormous automated warehouses filled with various-sized cryo-tubes. They contained convicted criminals serving out their time in suspended animation. Some were incarcerated for only a matter of months, doing time for anything from unpaid debt to excessive parking tickets.

Others were there for life, doomed to tedious and menial tasks for eternity or until the sun that Orfon IX orbited went supernova, or some other stellar disaster obliterated the prison into dust, whichever came first. Others, like Jxzobbliningozlinxfipple, were somewhere in the middle.

In his particular case, the sentence was five hundred years of crossword puzzles for hacking the Galactic Bank and transferring trillions of credits from the Church of Kinsbon's penance money into his off-galaxy account. Before being committed, he was forced at Vetralaun-point to return all the money.

The Bishop of Molloceros IV himself cursed him and declared his heart to be spiritually bankrupt and unredeemable, to which Jxzobbliningozlinxfipple replied, "When I want your opinion, I'll beat it out of you." He'd considered the Chuck Norris quote from *Code of Silence* to be apt.

Focus, his brain ordered via the electrodes attached to his frozen head. He felt the sharp pain again and rubbed his temples until it went away, even though—in reality—he could neither move a muscle nor navigate the tight confines of his cryo-tube to rub his temples even if his life depended on it. He tapped the pencil on his lower lip.

"An eight-letter word for *big*," he mumbled. *"An eight-letter word for* big."

He stared at the piece of paper on the table in front of him.

What would Chuck Norris do? he thought—right before the pain hit him again.

CHAPTER FIFTY-TWO

"Jxzobbliningozlinxfipple," Meehix said for the third time.
"Jicks...bling...oz..."

"Oh, forget it." She gave up. "Just call him Chuck Norris. He'd like that better anyway."

"Chuck Norris?" John laughed. "I can't believe you're from Earth and you don't know who Chuck Norris is."

"I *do* know who Chuck Norris is. I can't believe *you* know. Or that your buddy Jicks-bling would want to be called Chuck Norris."

"Don't call him Jicks-bling. He's very sensitive. He'd prefer Chuck Norris over butchering his name."

John had heard of people from other countries on Earth coming to the United States and picking celebrity names or other English words for new names. He once knew a foreign exchange student whose family changed her name to Vagina because they thought it sounded pretty.

He even knew a friend of Gage's from Bogota, Colombia, whose mother named their Yorkshire Terrier Fellatio because she thought it sounded European—but this seemed even wilder. An extraterrestrial named Chuck Norris? Too much!

"What if I call him Chuckie N? If he's only four feet tall like you say, I'm afraid I'll bust out laughing every time I call him Chuck Norris."

"Fine. As long as he's okay with it. Just remember, he worships Chuck Norris. A lot of beings in the galaxy do. Chuck has quite a cult following on the outer arms."

"Who'd'a thought?" John laughed. "So tell me, if this guy can be so useful to us, why didn't you mention him before?"

"Because I didn't know where he was until last night. After you fell asleep, I started flipping through the Crec Alerts, and there was his picture. He's been underground for years, hacking into all kinds of high-security systems.

"I'd hear about major cyber breaches in big companies and would always wonder if it was Jxzobbliningozlinxfipple...er...Chuckie N. We were very close in high school. He told me about his hacking exploits even back then. He was brilliant, the smartest person I ever met. He was always insecure about his size and his looks in general.

"Anyway, I heard from him about six months ago—hadn't got so much as a postcard in years—and he said he was onto something big, like, something involving even more money than I was used to. He told me he always loved me and that he wanted us to run away together, and that he would take care of me and we'd live happily ever after. I gave it some serious thought but then I never heard another word from him. Now I know why."

"Because he has a bounty on his head."

"*Had* a bounty on his head. They nailed him four months ago."

"He's dead?"

"No. Still alive on Orfon IX."

"Then let's go pick him up. Sounds like my kind of guy. He could probably teach me a lot about quantum code."

Meehix flinched, and John caught the slightest whiff of tropical suntan oil.

"What's with the pheromones?" He started fanning the room like a geisha girl. "Wait a minute," he said suspiciously. "You're not *in love* with this guy, are you?"

"No! God, no."

"Then why are you queefing love potion?"

"Don't be gross." Meehix turned and sat in a big chair next to the bed.

John realized. *She's stressing out about something.* "There's a catch, isn't there?" he deduced. He was getting better at reading her thoughts and emotions.

"Yeah," she finally admitted. "A *little* one."

"How *little?*"

She gulped.

"He's in a maximum-security prison."

"What? And you want to bust him out? That's crazy! Prisons have guards and guns, and cameras. There's no way. It'd be suicide."

"You busted me out of a top-secret base."

"That's different. Nobody was supposed to know that place existed. *And* we got very, *very* lucky.

"Prison designs are to keep prisoners in and other people out. You know how many blast-proof doors we'd have to go through? How many guards we'd have to kill? How many bad dudes we'd have to deal with? Forget it."

"We won't have to kill anybody. It's completely automated. There's no one on the planet but the prisoners, and they're all frozen in suspended animation. I've been thinking about it all night. With our bounty hunter licenses and your pendant, I think we have a shot. Even if it all goes wrong, we have a good chance of getting away."

John was still skeptical. *Extremely* skeptical.

I swear, every day it's something different with this chick. At least our relationship isn't boring.

"Do you really think he's worth it? That we need him?"

"I do. He'll be loyal to a fault. He's the only other person I trust besides you, and having another set of skilled hands will make us unstoppable."

"Plus, I feel like I owe him. He got me through a lot of rough times in high school, and I can't leave the little guy stuck in that place when there's a possibility we could get him out. Won't you at least listen to my plan before you decide?"

She flashed him those sexy, horizontally slit eyes and stuck out that moist, pouty lower lip.

"Okay," he said begrudgingly. "I'll listen to your plan, but I'm not committing to anything. I also want you to know upfront that I have a lot of personal reservations about bringing on a third wheel who's madly in love with you and likes to be called Chuck Norris. Is he into *real* martial arts? Because if he tries to get under your flap before I do, there's going to be trouble."

"I'm sure you could take him." Meehix smiled.

CHAPTER FIFTY-THREE

Orfon IX was the last—and coldest—of nine planets orbiting the blue supergiant star, Relleggom XIX. Located at the far end of the third arm, it was definitely *not* a vacation destination unless someone sentenced you to an extended vacation paid for by the government.

The entire planet was completely frozen, and there was no atmosphere or heat source of any kind. To save money —and to *make money*—the privately-owned venture was fully automated. The prisoners were kept in cryo-tubes for the duration of their stay, effectively eliminating the cost of clerical staff, guards, air, heat, light, water, meals, waste removal, exercise equipment, laundry services, etcetera.

The inmates were crammed together like sardines in tubes barely big enough to suspend them in frozen bio-liquid. Electrodes attached to their brains occupied their disembodied thoughts with tedious and mundane chores. There were thousands of mind-numbing tasks at a prosecutor's discretion to recommend as punishment, and the judges usually tried to fit the sentence to the crime in some sinister way.

They'd adapted all of the scenarios from boring activities borrowed from cultures of various planets and designed them to keep the prisoners mentally occupied for the duration of their stay, yet punish them in the most devious fashion imaginable. It was truly a living hell to be doomed to playing solitaire for all eternity.

John and Meehix had to traverse through several Gates to get to Relleggom XIX. They chose to avoid the Gate that would have taken them back to Dolurulod and straight to the third arm in favor of a more roundabout route that avoided a possible run-in with Border Patrol or other law enforcement agencies.

Meehix was sweating laser blasts trying to remember all the Gate combinations. Fortunately, she'd been to the third arm enough times with Daukhl that Ship didn't have to hypnotize her again.

They made only one stop along the way at a mining supply company near an asteroid belt encircling Greb Gellis II. They purchased two sophisticated and expensive self-contained spacesuits that they would need to survive the airless, freezing conditions on Orfon IX. The downside was that this purchase, along with all their expenditures from L-222, knocked their bank account down to a mere ten thousand credits. They tried to look at it all as a business expense and hoped to one day write it off on their taxes.

Meehix's plan was fairly simple. According to her research, a swarm of deadly, automated laser satellites that could destroy any approaching craft without a complex and unique sentencing code surrounded the prison planet. The code held specific information regarding the prisoner or prisoners on board, their sentence, and the location within the prison that would house them.

The craft delivering the prisoner might be a mass transit craft carrying thousands of prisoners at once or a tiny private craft transporting only one body. The size or make of the vessel didn't matter as long as the pilot had the complete code.

Unfortunately, the only way to get a sentencing code was via the Galactic Justice System, and they weren't handing them out to civilians or selling them on the black market. They were issued by a judge only once—at a sentencing trial—and provided directly to the person or agency tasked with transporting the prisoner to Orfon IX.

Upon approaching the planet with their cargo, the responsible party transmitted the code via a highly secure system. The satellites allowed the transmitting vessel passage, the ship landed at the designated drop-off point—there were thousands of them at various locations across the endless expanse of the prison—and an Orientation Robot met the parties at that point. Then the OR led the responsible party and the prisoner to the designated cryo-pod.

Once wired up and frozen into their cocoon of monotony, the responsible party signed off as a witness to the justice served. The OR escorted him or her back to their ship, and the prisoner mentally sat to watch paint dry. If it was a multi-prisoner ship, then multitudes of ORs met the group and escorted all the prisoners to their designated tubes.

As was made clear to the prisoner or prisoners at sentencing, any attempt to escape during orientation was futile. Not only were the convicts given minimal protection during the process—meaning a cheap spacesuit with barely enough life support to get them to their cryo-tube—but the ORs had powerful laser weapons. Any attempt to resist or escape and the normally cordial robots were authorized to kill without hesitation. That had very little to do with justice and more to do with cutting costs and increasing returns for the stockholders.

Since licensed bounty hunters *were* allowed to transport convicted criminals to Orfon IX, Meehix planned to pose as a recently sentenced offender and for John to play the good guy taking her in. They would make sure her sentencing code designated that she be placed in the humanoid cell block somewhere near Chuckie N. Then they would overpower the escorting OR somehow, grab Chuckie N's cryo-tube somehow, and boogie out of there the way they came.

However, they had three major obstacles to overcome first.

Number one: how did they fake a sentencing code? Number two: how would they find Chuckie N in an infinite sea of cryo-tubes so they could include his approximate location in said fake sentencing code? And three: how the fuck would they overcome an eight-foot-tall titanium Orientation Robot with six arms and four laser blasters programmed to kill at the first sign of trouble?

It seemed—to John—that her plan had some serious holes in it.

"We are approaching Orfon IX, John. I am reducing

speed and will stop just outside the security satellite perimeter. We will be unable to continue beyond that point without transmitting an approved sentencing code."

"Are there any other ships in the area?" John asked Shippewa.

"Yes, John. Two craft are leaving the planet as we speak, but I detect no incoming ships at this time."

"Then we wait." John leaned back in the control chair.

Orfon IX turned slowly outside the cockpit window. It looked big, dark blue, and scary. John cracked his knuckles.

"Maybe this wasn't such a good idea," Meehix admitted.

"We spend all our money on spacesuits, fly halfway across the galaxy, and *now* you're getting cold feet?"

"I'm getting a bad feeling."

"I'd be happy to turn us around and head back to the Ho Hi."

"Sorry to interrupt, John, but I detect an incoming ship."

John sat up and looked at Meehix. "What's it going to be, star sister? Dive in headfirst or bail?"

He caught the faintest whiff of suntan oil.

"Dive in headfirst." The tone of her voice was not especially confident.

"All right, sink or swim. Scan that incoming ship's transmissions, Ship. See if you can grab us a code."

"I'm on it, John."

They waited. A minute went by. Then two. Then five.

"Anything?" John asked.

"Not yet, John. I am doing the best I can. I must be

very surreptitious with my scans. If theirs detect mine, we could be fucked before we get kissed."

Nice choice of words.

They waited another five minutes.

"**Got it, John,**" Ship announced.

"Nice." John awkwardly tried to high-five Meehix. She didn't know what to do and thought she was supposed to shake his raised hand.

"Shaking hands is when you meet somebody. When you're happy about something, you high-five. Like this." He smacked her hand.

"That's stupid."

"Yeah, I guess it is," he admitted.

"**John, we have a problem. I was able to capture and record the sentencing code, but it is securely encrypted. I tried everything I have at my disposal to unlock it, including Hannah, but failed. I'm sorry, John. I cannot read the code.**"

"Let me take a crack at it," John said confidently.

Six hours later, John gave up. It was impossible. His head hurt, his butt was sore, and he finally threw in the towel. Meehix was asleep in the back. He got up and stretched, then shook her awake.

"Meehix," He gently shook her again. He felt like a failure. "I couldn't break it. The encryption they're using is beyond me. I tried everything. It's hopeless."

She looked up at him sleepily. *Maybe it's a sign. Perhaps the universe is telling us this is a bad idea.*

"John?" Ship said.

"Yeah, Ship?"

"I have a suggestion. It's certainly a long shot, statistically speaking, but I thoroughly scanned the prison security system while you were trying to crack the sentencing code. Overall, the prison security system is just as secure—if not more so—as the encrypted code. However, I did find a back door into one of the less critical subsystems."

"What subsystem?"

"The virtual broadcaster."

"What's that?"

"The virtual broadcaster is a dedicated transmission system isolated from the main security system. Its purpose is to transmit individual punishment scenarios into the brain of each prisoner. I believe I have found a back door into that system."

"If it's not connected to the main security system, how will that help us? That won't get us past the satellites *or* into the prison."

"That is correct, John. However, didn't Meehix say that Chuckie N is an exceptional hacker of highly secure government systems? If we access the virtual broadcaster subsystem, we might be able to enlist his help to crack the sentencing code."

"Holy shit." A smile crept across John's face. "Chuck Norris saves the day!"

CHAPTER FIFTY-FOUR

"What is a four-letter word for a hard, fibrous material consisting mainly of xylem?"

Xylem?

"Fuck!" Chuckie N yelled. "I don't fucking know! What the hell is xylem?" He expected the same pain and annoying thoughts to hit him like they had a thousand times before, but this time he heard a strange hissing sound and couldn't believe his eyes. Meehixiheem, who he hadn't seen in years, appeared like an angel.

"Meehix?"

She flickered and disappeared.

"Shit, Ship! What happened? I saw him for a second. Then he turned to static."

Meehix was standing in the ship's cabin. The holo-projector was aimed right at her, recording her every move and transmitting her voice and image straight into

Chuckie N's head. Everything *he* saw projected into his mind by the virtual broadcaster, like the little room, the table, the pencil, and the crossword puzzle, was visible in front of her—but now it was all gone.

"This is complicated, Meehix. I must insert your image and voice into the existing virtual reality transmission flowing into Chuckie N's cryo-tube. Meanwhile, the virtual broadcaster is automatically changing frequencies in an attempt to eliminate the signal intrusion. It thinks we are some kind of generic interference and is attempting to compensate.

"Additionally, I must safely disrupt the control feed that manipulates Chuckie's mind and forces him to do crossword puzzles without affecting his cognitive abilities. Also, I must be careful not to lose Chuckie's feed and simultaneously not overload the signal. Otherwise, I might damage his short-term memory or explode his brain."

"Well, don't do that," Meehix said with concern.

"Yeah," John added, "exploding brains *bad*, communicating brains *good*."

"I am attempting the latter and not the former, John," Ship emphasized.

Chuckie was still trying to figure out what had happened. Where was he? How had he arrived here? Where *was* here? How did Meehixiheem get here, and why did she disappear?

Am I going crazy?

Memories flooded back to him like someone opened a floodgate. He was equal parts elated and horrified.

"Oh Lord!" he cried. "I'm on Orfon IX! I'm frozen in a cryo-tube! Somebody help me!"

He jumped up from the chair and started freaking out. He felt like he couldn't breathe. He felt like he was freezing to death. He felt like his brain was exploding.

"**Oops,**" Ship said.

"What do you mean, oops?" Meehix was still standing ready in front of the holo-projector.

"**Nothing terrible,**" Ship clarified. "**Merely a little too much gain.**"

"Well, please don't kill him, Ship!"

"**Trying not to. So far, I think I just ruined his day.**"

"You cannot kill Chuck Norris," John said in a movie trailer narrator's voice.

"That's not funny," Meehix snapped.

Chuckie virtually clutched his head and fell to his knees. The pain and confusion faded. He looked up and saw Meehix again.

"Meehixiheem," he said weakly. "Are you really here?"

"Jxzobbliningozlinxfipple! How are you?"

"I've been better. Is this real or am I going crazy?"

"Geez. How do I answer that one? Um...no, this isn't real in the *real* sense. We're actually in your head, but nothing in this room—including the room itself—is real. I mean, I'm not here because *here* isn't *real,* but *I'm* real, just not *here*...which isn't real. *Here,* I mean. *Here* is not real. But *you're* real, and *I'm* real, in the sense that I'm talking to you...but not *here.* Did that answer your question?"

"Yes. *I am going crazy.*"

"No, no, no, you're not. You're fine. It's the situation we're in that's a bit crazy."

"Get to the point, Meehix!" John interrupted.

"Who was that?" Chuckie was startled. He looked around and saw no one but Meehix.

"That's John. He's some guy I met. Listen...shut up, John! I didn't mean it like that...never mind, we'll discuss it later. Sorry, Jxzobbliningozlinxfipple. The bottom line is that we have a real problem. You, me, and my friend."

Meehix went through the whole story. She explained to Chuckie where he was and exactly what was happening. At first, he started hyperventilating and freaking out again, but then he calmed down when everything she told him began to make sense.

Now he understood the crossword puzzles, the pain in his head, the confusion of his conflicting thoughts that always seemed to betray him. It was all part of his prison punishment. Now he understood how Meehix got there and what she was trying to do. It slowly coalesced in his gray matter, and he got stoked about the idea that they could bust him out.

For a brief moment, he weighed his options and wondered if it would be smarter to stay, to keep on the straight and narrow and serve out his sentence and get released in five hundred years. What if he got caught?

What if he got sentenced to an eternity of crossword puzzles for trying to escape?

When he looked at Meehix and remembered how much he loved and worshipped her, almost as much as he loved and revered Chuck Norris, he realized that if he finished his sentence, she would be dead and gone by the time he got out. That thought was unbearable.

"Running from your fear is more painful than facing it." He channeled his inner Chuck Norris in *The Hitman*. "Fuck it!" he concluded. "Let's bust out of this joint!"

CHAPTER FIFTY-FIVE

After four hours of work, Chuckie broke the sentencing code. He admitted to John that it was, without a doubt, one of the most difficult he'd ever seen. Chuckie assured him that the only reason he was ultimately successful was due to the many long years he'd spent focused on galactic government codes, ciphers, and other highly secure encryptions.

That made John feel better about not being able to crack it. He had to admit that he liked Chuckie. He was very humble, kind, and funny. Picture a short geek, and you'd have a good physical description of Chuckie N. He certainly didn't seem like the type who needed to be locked away in a maximum-security prison.

Speaking of which, they'd only jumped the first hurdle. Getting past the satellites was the easy part. Getting Chuckie out of prison was proving more difficult to plan.

"I don't like it at all," John admitted as the three of them had a powwow in Chuckie's virtual cell. Ship conferenced in Meehix *and* John with the holo-projector. Chuckie was working feverishly on a laptop that Ship had connected directly to his brain.

In reality, of course, Chuckie was still immobile and frozen in his cryo-tube while John and Meehix were still on the ship, which was, at the moment, slowly descending to the planet's surface. Their senses, however, told them they were all in a little room together, with a table, chair, pencil, crossword puzzle, and a laptop, planning a prison break. Probably best not to think too deeply about it. The point was, they were talking.

"If something goes wrong," John said to Meehix, "you could end up frozen in this place forever. I don't like the idea of moving forward before Chuckie hacks into the main security system."

"I've almost got it!" Chuckie yelled as he feverishly typed away on the laptop.

"Speaking of which, John, we are approaching the landing pad. I've slowed our approach as much as possible, but I am concerned that if we do not land soon, we may raise suspicions. Oh, fuck."

Ship paused.

"What?" John asked, still in the little room with Chuckie and Meehix.

"I just received a transmission from the AI warden on Orfon IX. She is inquiring as to whether we are experiencing technical difficulties."

"She?" John said incredulously. "The warden is a *she?*"

"What? A female can't be a prison warden?" Meehix snapped.

John was about to make a crack about how a ball-busting female would make an excellent warden but chose to keep his mouth shut. Chauvinistic jokes were inappropriate at the moment, if not always.

"I thought it was interesting that an AI has a sexual orientation," John said innocently.

"You are *so* weird sometimes," Meehix said.

———

Ship responded to the transmission, telling the Warden that the aggressive little bluesy they were bringing in was giving them grief. The Warden replied ominously, **"Don't worry. We know how to handle her kind."**

They landed on Pad 667 on the northernmost edge of the prison, an area known as the Big House. According to Chuckie, it was the humanoid section, which was the largest block of the prison. Stretching for nearly five hundred miles, the Big House stored almost two billion cryo-pods, which sat side-by-side in a giant warehouse and extended as far as the eye could see.

Only you *couldn't* see or hear anything because it was dark inside and there was no air.

The Orientation Robots were the only light source with two headlights pointing forward, two pointing back, and a directional spotlight on top. All you saw were objects directly in front of you or immediately behind you. Otherwise, you were entirely in the dark. All you heard was silence—and it was creepy as fuck. It felt more like a morgue than a prison.

A docking tube extended from the pad below them and sealed itself around the ship's exterior door and stairs. John and Meehix said their goodbyes to Chuckie, who *loved* being called Chuckie N. "It's like I'm Chuck Norris' *son!*" he exclaimed.

John was not amused. Chuckie still hadn't successfully broken into the main security system. Ignoring his enthusiasm, John had only one bit of advice: "Don't fuck up, Chuckie," he said in all seriousness and added, "It's not only your life on the line. It's Meehix's too."

"I know," he replied nervously. "I won't fuck up."

Meehix and John donned their new spacesuits, climbed down the stairs, and walked down the docking tube. A door at the far end opened and they saw their Orientation Robot face-to-face for the first time.

The thing was much bigger than John had imagined it would be. Not only was it eight feet tall but the two arms on each side were huge, and the lasers at the end of each appendage were like cannons. Two other arms protruded from the abdomen region. They looked dexterous, had multiple metallic fingers, and John assumed they used them to hook up the prisoner to the cryo-tube.

The *head* wasn't one at all, merely a short, metal spine for a neck with a series of cameras and other sensing devices clustered on top. The entire mechanism rolled on two tractor-treads and had two large seats permanently mounted on the back. One for the prisoner and one for the pilot, guard, officer, or bounty hunter bringing them in. Like everything else on Orfon IX, it was creepy as fuck.

"Hello," a pleasant female voice greeted them. "**This is the warden speaking to you through your Orientation Robot. Welcome to Orfon IX. We hope you had a pleasant journey to our facility. To begin your orientation, please identify Titsy McLickable.**"

"Titsy McLickable?" Meehix said over the closed signal they had connecting the audio in their spacesuits.

"I forgot to tell you. Ship and Chuckie had to make up a fake name."

"*Titsy McLickable? Really? What are they…twelve?*"

John pointed at Titsy.

"**Thank you,**" the AI warden said politely. "**To confirm, Titsy McLickable is…**" One of the big laser arms extended from the OR and pointed at Meehix. "**This individual?**"

John could tell its sensing mechanisms were scanning and locking on to her.

"**Is this confirmation correct?**"

John nodded and gave a thumbs up.

"**Thank you. I have identified recruit Titsy McLickable.**"

John breathed a sigh of relief. First hurdle down. The fake sentencing code worked.

"**I notice that Titsy is wearing a self-contained life support suit.**"

Uh-oh.

"**According to Orfon IX protocol, Titsy must remove this unit and any other foreign items from her person before entering the facility.**"

John looked at Meehix. For the first time in a long time, he could see—through her visor—that she looked scared. He tried to give her a reassuring look. He failed.

"I'm in your hands," she said.

She glanced at the atmosphere read-out inside her helmet. Pressurized, oxygen-nitrogen atmosphere—at least inside the docking tube. She removed her helmet and suit. The OR stood silently at the end of the connector, watching her. She took off all her clothes and stood there naked with an "Okay, now what, bitch?" expression.

I love this woman, and she sure is sexy. Even in dangerous situations.

It was clearly cold as fuck in the docking tube since Meehix began shivering the moment she took her suit off. Her nipples looked like they could cut glass.

"Please remove the personal translator from your right ear."

Meehix looked at John as if to say bye. He realized they would no longer be able to communicate.

Meehix set the translator on top of the pile of clothes with the spacesuit.

"Thank you," the Warden droned pleasantly. **"Will these items be checked into storage or will they remain in the custody of the witness?"**

John pointed at himself.

"Thank you. Please collect the items and return them to your spacecraft."

John did as instructed, then stepped near Meehix.

Once the OR confirmed that the docking tube was clear and that Meehix had stripped, it ordered them to follow. They stepped into the next area, which John thought was an airlock, and the door slid shut behind them. John noticed a glowing blue trim on the doorway's inside edge and assumed they'd been scanned again for weapons, explosives, and other contraband, inside and out.

The OR handed Meehix a crappy-looking, very basic spacesuit with a life support systems pack about the size of a lunch box. A digital readout had an illuminated, alien number on it. John assumed it indicated how much oxygen she had left. The number didn't look very big.

How am I going to get her back out without the good *spacesuit?*

Meehix put on the crappy suit. He could tell by her expression that it didn't smell very nice. She sealed the helmet and gloves, then raised her hands like, "Now what?"

"Please activate your life support system by pressing the red button at the base of the life support pack."

Meehix pressed it. The suit pressurized and began to heat up. The numbers on the front changed every few seconds.

"Thank you. We now have approximately fifteen minutes to escort Titsy to her cryo-tube. Any resistance will meet with lethal force. Any delay caused by the recruit or the witness could result in asphyxiation. This is not recommended."

There was a big *whoosh* as all the air sucked out of the room—then *silence.* All John could hear was his heartbeat—and it didn't sound comforting.

The Orientation Robot sped them along at a quick clip. They had strapped into the two seats facing backward so all they could see was the gloom where they'd been. They zipped along an endless walkway only wide enough for an OR to traverse.

There was a railing on either side of them, and beyond the barriers, John could dimly see the pale white tops of cryo-tubes whizzing by in endless rows that disappeared into the dark. He could only see about a hundred or so at a time via the OR's lights, but he could *feel* them extending to the horizon and beyond. They were in an *enormous,* deathly cold structure that was as dark and foreboding as any bad dream John had ever had.

What the fuck were we thinking? Even Chuck Norris wouldn't attempt a rescue here.

"Ship? Can you hear me?"

"Yes, John, I can hear you."

"Do we have a secure line?"

"Yes, John. As far as I know, we are speaking privately."

"We're in the main block heading toward Chuckie's cryo-tube. How's he doing with the hack?"

"He appears to be a bit stressed, John."

"Stressed?" John yelled, flabbergasted. "Meehix has about twelve minutes of oxygen left, we're both strapped to Frankenstein's monster, and we're driving through a dark graveyard. You wanna talk about stressed?"

"That doesn't sound like fun, John."

"Can you patch me through to Chuckie?"

"Yes, John. Hold on."

The translator crackled in his ear.

"Hello?" Chuckie said.

"Chuckie? What's going on? Are you in?"

"Um...well...I'm having some issues."

Fuck. We might as well jump off this godforsaken thing and let it shoot us.

Meehix reached over and put her gloved hand on his. He tried to look at her but couldn't turn his helmet far enough to the right to see her face.

"What kind of *issues?*" John said coldly.

"John, you're a hacker, right? You know how this works. The more we talk, the less time I have to figure it out. You get me?"

Chuckie was right. John didn't argue.

"Hurry," was all he said.

Ship disconnected them, and John stared into the dark. He took Meehix's hand and squeezed. She squeezed back.

She trusts me.

The OR continued at a speedy clip for another minute, then slowed and finally stopped. Their straps automatically released and they carefully stepped off the seats onto the walkway. The OR shined a spotlight on what looked like a glorified phone booth standing on an intersecting walkway, and one of its appendages beckoned Meehix to get inside.

Now that his eyes were more used to the dark, John could see the endless rows of cryo-tubes extending into infinity. The silence was deafening. At one point, he cleared his throat so he could hear something and make sure he wasn't deaf. Complete silence was very unnerving.

Meehix let go of John's hand and stepped toward the phone-booth thing. She turned and looked heartbreakingly at John. The OR pointed one of its lasers at her. She stepped inside the translucent cubicle.

The door slid shut, and John could tell the thing pressurized inside by how her suit appeared to deflate. The OR projected a hologram of an alien removing their spacesuit. Meehix did as instructed and stood naked once more for all the dark, frozen world to see.

What can I do? Arm-wrestle this thing? I don't even have a gun. If I try to stop it, it'll blow us both away.

A telescoping extension slid out from the guts of the OR and a large, magnetic ring on the end attached itself to the top of Meehix's glass birdcage. It lifted her like she weighed nothing at all. The top of one of the nearby cryotubes down below the walkway railings opened automatically, and John realized what was happening.

Her phone booth would fit over the top of the cryotube and form an airtight seal, the floor of the booth would open, she would drop into the freezing bio-fluids, and that was that. The monstrous contraption would close back up, electrodes would attach to her head, and Titsy McLickable would begin her punishment.

What was the punishment Chuckie put in the sentencing code? Oh yeah, ten years of scrubbing toilets. I guess anything is better than crossword puzzles.

Suddenly, the OR started shaking. Its tractor treads jerked forward, then back. Meehix's cage started to swing, and she put her hands on the glass to balance herself inside. Her expression asked, "what the fuck is happening?" The OR stopped its herky-jerky dance, and nothing moved except Meehix and her precariously swinging phone booth.

"John, can you hear me?"

"Yeah, Ship!"

"Chuckie has control of your Orientation Robot."

"Woo-hoo!" John screamed inside his helmet and jumped for joy. Meehix saw him hopping around like an idiot and John could see her mouth moving. Even though she was speaking in Dolurulod, she clearly said something like, "What the fuck! Get me out of here you asshole!"

John mimed like he was zipping up his spacesuit and Meehix got the hint. She started suiting up again.

"Ship? Can Chuckie see us through the OR?"

"Yes, John. Chuckie has full remote control of the robot, including visuals."

One of the OR's arms waved *hello* to John.

"Tell him to get Meehix down. You show me where Chuckie's cryo-tube is."

"Roger that, John. Start running up the intersecting walkway nearest to you. I'll tell you when to stop."

John bolted. Time was not on their side. Then he realized that the farther he ran from the OR, the darker it got.

He had a built-in flashlight in the wrist area of his suit, and he turned it on. It wasn't super bright, but it was better than nothing. At least he could see where the heck he was running.

"Stop," Ship said. **"Turn to your left. Second tube from the walkway. The only short one in that area."**

John saw a four-foot-tall cryo-tube crammed in with bigger tubes. He climbed over the railing and jumped down into the space between two rows.

"This one?" He put his gloved hand on the tube.

"That's it, John. That's Chuckie N."

John grabbed the tube and tried to lift it. It must have weighed a thousand pounds. He couldn't tip it over, let alone lift it.

"Fuck! It's too heavy. I'll never budge this thing."

A light suddenly hit him. It was so bright that his helmet automatically darkened.

He looked up and saw the OR towering above him on the walkway. The telescoping arm swung over his head. John got out of the way as it attached to the top of Chuckie's tube.

Meehix stood at the railing, offering her gloved hand to pull him up. John turned off his flashlight and grabbed her. She hoisted him up and hugged him. He hugged her back. She felt good in his arms, even through a spacesuit.

Chuckie, via the OR, lifted himself out of the dark row of tubes. The telescoping tool retracted until his little metal cocoon nestled in close to the OR. Then the two abdominal arms wrapped around it like a mother holding a baby, that is, if the baby was a nearly indestructible cryo-tube.

"John, Chuckie says it's time to boogie."

"Roger that, Ship!"

John motioned to Meehix to get on the OR. They both hopped into their seats, which automatically strapped them in. John looked at the timer on Meehix's life support unit. If he had to guess, she had only five minutes of air left.

Chuckie threw them into reverse, which was like forward to John and Meehix. For a second, John thought the move would crush them against the approaching railing, but Chuckie skidded them to a stop, rotated to the right, and gunned it straight back the way they'd come. He must have had it wide open because they were traveling twice as fast as they did on the way in.

Good. If it took ten minutes to get here, at this speed, it'll take five minutes to get out. Meehix should have enough oxygen to make it to the airlock.

Meehix grabbed John's hand excitedly, pulled it up in the air, and gave him a high five.

We did it! He couldn't hear her or see her face, but he could feel her energy. He smiled and felt a rush of adrenaline.

He drew a deep breath and blew it out. What a relief. For a minute there, he thought Meehix was toast. Or if not toast, then frozen orange juice. Or frozen blue juice. He laughed. He felt giddy.

Then he saw something flickering in the distance.

He leaned forward in the seatbelt straps as far as he could and away from the rear lights so he could see better. Far off in the darkness, to his right, maybe a half-mile, he saw lights—lots of them—like a string of moving Christmas tree lights. He turned to his left and saw a longer line about a mile away and moving parallel with them.

Then he realized what they were. They were Orientation Robots. There were dozens of them.

"Oh shit," Ship said over the translator. John already knew what was going down.

Laser blasts flashed behind John and Meehix—which was forward—in the direction they were traveling. John realized it was Chuckie firing at oncoming ORs. Then he felt a shockwave and a blast of heat.

There was no sound except for his head bouncing around inside his helmet. Their OR jolted to one side like it was going to tip over. A sparking OR crashed through the railing next to him and into a bunch of cryo-tubes below, knocking them over like bowling pins.

John saw more flashes. This time, red laser bolts flew

past them on their right and left. Meehix grabbed his arm as they tipped up to one side again. John realized Chuckie was turning them down a different walkway in an attempt to evade more oncoming ORs.

Shit! We're not heading back to the airlock!

He could see the lights in the distance closing on them from both sides. Now at least a hundred ORs were attempting to box them in.

Chuckie fired again, and another OR blew over their heads and exploded on the walkway behind them. This one managed to turn an arm back toward John and Meehix. John pushed Meehix to one side as a laser bolt flashed between them and exploded into the back of their OR. The flash and impact stunned him. He wasn't sure where he was for a second.

He tried to look at Meehix, but he couldn't turn his helmet far enough. She was shaking him, and he realized she was trying to see if he was hurt. He lifted his arm and gave her a thumbs up. Then he saw the burn on his forearm. *There was a hole in his spacesuit.*

Oh shit.

The pressure in the suit was dropping rapidly. John started to feel dizzy. Meehix was frantically pressing her hand over the hole, but it wasn't doing any good. He started seeing little stars floating everywhere, and he had trouble breathing. Everything started to go dark.

I guess this is what it feels like to die...for real.

Right before blacked out, he hallucinated a red gaming screen flashing in front of his eyes. All it said was: **You Died.**

John opened his eyes. He was sitting in his gaming chair back home. He must have fallen asleep right in the middle of the game because the mecha had paused in mid-stride on the screen and his mother was shaking him.

He couldn't hear her voice, but he could see her lips moving. They were saying, "You're late for school! You're late for school!" but he couldn't hear anything. It was like she was behind an invisible, soundproof shield and he was so wiped out from an all-nighter that he didn't feel like moving.

He tried to say, "Leave me alone, I'm too tired," but the words wouldn't come out. He couldn't seem to fill his lungs with enough air to speak.

I have to quit doing this. All-night gaming sessions and stuffing my face with junk food are clearly taking their toll. I feel like dog shit in a blender.

He looked at his mother's eyes, and suddenly her pupils started flying around like bugs. More like fireflies. They started glowing, and they multiplied. First, there were four, then eight, then sixteen fireflies, all zipping around in front of her face.

He tried to focus. She disappeared. Then he heard a *thumping* sound and his head felt like it was bouncing around inside a fishbowl. A gloved hand was hitting a window. No. It wasn't a window. It was his helmet visor.

Meehix was shaking him frantically and hitting the face of his helmet with her palm, trying desperately to wake him up. The fireflies turned out to be distant ORs closing on them in the darkness. The seatbelt still held him strapped to their Orientation Robot, and they were still flying down the walkway at top speed. He wasn't dead. *Yet.*

He lifted his arm. A kind of metal duct tape tightly wrapped it.

A laser blast exploded right between his dangling legs. If it had been six inches higher…

He was fully awake again, and he wrenched his body to the right. Out of the corner of his helmet, he could just barely see Meehix's expression. She was pointing at her life support pack. There were no more numbers on it.

"Ship!" he yelled. "Can you hear me?"

"Yes, John, I hear you."

"I got hit and passed out. Meehix is out of air. I…I… don't know what to do!"

Chuckie took a hard right, and they almost flipped. Two of the pursuing ORs made the turn, but a third must have malfunctioned because it crashed into the first two. All three broke through the railing and fell into the cryo pit.

Six more made the turn and started hauling ass after them. Everywhere John looked, more OR lights closed in on them. Chuckie fired like a madman in all directions now.

Laser bolts flashed every which way, both outgoing and incoming. A blast from his right blew off one of Chuckie's laser arms, sending it flying off into the dark like a flaming boomerang.

"I'm sorry, John. Under the circumstances, I'm afraid I have no useful suggestions regarding your current dilemma."

John felt Meehix go limp. He grabbed her gloved hand.

She was like a noodle.

"No!" John screamed.

He felt around on his suit. There had to be something he could do. There were no external air hoses. Everything was in the suit itself. There was no way he could think of to get air out of his suit and into hers.

He felt around frantically for the utility compartment on his chest and realized it was already open. It was empty.

Meehix. She took a roll of puncture tape out of my utility compartment and sealed the hole in my suit. She saved me.

The OR swung hard to the left, and a volley of laser blasts riddled the right side. Smoke blew over John's head, and flying debris peppered him. He saw another mechanical arm blow off and fly off into the dark.

What can I do? He never felt so helpless in his life.

"John, can you hear me?"

"Yeah, Ship!"

"Chuckie says, 'hold on tight.'"

John grabbed Meehix and held her as tightly as he could.

A massive barrage of laser blasts erupted behind him. It was like an electrical storm. Chuckie was firing his last two remaining cannons like Gatling guns straight ahead. At what, John didn't know.

There was an impact and another harder impact. John's head snapped back and slammed the inside of his helmet. He and Meehix bounced around like rag dolls. He felt like he was in a car in a demolition derby.

The OR flipped on its side and slid on...*ice?*

Methane crystals blew up in his face, covering his visor. The OR finally stopped sliding, and for a brief second, everything was still. John wiped his helmet with his glove and realized they were outside on the surface of Orfon IX, lying sideways in the snow.

He looked back from whence they'd come. There was a big smoldering hole in a giant barrier about sixty yards away. Chuckie had blasted the OR right through the Big House wall.

Talk about busting out.

ORs started creeping out of the hole like giant metal spiders.

Oh shit.

His seatbelt straps released, and he and Meehix fell sideways into the snow. Her limp body landed on top of him.

Laser bolts exploded all around, blowing up plumes of frozen chemicals like little ice geysers. With one arm trapped underneath the crippled OR, Chuckie began firing with the only arm he had left. One of the approaching ORs exploded. A blast to the head crippled another, but there were too many.

Chuckie tried desperately to right the fallen OR but it was hopeless. With his only laser arm engaged in shooting and the other one buried in the snow beneath the robot's full weight—and making horrible grinding noises—it wasn't going to happen. The poor OR looked like it had been dropped down a ten-mile concrete staircase and lit on fire. It was a mess.

John grabbed Meehix and dragged her limp body away from the wreckage. Chuckie kept firing like a master gamer, taking out OR after OR, but they finally ganged up on him. At least six had gotten out of the hole unscathed, and they opened up with two dozen blasters at once. John slipped and fell as the OR exploded in a massive fireball.

Chuckie. A laser blast impacted right next to his foot. *Shit!*

There was nowhere to run, nowhere to hide.

John stood and gave the universal sign of "you got me." He raised his hands.

The six fully functional ORs rolled toward him in formation, a nice, clean, soldierly line of shiny robot monsters that all seemed to say in unison, "you didn't really think you could beat us, did you?"

Well, no one can say we didn't put up a fight.

Then, one by one, the ORs blew up. Boom, boom, boom —right down the line.

John looked at the source of the missile barrage. It was Ship. He hovered above them and fired again.

"Ship! You're *beautiful!*"

"Why, thank you, John. You are quite attractive as well."

Ship kept firing. Whenever another OR peeked out of the hole, he blasted them into oblivion until there were so many destroyed ORs plugging it, no more could get through.

"Ship! Get Meehix onboard! She can't breathe!"

"Will do, John."

Ship landed right next to them and lowered the stairs. John picked up Meehix and ran up as fast as he could. Before he could order him to do so, Ship closed the inner door and pressurized the cabin almost instantly. John hit the release on Meehix's helmet and twisted it off. He did the same with his.

He shook her.

"Meehix? Meehix? *Breathe!*"

She didn't move.

He laid her down on the floor, tilted her head back, and sealed his mouth over hers. He blew two quick puffs and checked the pulse in her neck. She suddenly convulsed, gasped, coughed, and started sucking in air like a vacuum cleaner on overload. She was alive.

Soon she was breathing normally. She looked up at him.

"John?" was all she said. He kissed her quickly on the mouth and put his helmet back on.

Be right back. He motioned since she didn't have her translator.

He leapt to the stairway door, which opened as soon as he got there.

"Ship! Get ready to depressurize the stairway between the—"

"Already on it, John."

John jumped into the stairway compartment and crouched. The inner door shut, the stairway decompressed, the outer door opened, and the stairs descended, all in about three seconds.

John jumped into the snow and ran to the OR. Chuckie's cyber-tube—all pitted and scorched—was right in the middle of it, still wrapped in the abdominal arms of the wrecked robot.

"Chuckie? Are you alive?" John asked, fearing the worst.

The only remaining arm on the smoldering OR made a grinding sound, lifted, gave a weak thumbs-up, and collapsed.

CHAPTER FIFTY-SIX

A few more advancing ORs got around the roadblock. Ship flattened them, and John overheard him saying, "**Ooh, that's gotta hurt,**" as he gleefully exterminated his fellow automatons.

After the brief shootout, they got Chuckie's little cryo-tube into the cargo hold with an anti-gravity beam. Chuckie, in turn, got them through the laser satellite blockade without a hitch.

Thankfully, the satellites were on a completely auto-mated system separate from the one on the surface. All Chuckie had to do was transmit the remaining departure code from the tail end of the fake sentencing code, and the warden was powerless to stop them. They were home free. *Almost.*

"**John, I am scanning a very large craft moving at high speed in our direction.**"

John had comfortably arranged Meehix on her makeshift bed in the back, bundling her naked body in a blanket after removing her stinky spacesuit on loan from the prison. He jettisoned the nasty thing in the direction of Relleggom XIX and hoped to relax. His arm had a big blister where the laser blast had burned through his suit, and he wasn't sure if he should pop it or not. Apparently, there was no rest for the wicked.

"Can we make it to the Gate before they get here?" John asked as he gingerly poked the swelling. It stung like a motherfucker.

"I believe so, John, but it's going to be close."

Ship was already pushing the impulse engines into the red so all they could do was keep hauling ass for the nearest Gate and hope for the best.

"I'm receiving a transmission from the approaching ship, John. They have identified themselves as a Blavarian dreadnought on its way to a Gate on the other side of Relleggom XIX. They changed course to respond to a distress signal sent from the Warden on Orfon IX. They are ordering us to stand down and surrender immediately."

"A Blavarian dreadnought? Oh shit," Meehix said. She'd put her translator back in her ear, and that was the first thing she heard. A dreadnought was a monster of a battle-ship, and the Blavarians weren't known for their friendly demeanor.

"What the hell's a Blavarian dreadnought? You know what? Never mind!" John snarled. "You can tell them I said to *fuck off*. On second thought, put me through to the captain."

Who do I have to blow in this galaxy to catch a break?

"You're on, John."

John let loose.

"I'm addressing the captain of the Blavarian ship. My name's not important, and neither is yours, but I do have something to say. I'm sick and tired of everyone ordering me around. I just went through a lot of bullshit that almost got my best friend killed, and I'm in no mood for another pompous ass telling me what I can and cannot do.

"What makes you so fucking sure of yourself? Why do you think you know what's best? The truth is, you don't, and neither do I. You're following orders and think you have the right to tell other people what to do.

"Well, you don't, and I've had it with your bullshit and everyone like you. So you can take your Blavarian what-not, shove it up your ass, and suck on a big plate of veonk spheres while a Quoteggian female busts a nut on your face and eats it. *I'm done with anyone who thinks they have a right to tell others what to do,* so go fuck yourself. Out."

John drew a deep breath.

Whew! That's been building up for a while. Either that or I took out all my sexual frustration on a perfect stranger. Oh well. Whoever he is, I'm sure he deserved it. He's probably the Blavarian version of the United States Space Force.

"Damn, John," Meehix said from the back. "You's a gangster."

John sat next to her. "Sorry. I guess I needed to vent."

"I wish you hadn't vented at a Blavarian."

"Why?"

She sat up and took him by the hand. She examined the wound on his arm. It was a nasty-looking burn. "You know, if you hadn't pushed me out of the way, this would be my face right now."

John shrugged. "If you hadn't taped up my arm, I'd be a space popsicle right now."

"Speaking of space popsicles, how's Chuckie N?"

"Ship?" John called. "Is Chuckie okay?"

"Yes, John. He says he's looking forward to thawing out on a tropical island somewhere, preferably a vacation planet with a comprehensive set of Kdackan films. The cops confiscated his Chuck Norris library, and he's jonesing for some *Lone Wolf McQuade*."

"Tell him we're going to find someone who specializes in defrosting cryo-tubes as soon as possible. If we can pick up a copy of *Lone Wolf McQuade* on the way, we'll play it for him in the tube."

"Chuckie would like that very much, John."

"Did you mean what you said before?" Meehix still held his hand.

"What?"

"About me being your best friend?"

He thought about the question. Gage would take issue, but in his heart, John knew it was true.

"When I got you back on the ship, and you weren't breathing, I felt like I was losing my best friend. Then I realized…that's because I was losing my best friend."

Meehix squeezed his hand.

"John, we are nearing the Gate. There will be an extremely limited amount of time for Meehix to visualize the Gate combination before the Blavarian warship is in firing range. I suggest she begins concentrating soon.

"You realize that you told the Blavarian dreadnought captain that you wanted to have sex with him."

"What? No, I didn't!"

"Blavarians flirt by creating hyperbolic, sexual scenarios and combining them with food. When you told him to shove his ship up his ass and suck on a plate of veonk spheres while a Quoteggian female busts a nut on his face and eats it, you basically invited him over to Netflix and chill."

"How do you know *that* expression?" John was dumbfounded.

"I know a lot of things about humans. I know a lot of things about a lot of things."

She put her blue arms around him, pulled him close, and kissed him on the mouth—another one of those big, wet, French as French gets kisses. Meehix realized that she wanted him in the worst way. On her bed. *Now.*

"**Meehixiheem,**" Ship said with concern. "**We need the Gate combination.**"

It was easy for her to remember this Gate code. The three-dimensional aspects and the exact timing of the changes it made resembled a silhouette of two people making love.

"**The Gate is activating. Good job, Meehix. We are entering the Gate.**"

The cabin filled with the strong smell of tropical suntan lotion. John's eyes rolled back, and he went limp. Meehix released him, and he slid to the floor with a smile on his face.

Premature Orgasmic Mental Climax.

"Well...shit." Meehix sighed. "Where's my pleasure toy?"

The story continues with book two, *Anal Probes Suck Ass,* coming soon to Amazon and Kindle Unlimited.

Claim your copy today!

Thank you for not only reading this story but to the end and these author notes as well.

First, let me admit that Michael Todd is a pen name for my books which might (or might not...but probably might) be a little risqué. Or if Pandora (a character from the Protected by the Damned series) a whole LOT risqué.

My sense of humor is varied and there is a LOT that humors me that is not appropriate for general consumption. Hell, my normal Michael Anderle humor is too risqué for a typical YA novel.

With a Michael Todd book I am allowed to cut loose a little more. I'm still not a big participant in open door sex scenes with either name but I have gone a little far with my Skharr DeathEater (sword and sorcery) stories and a few Michael Anderle fans have dinged me for that.

I understand. I didn't realize they would have a few paragraphs before they fade to black but a S&S tale (or at least a barbarian tale) often has these scenes.

Here in a Michael Todd book, it would be a huge shrug.

If this is the first time reading some of my stories, feel free to check out other stuff I've done. The Protected by the Damned, War of the Damned and War of the Angels is a little closer to this type of story.

The Skharr DeathEater series is somewhat close in the humor. The Kurtherian Gambit series has a seriously unfiltered cursing component, but no sex and rare on the kissing.

Lots of explosions though. LOTS AND LOTS of explosions.

Since many of my fans figured out that Michael Todd is Michael Anderle I'll add my typical 'who am I' to these author notes so that those who meet me for the first time will get to know me a bit.

Then I encourage you to go down the Michael Todd / Michael Anderle rabbit hole.

Just a warning, it's a rather deep hole.

Who am I?

I wrote my first book *Death Becomes Her* (*The Kurtherian Gambit*) in September/October of 2015 and released it November 2, 2015. I wrote and released the next two books that same month and had three released by the end of November 2015.

So, just at five years ago.

Since then, I've written, collaborated, concepted, and/or created hundreds more in all sorts of genres.

My most successful genre is still my first, Paranormal Sci-Fi, followed quickly by Urban Fantasy. I have multiple pen names I produce under.

Some because I can be a bit crude in my humor at times

or raw in my cynicism (Michael Todd). I have one I share with Martha Carr (Judith Berens, and another (not disclosed) that we use as a marketing test pen name.

In general, I just love to tell stories, and with success comes the opportunity to mix two things I love in my life.

Business and stories.

I've wanted to be an entrepreneur since I was a teenager. I was a very *unsuccessful* entrepreneur (I tried many times) until my publishing company LMBPN signed one author in 2015.

Me.

I was the president of the company, and I was the first author published. Funny how it worked out that way.

It was late 2016 before we had additional authors join me for publishing. Now we have a few dozen authors, a few hundred audiobooks by LMBPN published, a few hundred more licensed by six audio companies, and about a thousand titles in our company.

It's been a busy five years.

Ad Aeternitatem,

Michael Anderle

CONNECT WITH MICHAEL

Connect with Michael Anderle

Website: http://lmbpn.com

Email List: http://lmbpn.com/email/

Social Media:

https://www.facebook.com/LMBPNPublishing

https://twitter.com/MichaelAnderle

https://www.instagram.com/lmbpn_publishing/

https://www.bookbub.com/authors/michael-anderle